Dagger

An MC Romance

Charlotte McGinlay

Copyright © 2023 Charlotte McGinlay

All rights reserved.

ISBN: 979-8-8524-7955-6

Description

Dagger

Growing up in a clubhouse is supposed to be fun and I guess with my friends it has been,

But with my family, not so much.

My father's been basically absent while there for my blood brother.

And his wife has made my life hell.

I made sure to grow strong to stop the abuse, I made sure to grow in the club as a screw you and succeeded,

I'm now the Vice President,

I'm stronger than I was when I was a kid,

And I refuse to be vulnerable again,

Until I meet HER.

She makes me want to be vulnerable and show her a different side to me,

She makes me feel period.

But I messed up and she doesn't want to know,

She thinks I'm a player, not knowing my demons.

But she has some demons of her own,

And come heaven or hell,

I'll make sure we face them together.

Melanie

I can't remember the last time I felt happy,

Maybe before my father left when I was only four,

Or maybe when my momma overdosed, and I had to stay somewhere else for a few months until she was better?

Life hasn't been nice to me growing up and I've been living through the motions,

Concentrating on school,

I refuse to be vulnerable to anyone,

People always disappoint, people always leave,

And I prefer being alone dealing with the shadows,

Until I meet HIM.

He's a player but I can see the same pain in his eyes that I have in my own,

I want to help him, but I don't want to get hurt,

He'll be the end of me, I just know it,

But he's persistent despite my turning him away over and over,

He wants to fight our demons together, to burn them,

But how do I let myself fall into the flames with him when I've been burning inside from the memories of my past?

This can be read as a standalone, it is book 2 of 7 of Untamed Hell's fire MC series, with a HEA. Due to mature content and themes this book is recommended for readers aged 18+, this novel may contain triggers.

Prologue

Travis - age 11

I'm sitting on my bed crossed legged playing against Logan, the pres's son on the Xbox. I sigh when the small tv glitches again making me lose a life. The tv is quite old. It used to be my mother's before she died and dad gave it to me last year, much to his wife's dismay. Apparently, it was in club storage or something. The Xbox was my little brothers Jacksons until last month when it started playing up. He begged dad and his mum for an upgrade, and they gave in straight away letting him have a brand-new gaming system while I'm stuck with an old one that likes to freeze more than the tv.

I know I probably sound ungrateful for having this one, but my problem is, he always gets what he wants, always. I've resented him a lot as we got bigger. He wants new clothes; he gets them while I have to have the hand me downs from Uncle David's kids. He wants to go out for dinner; they take him while leaving me behind with Jewels. He wants to go camping; dad takes him and leaves me with his wife, and it sucks. You see, his mum isn't mine and she hates me because I'm a reminder of her husband's old life. For as long as I can remember she has made my life hell. If Jackson does something wrong, she tells my dad it was me and I end up with the belt across my ass. If somethings gone missing or something's a mess, again, I'm the one with a belt across my ass. My dad believes her every time even though I try to tell him it wasn't me, I'm not even home half the time she accuses me but as far as he's concerned my mum was a compulsive liar so I must be too and as far as Leslie, my father's wife is concerned, I'm the project of a stupid mistake on my fathers end and shouldn't be living with them.

When he started seeing Jacksons mum, my momma who was a sweet butt for the club decided to trap my dad, apparently. This is coming from him and Leslie. My mother died during childbirth so she can't exactly tell her side of the story now, can she?

Jewels, a sweet butt who has basically raised me so far, has told me several times now how my momma didn't trap my dad. She didn't understand how she fell pregnant but refused to get rid of me like my so-called father wanted. According to Jewels, she didn't even ask my dad for anything. She moved out of the clubhouse and got a job as a receptionist for a tyre place two towns over and the only reason why I ended up with my dad was because momma made sure the hospital staff knew he was the father when she realized she was dying so I didn't end up in care. She died of preeclampsia and apparently it took Logan's dad, Dead Shot, the president of the Untamed Hell Fire's MC to convince my father to keep me even though Leslie threatened to leave him if he did, it was her or me and Dead Shot made sure he chose me and I mean obviously he did, he kept me, and Leslie obviously stayed with him. Most likely because she fell pregnant after my birth causing the man who fathered me to barely pay any attention to me. Jewels has mainly looked after me. As far as Stormy's concerned, I don't exist.

I shoot and go to kill Logan but miss when the game freezes again and I groan thinking it's the Xbox or tv again until a voice sounds over the mic that Jewels bought me last week.

"AFK (away from keyboard) momma wants help in the fricking kitchen again. I nearly had you as well." I grin and shake my head. Momma Cammy is a bulldog. She can be sweet as pie one minute then a raging dog the next. She's someone you don't want to mess with. I sigh and turn the Xbox and old tv off before I lie back on my twin bed and look at the ceiling. Logan won't be back on now, Cammy will make sure of it, she loves me but she's best friends with Leslie and seems to believe the crap that she spews.

I look around my room and sigh again; it's small. It can only fit my bed and a small chest of drawers that I can't open fully because there's only two inches from itself and the end of my bed. It holds the tv and the Xbox and that's all I've got, it's all that can actually fit in here. My room is basically a storage cupboard. I slowly close my eyes and take a deep breath as my stomach grumbles.

I haven't eaten today.

Jackson accidently broke his mum's crystal vase with his football, she confronted him and when he admitted to it, apologizing over and over, she told him it was fine and gave him some money for some sweets before she went and told

Stormy that I did it instead. She told him I was laughing at her and calling her names as well so as punishment he punched me across the face, dazing me while also splitting my lip then told me I wasn't allowed to eat today and not to leave my room and like the good kid I actually am, I listened even though all I want to do is run away from here. I have several times now but have been brought back each time despite screaming and pleading with people to listen to me and send me away. They never listen, they all believe her, and I would bet my left toe that Leslie will lie later, and I'll get another punishment.

I close my eyes, trying to shut my thoughts off, trying to fall asleep, hoping it would help the hunger pains.

I don't know how much time had passed after I dozed off, but I wake to the door handle to my room jiggling and I tense. I know it's not Jackson because he's gone to Leo's for a sleep over because he's allowed them while I'm not, plus no other brother or old lady want me around their kids because of Leslie's lies and I know it can't be Stormy because he had club business to attend to until 4am, so that could only mean,

"UNLOCK THIS DOOR RIGHT FUCKING NOW SHITHEAD."

I swallow hard.

Whenever the house is empty, she does this. She'll get drunk then come in here and beat me black and blue on my body, making sure my face is bruise free. When I showed people the bruises on my body, she came up with a story of how I had myself beaten by a rival club, no one would look at me right after that. That was when I was five years old. I've kept them to myself since then, including the scars she's caused.

Leslie is a nasty, scorned woman and I'm the reminder, I'm the person, the kid who she decides who needs punishing for her husband's sins when they weren't even a real couple when I was conceived. She's getting worse, which I didn't think was possible until last year when she got two of her friends to rip my clothes off of me before tying me down on my bed while I screamed at them to leave me alone all while she laughed and recorded it as they put tape over my mouth before they started to touch me.

I squeeze my eyes shut as the memories hit me hard. They would touch all over my body while they squeezed their dicks before spurting out cum all over me. Now don't get me wrong, I'm 11 so I know all about sex no thanks to the club brothers but what they're doing to me is wrong and I hate it. I feel dirty all the time and when I tried to tell my so-called father what she had her friends do, he hit me hard in my already bruised stomach for 'lying' like my momma. She's done this every week since, until today. Today I managed to get the dead bolt installed after I told Tank, Zayne's dad, that my brother kept pranking my room. He made sure it was on properly before he left me on my own after scowling at my box room.

The brothers don't know how bad I'm treated here, they never believed me, if they did, I don't think Stormy would still be VP. I think Tank is the only one looking at me fully now, everyone else keeps away from me.

Banging brings me back to the here and now and I tense even further, they won't touch me again, even if she lies to Stormy, I don't care. If he kills me then so be it.

"OPEN THE FUCKING DOOR TRAVIS." I don't listen, I lay down

and bring my knees up to my sore stomach where she hit me yesterday with a bat. I felt a crack and my whole side hurt and it's now badly bruised.

"Why the fuck is his door locked Les? I'm fucking horny and if you don't open up the door then I'm fucking you instead." I tense even more while she growls,

"You know I won't cheat on my husband Shack. I'll suck you off but that's it. Tomorrow I'll make sure Stormy punishes him for this little stunt. Come back next week, I'll make sure the locks are removed from the door. The boys a whore just like his mother."

I hear them walk away as tears fall from my eyes and I sniffle wondering if I'm better off never leaving this room again.

I can't wait until I'm older and no longer have to see them because I'll leave, and I'll never come back.

Melanie – age 4

I yawn and look around. Where's mommy and daddy? I furrow my brows. I fell asleep on the comfy sofa after dinner. I didn't mean to though. Are they mad at me for sleeping?

I get up and go to the kitchen but it's empty, so I go to the stairs. I hear a bang, so I climb the stairs and follow the banging noise. I'm scared and I want my daddy. He hasn't been home a lot lately.

When I get to mommy and daddy's room, I see daddy putting his clothes in his bag.

"Daddy?" I whisper, still sleepy, and his head shoots up, his eyes are angry and red, but they soften when he sees me,

"Baby, did you have a good nap?" He questions while he walks over to me and picks me up making me grin as I put my head in his neck and nodding.

"I scared daddy, I didn't know where you were, where's mommy?"

He rubs my back,

"I'm sorry princess, I lost track of time, mommy's just nipped out." I nod again and squeeze his neck but pull back when my neck feels wet. Daddy's eyes and cheeks are wet, and I grab his cheeks with my hands,

"don't cry daddy."

He sniffles, "sorry princess. Daddy's got to go. Mommy and I, well, mommy and I have decided to live apart and I need to leave before she comes home. I need you to be a brave girl and stay in your room for me until she gets back, ok?"

My eyes widen then tears fall, fast and I sob.

"Daddy can't go, p-please d-daddy. I'll be good, p-please." He hugs me tight and carries me to my room before placing me on my bed. He kneels down, "I'm sorry princess, I can't stay. I love you. Please stay in your room." He gets up and walks out of my room, shutting the door without looking back and I scream out, crying for my daddy.

What did I do? Why is he leaving me?

I quickly jump off my bed and run to my door, trying to open it but it won't. Why won't it open? I bang on it screaming,

"DADDY, DADDY, DON'T LEAVE, DADDY." I hear another bang then mommy's voice, she sounds worried,

"Why is our daughter screaming from her room Callum? What happened?"

"You're not supposed to be home for another hour Beth." His voice has gone angry. Why's he angry with mommy?

I bang on the door again crying out, but they don't listen.

"Callum? What's going on? Why are your bags packed?"

I hear daddy chuckle,

"Maybe because I had just found out that MY daughter isn't even MY daughter. You cheated on me with a fucking biker!"

My tears still fall not understanding what they're talking about. He sounds so angry.

"Who-who told you that?" Mommy sounds scared, why is she scared?

"The biker's wife, she offered me $100,000 for me to hand Mel's over to her." I hear my mommy gasp,

"C-Callum, I-listen to me. It was a mistake. We both agreed to forget it ever happen, please, please, she's yours, please."

He scoffs and I bang again, "DADDY, DADDY." They both ignore me still and I sniffle.

"Honestly, I don't give a shit if it was a mistake, THAT'S NOT MY KID."

I jump at his shout,

"I've been looking for an excuse to leave your skanky ass, you cheated which means everything's fucking mine per the agreement of the prenup. Enjoy being penniless bitch. You have 48hours to vacate the premises. The house has been sold." I hear mommy scream, "CALLUM" before there's a bang from the front door and I run towards my window. My tears fall harder when I see daddy climbing into his car and I bang on the window, "DADDY" he looks up and waves with a small smile then leaves, driving away.

"DADDY, DADDY."

My door unlocks and mommy comes in with her cheeks wet and I go to run towards her wanting a mommy cuddle because they make everything better but when I get near her, a loud slap sounds into the room and I scream falling to the floor, my cheek hurting, and I cry. She grabs a hold of my hair and makes me look at her while I sob in pain, "no dinner for you tonight. This is your fault why he's left." Then she spits in my face before throwing me on the floor, slamming my head against it. She slams my door shut and I hear it lock again.

I don't move. I can't.

What did I do wrong?

Chapter 1

Dagger – 30 years old – current day

I sit in church next to Axel as our brothers take a seat around the solid oak table. Ink, my blood brother sits next to me as our club secretary while Gunner our enforcer sits on the other side of Axel. With Slicer our treasurer sitting next then Flame, our road captain, and tech guru before Hawk our Sergeant at arms sits down. Then we have the old timers, Dead Shot, Butch, Stormy, Tank, Doc and a few more take a seat on the other end of the table. They used to be council which is why they're in church. We all sit and listen as Flame goes over this month's gun run up to Wincher. This month is Axels turn to go. We take it in turns each month, ensuring one of us is left behind in case there's an emergency. If something was to happen to Axel then I would take over the club, it's a system he lives by and a job I don't fucking want.

"Axel, Hawk, Gunner, and Buzz will be on bikes, while the prospects, Shane and Bill will be driving the lorry. Slicer will drive with until the end of town before turning back home." Flame finishes and we all nod before Axel asks about each of the businesses. Flame starts out,

"the garage is doing really well, I think we need to start hiring some more mechanics, works piling up." Axel nods, "set up wanted ads and see if any other brothers want some extra cash." Then he looks towards Slicer who continues,

"The bar's good, no problems, we're busy every night." Axel turns to Ink who grins, amusement flashes in his eyes, "Fire's Ink is fucking awesome, more clients have been coming in, Hawks especially busy with the ladies." Hawk gives him the middle finger while Ink snorts out a laugh and we look at them confused. Hawk points at Ink, "don't you fucking dare." He just grins and looks around the room,

"Seems Hawk has gotten himself a 17-year-old admirer who thinks she's old enough for him."

We all burst out in laughter while Hawk huffs, crossing his arms over his chest.

"It's not fucking funny; she comes in everyday trying to book a tattoo knowing she's not old enough yet wearing these skimpy fucking outfits and too much fucking make-up trying to be seductive making my skin fucking crawl. She won't take 'no' as a fucking answer." We all laugh harder while he scowls at us all. Axel shakes his head and bangs his gavel,

"Alright fuckers quieten down; I'd like to hit the road soon so I can get back to my woman. Hawk, try and stay away from jailbait will yah, ban her from the shop if you have too. Dag, you were last doing the books for the club, how we doing?" Hawk growls while the rest of us laugh. I shake my head and speak up, "the club is doing good, making good profit, although Louisa dropped by yesterday." Axel sits up straight, rage enters his eyes, and I don't blame him. His woman Annalise suffers from anxiety and not long-ago Louisa, who was another baker working for Annie, not only left the bakery in a mess, not doing her job properly but she also stole $400 out of the till, only a few months after that Annie was attacked by her ex-boyfriend David who enjoyed being chopped up by Axel, apparently Buzz, our newly patched brother, nearly threw up and it was a sight to see.

I put my hands up, "she came in looking for a waitressing job, but I told her we don't hire thieves. She tried saying Annie was lying and she'll end up homeless without a job." Dead Shot growls and I smirk, continuing, "she soon ran out the door with her tail between her legs though when I told her Annie was your woman and we've seen the CCTV." The brothers grin while Axel nods, "good, I don't need her stressing my woman out." He looks around the table, "anything else?"

Stormy stands and I tilt my head, "wanted to make sure everyone would be here for Leslie's birthday tomorrow night?" I try, I really do try but I can't help the eye roll but I manage to keep the snort in though so I should get points for that, right?

Axel looks around the room and all the men grin and nod, they all love her. To them I'm the ungrateful one, hating his innocent stepmom who took him in as a baby and raised him, all oblivious to what she put me through, and it was in fact Jewels who brought me up. Tank looks at me with concern but a give him a subtle head shake. He doesn't know a lot, only what he saw of my room really and how Ink had received more things compared to me, but he's guessed I wasn't treated right which I've never confirmed nor denied but the fact I never go to family occasions or dinners after returning home to take on the VP patch which Axel and Dead Shot begged me to do has only increased his suspicion but I'm 30 years old and a retired Navy Seal, they can't force me anymore and if they tried, well, let's just say, I can fight back now. Stormy lays one hand on me and father or not, he's a dead man. I didn't get the road name Dagger for shits and giggles.

Axel looks at Ink who scoffs rolling his eyes, "I'm her fucking son of course I'm going to be there, she'd have my balls otherwise." Everyone chuckles except for me, and Tank before Axel looks at me and raises a brow. I give him a small smile, "sorry, can't make it, got a meet with my squadron." That's all I say, it's all he needs for him to nod. He knows when they call, I answer, that was the deal for me retiring from a team that I'd been with for 8 years, even if we're only doing a group call, they come before a woman who abused me growing up.

Axel doesn't know what happened over the years. He was never allowed to stay over so he never saw my room or the lack of food I was fed, and he never saw the scars on my body, no one has, and I want to keep it that way.

Ink looks at me with furrowed brows but keeps his mouth shut. He never saw what happened growing up either. He'd question why he had a bigger room and more things than me or why Stormy had hit me, and they'd always tell him I was a fuck up, that I'd hit his mom or ruined some of his shit. I barely talked to him growing up, I resented him but as I got older, I realized it wasn't his fault, it was our fathers and his mothers. We've become closer since I returned from active duty.

I hear Stormy growl, but I ignore him, and Axel bangs the gavel down, "alright fuckers if that's it, meeting done. Hawk, Gunner, let's get Buzz and the prospects and go, we're wasting day light." The men chuckle while they all start to head out of the Chapel into the common room. I stand and walk around the table briefly standing near the photo of my momma and Jewels on the wall and smile a little. She was beautiful. Dark red hair and bright green eyes.

I wish I knew her. And I wish I had more of her features and not the bastards.

Sighing, I continue to leave the room when Stormy grips my arm making me tense. I look at him and see concern in his eyes as they flicker to the picture of momma. He clears his throat, "Son, your mother, she misses you. It's one party, can't you tell your men this is the one call you can't make? You never celebrate birthdays or holidays, haven't done so since you left and even before that, you spent your evenings bolted in your room. Please son, do this for your mom and me. She brought you up as her own." His eyes flicker to the picture again before he looks back at me, "it'll be the best birthday surprise."

I smirk an evil smirk. I love how he calls me son now like he didn't beat me growing up and didn't listen to my abuser. I look at the photo again before moving my arm out of his grip and nodding my head towards the wall, "She is my momma and always will be. But my mom, the one who raised me, I spend every Sunday at her house as well as every holiday. Jewels, she's my mom, not your wife and like hell would I cut off my squadron who risked their lives for me and vice versa for you and that woman. See you later Stormy." Then I turn and walk out while his face goes red with shock, confusion, and anger but I don't give a fuck. I don't even fucking call him dad anymore, haven't done since I was three years old when Leslie burnt my back with the fire poker, yelling at me not to call him it.

The day I got a hawk tattooed on my back covering the scars from her was a good fucking day, I understand some are still visible but at least most of them cannot be seen.

As I get into the common room a loud bang comes from the Chapel making the brothers that are still around look that way in concern, but I ignore it heading towards the door, I've got to get to the club and being around the man who was supposed to protect me but failed is going to send me in a spin. Being back, even five years later, it's a struggle every day and every day I wonder if I made the right decision to come back. As I get to the front door Ink nudges my arm and I look at him, "what's up brother?"

He clears his throat before looking towards the common room then back to me, "its one-day Trav. Momma, she hurts. You've been home now for 5 years and yet you haven't said one word to her. If she walks in the clubhouse, you slink away, this will make her whole day Trav." I shake my head and he squeezes my arm, "one day Trav, just one day, she misses her son."

I give him a smile, "Jackson, your my brother, my blood and I love you but don't do this again. My squadron comes first, end of and I'm not her son."

I hear him sigh as I turn and walk out of the door. Like fuck would I be anywhere near that woman.

I climb onto my blue tank Harley and rev her up, listening as she purrs making me grin while I place my shades on. Just as I pull out of my designated space near Axels spot I see Stormy standing in the doorway with his arms crossed over his chest, his grey eyes that are so much like my own assessing me, but I ignore him like I always do and spin out of the compound, heading to the club. When I left I had been free, and I was adamant I was never going to return until Axel called and now I don't feel free anymore. I'm back where my demons live and most days I wonder why in the fuck I even came back in the first place, I mean fuck, my so-called father didn't even teach me how to ride or help me buy my first bike. He helped Ink but not me, Tank had helped me with Jewels. Being here isn't good for me, I think it's time I speak to my men about my return.

I get to the club ten minutes later and walk through the doors, placing my shades on my head. Sunny approaches me instantly, her brown eyes sparkle while she gives me a seductive grin making me smile and I nod my head towards my office making her eyes shine with lust before she struts down the hallway with me following, watching her juicy ass jiggle in her black thong. I unlock my door and she walks in, sitting herself on my desk, spreading her legs while moving her thong to the side, showing me her waxed wet cunt that glistens with need and I grin as my cock hardens in my jeans,

"lean back on your hands darling, you know the rules."

She pouts a little but does as I ask while I unbuckle my belt ready to fucking forget this morning

Chapter 2

Melanie – 23 years old – present day

My phone vibrates in my pocket, and I sigh, knowing it's probably mom again. I quickly cancel it and rush into work.

I'm late, crap.

I rush up the stairs and head into the staff room when I bump into Meghan the resident doctor. Her black hair is up in a messy bun with parts of her blue highlights framing her face. She arches her eyebrow at me, her blue eyes assessing me, and I bite my lip. I want to laugh so much but I'm late and I have rounds.

Fuck.

She furrows her brows when she sees my reaction to her, and I can't help it, my laughter bursts free making her look at me confused only making my laughter grow. Fuck, how has she not seen it. I try to calm down, breathing deeply before I grab her hand and drag her back into the staff room and place her in front of the mirror. Her eyes widen and I laugh again as she growls,

"fricking Lilah Rose."

Then she proceeds to get her phone out and take pictures of her now drawn on glasses, moustache, and beard before laughing too. Shaking my head I hand her the wipes before going to my cubby, placing my things in there, "I must admit, your daughter is a genius and how you didn't notice it this morning is a mystery to me."

She snorts shaking her head, "I was in a rush, I literally just through my hair up without even brushing it and you won't think that when she does it to you, the girl is slick I tell you."

I grin, "and when do I get the honor of having it done because I don't think I'd complain."

I raise a brow at her. We met about 3 months ago when she got transferred here to finish off her residency but I've yet to meet the little mischief.

"Probably when your actually not working." She raises a brow back at me.

I chuckle because it's true, I do work a lot, I think it's ingrained in me to do so after living in a damp trailer with my mom. She walks over and kisses my cheek saying she'll meet me at lunch in the dining hall before leaving and I pull my brown curly hair up in a messy knot before heading out to do my rounds before the charge nurse notices I'm late. I graduated last year from nursing school after working my butt off. After my father left when I was small my mother took to drugs, booze and men while ensuring I knew it was my fault why he left. We ended up downsizing from the house to a trailer and I was adamant I wasn't going to end up like my mother. I graduated high school a year early before heading to college on a scholarship. Leaving home was the best thing for me, it meant the abuse stopped, although it hasn't stopped her continuous calls for money which I try not to give into.

I'd had spent 12 years of my life with my mother verbally and physically abusing me while the men she brought home would leer at me and after one tried to touch me when I was only six I ended up locking my door, staying in my room until they were all gone which sometimes lasted a few days leaving me hungry and my room smelly because I had to use my trash can as a toilet. I did try to tell a teacher once when she asked me how I cut my lip, I think I was eight at the time and they ended up calling mom into the school who then proceeded to let out a sob story how I'm broken since my dad up and left and I was hurting myself for attention even though she is the one who hurt me the night before because I made a little sound closing the door. Since then I hadn't told a soul especially after I went back the next day with a cast on my hand after mom broke my wrist and the teachers shook their heads at me.

Pathetic, the lot of them.

I head into Mrs. Burns room and smile at the 58-year-old woman. Her blonde hair is up in a ponytail and her green eyes look at me as she grins, "Finally come to put me out of my misery."

I snort shaking my head, "you had your gallbladder removed and your finally being discharged. Why would I put you out of your misery? Unless you mean finally getting you out of here"

She scowls, "no, I mean, come to off me because if you discharge me then it means I'm back to being the cleaner, the cook, the laundress, the know it all, and the person who has to remember where everything is."

I burst out in laughter, "you mean a wife?"

She pouts and nods her head and I laugh louder shaking my head as Meghan walks in. She looks at me with a funny look then turns to Mrs. Burns, "alright lovely your being discharged in an hour." Mrs. Burns groans and I laugh again before stating to a confused Meg,

"she's wondering if we could put her out of her misery and not by discharging her either."

Meghan furrows her brows, "what on earth? She only had her gallbladder removed nothing life threatening." I snort, then laugh even harder as she repeats what she just told me,

"of course it's life threatening, just tell my husband you couldn't save me, there was a complication. Come on, do a lady a favor. I've had four blissful days of being waited on hand and foot, I don't want to go back to being a live-in maid and know it all."

Meghan looks at her for all of three seconds before she loses it too while Mrs. Burns scowls. I try to keep myself up right while Meghan has basically sat on the floor in laughter when Doctor Thomas walks in. His brows shoot high in his hairline, "do I want to know?" we laugh even harder while Mrs. Burns growls out,

"they seem to think my predicament is amusing and I'm telling you, it's not!" she sounds angry, but you can't hide the laughter in her eyes. This is what I love about this woman, she has a sense of humor.

The doctor looks at us with a frown and I clear my throat and rasp out, "Mrs. Burns would like us to put her out of her misery so she can be relieved of her wifely duties."

He bites his lip and nods his head trying to keep his laughter in, "but if we did that then what would happen to your husband? I'm pretty sure he'd be lost in the house to find anything at all without his better half."

Me and Meghan lock eyes and laugh again then even harder when Mrs. Burns states, "that is true. Maybe you can put him out of his misery instead." Doctor Thomas loses it this time and laughs and our patient grins, "I'm going to miss you three," we grin at her.

"Not as much as we're going to miss you." Doctor Thomas states before he looks at me then Meghan smiling, "alright ladies start her discharge papers please." We nod, still smiling and start the process before I go off to my next patient. I love my job!

About two hours later I've discharged three patients, changed two catheters, drawn several patients' blood and I'm finally about to head to one of my favorite patients' room who is unfortunately dying of liver failure after his transplant failed. Just before I get to his door my phone buzzes again and I sigh. I quickly head into the supply closet and grab my phone, answering it.

"Mom I'm at work."

I hear her growl, before she rasps, "then maybe you should have answered earlier when I called."

I shake my head, "what do you want mom?" I can't be dealing with her today. I know what she wants, it's what she always wants, and I've only ever given in once because she made a huge scene on campus last year, since then I dodge her.

"Is that the way to speak to your mother? if it wasn't for you then my husband would never have left!"

I sigh again. It's the same dance and accusation every time she tries to hurt me. I have no idea why dad left but I know I wasn't to blame, especially when she's a bitch.

"What do you want mother." I've had enough of her games and Mr. Samuels is expecting a game of gin.

"I'm short."

I chuckle, see. "your always short mom, I'm not doing this again, you're not my problem. Call one of your many boyfriends." I hang up the phone and put it on silent before heading back onto the ward ready to see my favorite patient.

When I get into his room, I smile. He's already got the game set up. Mr. Samuels is an 86-year-old man with white hair and bright green eyes, and the sweetest smile. He lost his wife a few months ago to a heart attack and has struggled since. I've known him since last year when I started at the memorial General hospital when he started his treatments for his liver and he's the sweetest man I've ever met.

I give his door a quick tap.

He looks up and smiles tiredly, his eyes lightening up, "well, it's-it's about time you-you got here sweetheart, I've got every-everything ready to-to kick your-your butt then you'll-you'll finally let my-my son take you out-out on-on a date." I grin at him shaking my head, he'll never give up on that notion even though his son is in his 40s and I'm only 23. I notice him struggling with his breathing and go to take his observations.

I furrow my brows when I see his SATs are below 85%,

"How you feeling Mr. Samuels?" He nods but doesn't speak and I look at him and see he's starting to nod off and I smile a sad smile while continuing with my observations for the next 15 minutes. His sats keep dropping. I page Doctor Thomas then grab the oxygen mask and gently place it over his mouth and nose before turning the oxygen up by 75% to see if it makes a difference.

There's a knock on the door a few minutes later and the Doctor comes in with a furrowed brow, "you paged Mel."

I nod, "Mr. Samuels is short of breath, SATs continue to drop below 85%, I've placed him on 75% oxygen to see if it makes a difference but so far it hasn't." He nods then comes over and starts his checks humming along the way before he looks at me with a sad smile,

"He hasn't got long left; I'll go give his son a call. Put the oxygen up to 100% and let's just help keep him comfortable." I give him a sad smile and turn to do as he asks as I struggle to breathe myself. He walks over to me and squeezes my shoulder as I wipe a tear away, "you're doing good Mel." I nod my head before he leaves. I sit with Mr. Samuels until I need to go do my rounds again. This week I'm on the Jay ward which is mainly the elderly and I love this ward; the patients are amazing. Next week I'll be in the ER then the week after that I'll be on the children's ward.

I love the rotation; it keeps me grounded in all areas.

Once my checks are done and I've checked on Mr. Samuels again who has now slipped into unconsciousness and is being accompanied by his son Thatcher, I head to the dining hall to meet Meghan already feeling drained. I quickly get a chicken salad and a diet coke before finding Meghan at the back table and take I seat. I huff a sigh.

"Bad morning?"

I shrug, "Mr. Samuels is no longer conscious." I wipe away a tear and she squeezes my hands, "this is why I tell you not to get attached." I chuckle a little before taking a bite of my salad. She did warn me, I'll give her that, but I like to think having a connection helps the patient especially if they've been here awhile which is unheard of unless you're an infant but if your family has money then the hospital will do anything.

Meghan sighs and puts her phone to her ear, and I watch her while eating my salad.

"Hi yes, uh, um, this is going to sound random, but I was wondering if you have a brother with the legal name of Noah, unknown last name but was on a club run to Wincher, Louisiana about five years ago?" she drums her fingers on the table then sighs, "and you don't know of any other club who do runs there?"

A small tear leaks out from her eye, and I wipe it away for her, making her smile at me, "ok, thank you anyway." She hangs up before sniffling.

I squeeze her hand, "no luck?"

She shakes her head. "I've tried over 13 different motorcycle clubs since she was born. I even stayed in Wincher for a year just in case he came back to the café before moving, it's like he's vanished. If I didn't have a permanent reminder of him in my daughter right down to her Hazel eyes then I would have thought I'd dreamt him." She met a guy who belonged to an MC about five years ago and had a one-night stand, to her she felt a connection but was told he didn't do relationships. When she had found out she was pregnant, she'd been doing everything in her power to find him but with no luck.

I chuckle then a thought comes to mind making me sit up straighter, "what about Doctor Thomas? He's in a motor cycle club isn't he?"

She gives me a slight smile, "already tried. Some woman answered and said she's never heard of him, and they don't affiliate with the Wincher club."

I sigh, "Dammit."

She nods, "Dammit."

We continue eating while I check my phone to see several missed calls and texts.

Mom – that was very rude, answer your phone right now or

else.

Mom – how dare you treat me this way. I'm like this because of you.

Mom – you stole your father from me. This is the least you can do. Answer your fucking phone.

Mom – MELANIE.

I sigh again and turn my phone off not willing to deal with this before I get back to my back-to-back shift, the woman is a menace.

Chapter 3

Dagger

I'm in the common room in the clubhouse with Clitter sitting on my lap while we watch the show of Axel and Annalise and I'm trying my hardest not to laugh my fucking ass off.

"I DON'T NEED TWO BABY SITTERS LOGAN." I snort and cover it with a cough before she glares my way, I don't need her anger turned to me because a pissed Annie is a scary fucking Annie but a pregnant pissed Annie? Hide the fucking knives.

Axel sighs, shoving his hand through his hair while Cammy smirks, holding Annie's puppy that Axel bought her. Fuck, maybe a dog will help me be comfortable around here again?

"Annalise."

My eyes shoot to flame, oh shit, the dude has a death wish, bull dog 2.0 is well in affect right now why would he get involved?

"It's not for long sweetheart. It's just until Grant is no longer a danger to you and the baby. We're just trying to keep you safe." Flame tries to placate her, and it seems to work when she pokes Axels chest causing him to look at her with wary, "why couldn't you just explain it like that instead of telling me I had to have two men stay with me at all times." I bite my lip to stop the laughter from escaping while everyone else lets it all out. I shake my head while ensuring Clitter sticks to the rules of no touching as Axel apologizes, "I'm sorry darling, next time I'll explain better, now let's go see our baby, yeah?" they turn to leave with Trigger and Jizz following who are chuckling.

"Fucking hell, if this is what a hormonal pregnant woman is like then remind me to double up on condoms." We all burst out in laughter again at Slicers comment.

Amen brother.

Clitter turns around a little while rubbing her ass against my hardening cock. She goes to touch my chest and I grab her finger while raising a brow,

"you know the rules Clitter."

She pouts, "but Dagger."

I shake my head at her about to remind her my one rule otherwise they don't get me anymore when someone stands next to us. I look up and my dick instantly deflates.

"Is there a reason why you missed Leslie's party last week Dagger?"

I sigh and tap Clitters leg to get off and she growls in frustration but does as instructed. She stomps off into the kitchen and I shake my head before I get up and tilt my head looking down into momma Cammy's brown eyes. She raises a brow at me when I just cross my arms over my chest, not answering her. I've always respected her despite never trusting me around her son.

"She is your mother Travis not the club whore who tried to trap Stormy and ruin his relationship. She raised you, loved you, fed you and clothed you. She took you in when you're a reminder of her husband's past despite how you treated her growing up. How hard is it for just one day to make her feel special. Just one day. You're being ungrateful which is surprising. I honestly thought you'd grown out of your horrible ways treating your parents like crap but I'm obviously wrong, I don't even know why you bothered to return 5 years ago when you're still acting like an ungrateful child."

My anger grows as she keeps talking while the clubhouse quietens as an old lady puts down their VP in front of them. This is the problem with Cammy, she doesn't stop and think about the consequences to her words or actions. She has no fucking idea what that woman did to me growing up or how Stormy acted despite me trying to tell everyone what was happening behind closed doors. She never believed me, and it took Dead Shot everything in him to convince her to let Axel still be friends with me growing up but still manage to minimize our time together. Yet I still showed her respect. Respect that she is not showing me in front of my brothers.

I shake my head. Her bringing up my momma is out of line too and she knows that. My momma can't defend herself and the only reason why Cammy hates her is because she slept with Dead Shot once. I bend so my face is in hers and she can see my anger making her eyes widen because not once have I shown any anger towards her, I've always thought of her like a mother to me despite her jabs here and there growing up about my so-called behavior so this fucking stings. I get she's sticking up for a friend but said friend is an abusing whore.

"I'm here because YOUR son begged me to return to be his VP. I never came back for Stormy or his wife, I came back, leaving my squadron for YOUR son. You are just an old lady. I don't give a shit if you're the presidents mother or a woman I USED to fucking look up to, I am the mother fucking VP in this club and while in these walls you show me some fucking respect and DON'T ever bring up my momma again. So fucking what she fucked Dead Shot ONCE, it was before your time, and it wasn't him who knocked her up so keep your trap shut. Oh, and from now on Cammy, stay the fuck away from me or I'll ensure to raise your punishment in church."

Her eyes turn glossy, but I ignore her and move to go around her. Several brothers are looking at us wide eyed while Tank gives me a nod and I know he'll inform Dead Shot exactly what his wife just said to me. If him or Axel want to have a go and try and vote me out of the club for talking to Cammy that way then fucking bring it on, she should never had said a fucking word and should have kept out of it. Leaving this fucking place is looking better and better as the days go on.

I get to my Harley and climb on, revving her up before heading towards Untamed girls knowing I have paperwork to do. It doesn't take me long before I'm parking up and heading inside. Sunny tries to flag me down, but I wave her off, not in the mood right now after my talk with Cammy and head into my office leaving a pouty Sunny near the bar. I see all the paperwork and I sigh, placing my hands on my hips. I look towards Axel's office then to my desk again.

Fuck it.

I grab half and make my way over to Axel's office. I unlock the door and put the paperwork on top of his on his desk before locking his door again and going back into my office which is definitely much lighter than Axels dark brown walls. I had the painters paint mine grey at the bottom and white at the top with a dark grey boarder then some black square shelves with all the books on them for the club. I smile and take a seat behind my dark grey desk looking at the picture of Jewels and my momma before I crack on with the inventory before I do the shifts wanting to lose myself for a little while.

About an hour later my phone rings and I look at the screen and grin,

"Hey mom."

I hear the smile in her voice, "hey baby boy, Peter and I just wanted to make sure you're still coming to dinner on Sunday."

I snort, "like you could keep me away, how is Peter doing?"

She hums, "he's good sweetheart. Is there any chance you could help him with the shelving unit? He's adamant he can do it this time."

I chuckle. Jewels and Peter married just before I was deployed and he's a good guy, just really fucking shit with DIY, "course, I remember the last one he tried to do."

She chuckles, "yes, that unit only lasted me two days before it broke."

I chuckle again and sit back, relaxing while we catch up. I haven't seen her in a week, so it'll be good to go round there, plus she and Peter are going travelling next month for a while, I need my time with her before they go. When we hang up my door opens and I look up to see a disappointed looking Dead Shot and Flame walk in and I sigh, crossing my arms over my chest.

"Look, I understand she was wrong but..." I cut him off instantly, "wrong? She brought up my momma, calling her a whore. Now unless you were bullshitting me all those years ago when you told me she only slept with you ONCE and only slept with Stormy a few times because she was more with the club for the money so she can go back to school than for a patched brother then she had no right opening her mouth."

Flame looks down not willing to look Dead Shot in the eye because he knows I'm right, Cammy over stepped.

"I'm the VP."

He nods while Flame looks at me again,

"I'm here because your son wanted me here, he wanted me as his VP, my best friend. I left my squadron. Men who risked their lives for me, men who I risked my life for. Who were with me, day in, day out for 8 years to be here for Axel. Your wife overstepped big time. She is only an old lady. She stopped being the first lady when Axel took over as president. Annalise is now first lady and Cammy overstepped, and she did it in front of the brothers, disrespecting me, the VP and you know as well as I, if it was anyone else she would have been banned from not only the clubhouse but also club activities for a month as punishment."

He nods again understanding flashes in his eyes. I didn't punish her; I didn't raise the alarm to the council. I walked away.

"It won't happen again."

I nod back before looking down, squeezing my eyes tight hating having to do this before I look at him again, I clear my throat, "it would be best if she stays away from me for a while." Flames eyes widen while Dead Shots mouth hangs open. He goes to say something to me, but I put my hand up, "she said something she had no right to Bruce. My momma doesn't deserve crap being said about her when she can't defend herself. I've always looked up to her despite her trying to minimize the time I spent with her son, I always saw her as a mother figure, but she overstepped, and I need space even if she is family to me." He sighs and nods his head in understanding knowing I could enforce for a club vote to have her banned for the month and I'm trying to do the right thing for everyone around. Flame goes to say something when we hear Axels office door open and him growl. I grin while Flame and Dead Shot look at me in confusion.

I get up and nod my head for them to follow heading into his office.

When we get in there we see Axel sitting behind his desk and he growls, pointing his finger at me,

"You."

I smirk at him while Dead Shot and Flame look between us

then to the pile on his desk making them both try to hold their laughter in, "it's not fucking funny, I have plans tonight and they don't fucking include the extra paperwork on my desk."

I just shrug, "I'm sure your old lady would wait until tonight for you to fuck her." He narrows his eyes at me while Dead Shot smacks me on the back of my head.

Fuck that hurt,

"shut up that's my fucking daughter."

I bite my lip to stop the laughter that's bubbling up in my throat from coming out, yeah, I can understand him not wanting to know about his blood son fucking the woman he brought up from 3 years old after her biological father beat her mama to death right before he tried to kill her. He's currently out of prison and threatened her about a month ago, wanting her mama's inheritance which she no longer has. She donated most of it to charity after buying her bakery and giving some to family and much to her disagreement that we saw this morning in the common room, she's being guarded by two brothers especially since she's currently pregnant, a conception that never should have happened. Fucking Bubbles had poked holes in Axels condoms hoping to try and seduce him. Fucking sweet butts are more hassle than they're worth.

Once we find Annie's father and put him out of his misery, life will be back to normal for Annie. Well except for the surprised pregnancy anyway.

Flame tilts his head, "is it incest if technically you had legal rights over her growing up?" my eyes widen. What the fuck, that's not true, right?

Dead Shot sighs and shakes his head before hitting all three of us on the back of our heads making us all grunt, "no you dipshit. She's not blood related, and they didn't grow up together, it's all fucking normal, but she is still my daughter and not because I technically brought her up but because she's now Axels old lady." Then he looks at Axel, "if you're about to tell me Daggers insinuation is correct then I'm going to beat your ass."

Flame and I laugh while Axel smirks before getting a small box out of the draw and opens it, my mouth drops open as he states, "actually I was planning on taking her and diamond to look out point where I first took her to convince her to give me another chance after I fucked up with Sugar. I was thinking about putting it in Diamonds collar." I grin fucking wide, happy for my brother. He had no idea Annie even existed until Cammy and Rosie, Annie's Grams, decided to set them up a few months ago. The parentals and her Grams were worried about her safety and Axels because of Grant, Annie's father who was trying to find her which is why no one knew who she was.

I look to Flame, and I sigh. He has confusion and heartbreak shining through his eyes and I shake my head. The fucker needs to catch Star, our club princess who also happens to be the love of his life before she finds someone who will catch her. This whole she's too good for him crap needs to stop before he loses her for good, there's only so much a woman can take watching the man she loves fuck around before she walks away. Axel tilts his head and says,

"Star helped me pick it out."

He looks up at Axel and nods his head while I look at the paperwork. Fuck, I'm going to have to do it. I sigh and stand up from where I've taken a seat and pick up my paperwork that I placed on his desk back up snapping Flame out of his head. They all look at me with raised brows and I shrug, "what, he's going to fucking propose, I'm not stupid enough to get in the way of that. Bull dog is getting everything she ever wanted. A daughter in law who happens to be her daughter in every way except blood, a grandbaby and now a wedding. I value my balls thank you very fucking much." They all burst out in laughter, and I start to head towards the door hoping they don't realize I just don't want any contact with Cammy for a while but with the way Flame tilts his head, I'm guessing he's quickly figured it out, but I give him a small head shake.

Just as I get to the door I hear Dead Shot speak, concern etching his voice and I turn back around with furrowed brows,

"Axel?"

I look at him and see he's gone pale, and I step further back into the room while he answers his phone, putting it on speaker.

"Trigger?" everyone in the room freezes. There would be only one reason he's calling.

Somethings happened to Annalise.

Chapter 4

Melanie

I've just finished getting my coat on when there's a knock on my door and I furrow my brows. Who in the hell would be here at 6:30 in the morning? I check the peek hole and instantly suck in a breath, stepping away from my door after seeing my mother's Hazel eyes. Her black hair is greasy and a mess while her clothes hang off her thin frame and I swallow hard looking around my small all in one, living area, bedroom, and kitchen. It's not much for a newly registered nurse trying to save up to buy a home but it's perfect for me, plus it came furnished and the small bathroom is behind the door.

She knocks again, "I know you're in there Mel's, open the door now."

I flinch at the nickname that my father used to call me. I haven't heard from him since he walked out the front door while I screamed for him at only 4 years old.

I turn and look towards the small window and bite my lip. I'm on the second floor so I know I won't be able to jump through it and its already past the time I need to leave to make it on time for work and I'm in the ER this week.

Shit.

If I go out there she could follow me to work, if I don't I could get a disciplinary.

Double shit.

Just as I'm about to open the door I hear another voice and I tense. WHAT THE FUCK.

"She's obviously not fucking there Beth. Let's just go and try again later before the neighbors call the fucking pigs."

It sounds like Harris, mom's drug dealer and pimp. I furrow my brows as anger grows. She brought her fucking drug dealer to my fucking flat.

"No, I refuse to fucking leave, if she won't give me the money we need then you'll pimp her fucking out like you should have done when she grew fucking tits." My mother, my fucking mother sneers as my eyes widen in shock. She wants to sell me out. SERIOUSLY.

I hear him sigh, "we'll try again later and bring some men with us to grab her. Come on, I've already seen three people looking out of their fucking doors."

I hear her huff as they both walk away but I don't move. I stay here for another twenty minutes until I leave my place feeling fucking shocked. She wants me to be pimped out to pay for her fucking drugs. My minds all over the place and I wonder, what the fuck happened to my mother? She was amazing when I was small but as soon as my dad left she turned into this spiteful, hateful woman. I shake my head and get into my car. It's an old baby blue beetle that I got for a steal a few years ago and I absolutely love it.

I take a deep breath and decide to make a detour on my way to work, grateful for placing one of those ring doorbell cameras to my door even if it did cost me half my paycheck and I head to the police station. I won't let her try to ruin my life like she has hers.

An hour later I quickly head to see the charge nurse Mary and she raises her brow at me for being forty-five minutes late and I give her a small smile, shutting the door to her office and I get right into it,

"My mom is a drug addict and this morning she showed up at my flat with her drug dealer. I didn't open the door but I overheard her telling her drug dealer to pimp me out against my will so she can get her fix. I've been at the police station, it's why I'm late. I did message Dr Thomas because I'm on his service today, but he's said he's running late because of a meeting anyway." I pull the letter from the chief and hand it to her, "this is from the Chief." She gives me wide eyes before rage takes over her features,

"What kind of mother...If I ever see her I swear to God." She takes the letter and I give her a smile, loving her protective nature for me taking over, she looks at me again,

"Are you ok to work? And do we need to inform security?"

I sigh, "I am ok to work. She's not aware that I'm a nurse, she knew I went to college, she just didn't know my major but tell security as a precaution." I hand her the next piece of paper with a printout of my mother from my door this morning with Harris, "this is my mother and her drug dealer, if you give it to security I would appreciate it."

She nods her head, "alright head back to work, come get me if there's any problems." I give her a smile and thank her before heading into the staff room to my locker. I then go and see who needs assistance in the E.R. happy to be back in work and not in my own head.

I don't know how long it's been, but I know I missed lunch with how hectic the E.R is today when my name is shouted from across the room,

"MEL, YOUR WITH ME NOW."

I turn to see what's going on and my eyes widen as a bunch of bikers rush in behind Dr Thomas who is rushing after some colleagues into the triage room. I run after them, the bikers parting ways for me to go through the door. When I enter the triage room I come to a stop with shock.

A young woman is lying on the gurney covered in blood. Her face is black and blue, and nose obviously broken but it's the blood between her legs that's absolutely heartbreaking.

Miscarriage. Fuck.

I snap into it, "what do you need?"

"Central line stat. The patient is Annalise Lawrence, 25 years old and at high risk of paralysis from a previous injury, she is also pregnant, roughly 8 weeks."

I nod to Dr Thomas's order while listening to the details of the patient and get to it while he checks her face then stomach. He looks at me,

"We need an MRI, head CT and OB." I nod and get to the phone. I call OB first and ensure they come now after explaining all the blood. I then call MRI then CT before going back to the patient. I quickly but gently pull her blonde hair to one side, away from her face and I look to the Doctor. He nods, grabbing her arms in case she wakes, and I take a deep breath,

Using an anesthetic spray, I numb the area. She may be unconscious, but I don't want to cause her much more pain, especially if she was awake when this happened to her which I am assuming she was, then I get a speculum and place it in her nose and with a nod to the doctor I realign it, she doesn't move. I quickly pack the nose to catch the blood before I order her iv antibiotics to prevent infection then place an oxygen mask on her face as Dr Thomas starts talking,

"Three ribs are cracked, I don't think they're broken, but the MRI can determine that as well if any more damage is done to her back. She definitely has a concussion so will need to be admitted for a few days at least, where's OB?"

Just as he asks OB comes in, Sarah looks at the patient and she squeezes her eyes shut seeing all the blood.

"she's definitely lost the baby, but she's lost too much blood. Let's give her a scan to make sure the baby has fully been flushed from her body and ensure she doesn't have any internal bleeding."

I swallow hard, pain for this woman shooting through me. Dr

Thomas looks like he's about to cry. He obviously knows her. I walk to her other side and gently wipe her head with a towel, sweat breaking out on her forehead while the doctor gives me a small smile. Sarah performs the scan and confirms the baby didn't survive and is free from her womb.

We couldn't have been in this room for more than ten minutes when the monitor suddenly flat lines and Sarah shouts out,

"WE'RE LOSING HER."

Shit!

We all get into action. I grab the crash cart while the doctor starts CPR. I quickly put the pads on her chest and side before grabbing the paddles, handing them to Sarah.

"CLEAR." She shouts. The machine shocks the patient, and her pulse comes back making us all sigh in relief,

"she's lost too much blood; we need to move her now. Mel can you please inform the family. It's all the bikers out in the waiting room but don't worry they're all friendly I promise, they won't hurt you, Axel is her man."

I nod my head then turn to Sarah,

"how did her womb look?"

It's a question the father may ask so I need to know. She gives me a proud smile for asking before stating,

"it's intact. If she wishes, she should still be able to carry again and to full term."

I nod my head then head towards the waiting room while they take her upstairs when someone grips my arm tightly, digging their fingernails into it. I turn to see Cassidy, the bitchy nurse who thinks she's above all scowling at me. I raise a brow at her,

"Unless you want me to report you to HR for marking my arm, get off me now."

Her eyes widen and she does as I ask while looking at me with hate. I don't know what I did but since I started here, she's had it out for me which is ridiculous when I've barely said two fricking words to her.

"I'll handle the family. You take Mrs. Lars." Then she proceeds to slam a clipboard into my chest while snatching mine and before I can protest, she's already marching into the waiting room. I shake my head. That woman shouldn't even be a nurse, she has no compassion whatsoever.

I go to cubicle four not willing to allow this patient to wait any longer than she's probably already made them wait and announce myself, "knock, knock."

I go in and smile at the elderly couple sitting on the bed.

"Hello, my names Melanie and I've come to take a look at the laceration on your head."

Mr. Lars smiles at me, "well, you're a much nicer nurse than the other." His wife smacks his arm and I giggle before I look at her forehead to see a deep gash there,

"Ouch, how on earth did you manage to do that." I ask as I put my gloves on and start to gently prod around it to ensure there's no nerve damage. She winces so that's good. Mrs. Lars gives a sly smirk to her husband, her brown eyes shine with mischief, and I look at him to see him grinning and my eyes widen,

"I don't want to know do I?"

They both chuckle and when Mrs. Lars states, "deary, were old, not dead. Got to keep the spark in the bedroom alive. Just don't do a 69 on a swing, it's definitely more dangerous than the books say" my face turns beetroot red, and they both laugh at me while I pat my cheeks with the backs of my hands, and they laugh harder while I shake my head at them.

"Alright you two laughing hyenas, I'm going to go and get the kit I need to stitch this up for you." They laugh harder and I smile going to Cassidy's trolly, but the smile soon drops when I open the draws.

I scowl. It's basically empty. That fricking woman I swear.

Sighing, I shake my head before going to the storage cupboard where we keep our kits but end up with more than I bargained for when I get the shock of my life.

Well, no wonder why she wanted to speak to the family.

Cassidy is bent over, nurse dress over her hips, hands gripping the metal shelving unit while a man who must be over 6-foot, hair in a man bun, wearing a tight t-shirt and a leather vest over it, is fucking Cassidy from behind. His jeans are only halfway down his ass as he thrusts into her while he looks my way when I enter and his grey eyes sparkle when he sees me.

"Hey beautiful, what's your name."

I can't help my eyes widening. He's still thrusting into her all while she moans like a fucking porn star and he's…. hitting on me? Are you fucking serious right now. I look around the closet and notice the kit I need on top of a blanket and decide I can grab that too so I can place it on Mrs. Lars' lap. Scowling, I turn to the man with sarcasm dripping in my voice and state, "not hers, please continue" before I grab the blanket and kit I need and walk out without looking back all while my face is red with a blush and my heart is racing.

His voice did something to me, it called to my body and heart like I was meant to belong to him. What the fuck. I shake my head, he's either a player or now with Cassidy so I need to stay clear. I decide to ignore the feelings and go back to the patient.

Ten minutes later I've just finished filling in Mrs. Lars' notes when Cassidy storms over to me and I raise a brow at the scowl on her face,

"The fucking idiot didn't make me cum, you distracted him."

I just snort and shrug, "well maybe if you were doing your job correctly and filled your cart up then I wouldn't had of interrupted your sex fest during rush hour."

Her eyes widen before she clears her throat knowing she fucked up, "the family of the patient I took from you want an update."

I furrow my brows, "but you gave them the update. You took my clipboard."

She swallows hard and I shake my head, slamming her clipboard into her chest, "bed 5 needs an enema." And I head to the waiting room ignoring her gasp. How fricking dare she. She didn't even update the family when they're family member is currently getting an MRI and head CT, that she lost the baby, what an absolute bitch.

Argh.

I take a deep breath trying to control my anger before I enter the waiting room. I look around and make eye contact with a man who is in absolute agony, pain radiates from him, and I know this is her man. I look beside him and see the man from the closet and my cheeks heat, and I swallow hard, not willing for him to see he's gotten a reaction from me, and I make my way to the man who I'm guessing is Axel. The other man grabs his hand and says something before the other men in the room clear their throats before some make their way over to me. They meet me halfway and I fiddle with my fingers, ensuring to keep my eyes connected with the sorrow blue ones.

"Are you Axel?" I ask in a soft voice while someone sighs.

Oh, geez, I'm nervous.

"I am, you have news about my woman?" I give him a gentle smile as my fingers tremble a little, more men have come up and I'm scared, I'm not exactly tall and they all tower over me. Growing up with men coming and going because of my mom has not helped my situation right here at all.

I clear my throat, pain shooting through me having to tell him this, "Dr Thomas asked me to give you an update on Annalise Lawrence." He gives me a gentle smile when another man comes up next to him and smiles at me too. He's full of ink around his neck and hands and I tremble some more. He actually looks like the guy I caught fucking Cassidy, "just tell us sweets, I know we look scary but were not; rip the band aid off." I him a small smile while the guy from the closet growls like a bloody dog but I ignore his weird behavior.

"Ok." I look at Axel again and I know my eyes show compassion because panic enters his eyes and I give him the news he desperately wants.

 "After we got her into her private room, she coded, and her heart stopped beating." The two men who look alike grab a hold of Axel quickly when he goes to collapse to the floor while someone sobs and I swallow hard, "we gave her CPR, managing to get her heart started again." I gently put my hand on his arm, keeping eye contact with him despite feeling several eyes on me, "she had lost a lot of blood and had extensive trauma to her lower stomach and I'm so sorry but after a scan, a heartbeat was not found and her womb was empty, it was determined that she had lost the baby." the men curse while I keep my eyes which I know are starting to tear up on Axels, knowing this has to be harder for him and a few tears fall from his eyes proving my point, he's a biker and he's showing his emotions, making it hard to keep mine at bay. "The good news is that her womb is still intact. No permanent damage was done, she'll still be able to carry more children if she chooses to do so in the future." He closes his eyes as more tears fall and I give his arm a squeeze before letting him go. He opens his eyes when I talk again, "Dr Thomas believes her ribs are only cracked but he wants to make sure. About half an hour ago she was taken for an MRI scan to determine his diagnosis but to also check her spine, we need to ensure she hasn't received more damage to her back due to her previous injuries and it'll also show any internal bleeding. He is also taking her for a head CT as a precaution due to the extensive injuries to her face and nose, her head has received some trauma, so we want to ensure she has no bleed on the brain. She does have a concussion and will need monitoring for a few nights. Dr Thomas will keep her admitted for the duration."

He nods and rasps, "thank you." I nod back before he asks, "is she awake? I mean does she know about our…." He's unable to finish his sentence but I smile gently at him, "she hasn't woken since being admitted, she doesn't know as of yet that we're aware of. During the incident she may had already noticed, I'm just not sure how much of awake she was during her trauma." I squeeze his arm again before turning to leave when someone clears their throat and Axel asks in a rasp, "what's your name?"

I turn and give him a gentle smile, "Melanie Wilson. If I hear anything else, I'll come to you straight away but otherwise if you need anything I'll be around this area." He nods again thanking me and I give him a smile, ignoring everyone else before walking out the door with my heart beating fast in my chest while some of my tears fall for the heartbreak this couple are facing and I wipe them away quickly, damning my empathy for others.

Chapter 5

Dagger

I watch the woman I want more than life itself, who I feel an instant connection with, walk out without a backward glance and I curse. How could I be so fucking stupid to hit on her while fucking that other bitch.

Fuck.

"Axel?" I hear Star whisper and I turn to see she's holding his hand while he stares after my nurse, his face full of pain and I lose the air in my lungs.

"My baby's dead." I slowly close my eyes as his tears fall, "how am I supposed to tell her."

I mutter, "fuck," hating the pain in his voice and grip the back of his neck, pulling him to me, ignoring the feeling of being dirty instantly by his touch while Star sobs.

Dead Shot stands next to him on his other side gripping his shoulder with tears in his eyes and rasps, "you hold her close. She's going to struggle for a while son, she'll need you now more than ever and you don't fucking let her push you away. We both know she will, she'll blame herself, but you don't let up, give her some space for a few days but then go all fucking in." I feel him nod against me and I squeeze him tighter to me before Dead Shot and Star help me move him over to a seat. I sit right next to him with my arm over his shoulder gripping him tightly to me, the feeling of being dirty intensifying but I push it down for my pres, my brother, my best friend.

The more his body shakes with silent tears the more my anger grows, I can't fucking believe that bastard kicked her baby out of her. The fucker is a dead man!

I don't know how long we sit here but Axel's tears had just dried up when Cammy comes in looking distraught.

Fuck.

I go to stand knowing it's still too raw to be near her when Axel shakes his head at me, "I know momma said some shit and she will be punished for it but please, don't leave me alone with her right now. She'll try and take over and I can't, I can't." He can't finish his sentence, but I understand, he can't fight her right now. I nod and stay where I'm at as she rushes over, her eyes watery,

"Any news?"

I clear my throat but don't look up. I don't want to talk to her, but I know Axe can't speak right now, his voice is already scratchy from his tears,

"She's having an MRI and head CT. Doc believes she has a concussion and a few cracked ribs. She was lucky."

She lets out a sob, "and the baby?"

I sigh and shake my head just as Dead Shot walks in. He sees his wife and guilt shines his eyes when he sees I'm the one having to talk to her for my friend, my president.

She lets out a wail making Axel flinch and I grind my jaw. I understand she's upset she lost her grandchild, but Annalise had just lived through her ordeal, most likely feeling the blood, her baby leave her body and Axel has lost his child. I shake my head and look Dead Shot in his eyes tilting my head to his son and understanding shines through his eyes and he takes his wife's arm, "baby, let's go outside, Axel doesn't need this right now." Axel flinches some more while Cammy's eyes widen,

"he's my son, he needs me-me." she's still sobbing.

"No Cam, he doesn't, not when your like this."

Her eyes widen some more at her husband's words, and she clears her throat, nodding her head and leaves the waiting room and we all sigh in relief while Axel physically relaxes against me.

Not even ten minutes later Melanie returns making my breathing increase and my heart to jump in my chest. Fuck she's beautiful. Her nurses dress hugs her figure nicely showing of the curve of her hips while her brown curly hair up in a messy bun shows off her cheek bones. Her gorgeous blue eyes shine with sorrow for my friend, and she heads straight towards him, not looking in my direction once which pisses me the fuck off but also makes me proud that her focus is her patient and their family.

She kneels down and places one hand on Axels and I instantly feel pissed at my brother. ***Don't kill my friend, don't kill my brother, don't kill my president.*** I chant in my head over and over.

Fuck, I want to kill him.

He shoots his head up and she gives him a gentle smile and the killing chants start again. Fuck sake!

Dead Shot and Cammy enter as she starts to speak in a gentle voice, "Dr Thomas asked me to come and get you. Annalise is back from her scans, and it's determined she has no internal bleeding. She's still unconscious but you can sit with her, but only you unfortunately for now though."

A few tears fall from his eyes, and he nods his head. She gives him another gentle smile and squeezes his hand before standing up while I swallow a growl making Axel side eye me with a raised brow and I clear my throat. Just as he stands to follow Melanie, Cammy oversteps a fucking gain, and I can feel the tick in my jaw I'm that pissed.

"I'm her mother, I'll be going in first, Axel can see her once I have. I need to see my baby; I need to make sure she's ok."

Dead Shots eyes widen, shocked at his wife's audacity, and I growl while Axel sighs, dropping his chin to his chest shaking his head knowing he's going to have to have that fight because like hell would he let her in to see his woman first. I understand she's a mother figure to Annalise, but Axel is her man, he's getting ready to propose and they've just lost their baby, Cammy is overstepping again. Axel's eyes widen though when Melanie steps in front of him and crosses her arms over her chest with anger flashing in her eyes while she raises a brow at Cammy,

"Are you her next of kin?"

Cammy's eyes widen, and she gets in Melanie's face. Rage takes over my body and I go to take a step between them, but Axel grabs my arm, stopping me from intervening. I go to snap at him, but he looks at me with pride and I look back to see the scene in front of me. Melanie hasn't deterred or backed down, she's taking on the bulldog,

"On her medical records it states a Logan Ramirez is her next of kin, then a Rosie Lawrence and that her paternal mother is deceased. And I'm guessing you are not in your 80's, nor are you male and you haven't risen from the dead so you will not be going in to see her first. Dr Thomas has requested Axel, who I am guessing is Logan Ramirez and that who's going in first and for however long he feels comfortable for. They've just lost their baby, so I'm sorry but you do not come first in this situation. Annalise and Axel do."

Cammy's nose flares while the brothers smirk liking her sass and spunk, especially Stormy and Ink who keep looking towards me with wide grins and I give them a subtle middle finger making them snort. The woman's taken on the bulldog, she has some brass balls and gained the brother's respect.

"How dare you speak to me like this, I'm going to report you to your supervisor."

I go to take a step towards them again not liking Cammy's fucking attitude but Axel's grip on my arm tightens and he shakes head before nodding it towards Melanie again who has a smirk on her face and I grin at her next words,

"Go right ahead. Her office is on the 3rd floor, door 476. Her name is Mary Sanders. Please ensure you have proof of paternity or kinship before you waste her time." Then she looks at Axel, "let me take you to your woman." Her eyes are gentle, and he nods, ignoring his momma while his dad smirks. I grin wider when she side eyes me causing her to blush while Axel raises a brow at me giving me a subtle half smile before following her out of the dull white waiting area.

Once they leave Dead Shot turns to his wife with a scowl his smirk well and truly gone, "you go anywhere near that office then I'll be staying in the clubhouse until the foreseeable future. How fucking dare you try and push our son, who has just found his woman beaten and bloody, seeing that she's lost their baby aside like that. I have never been more disappointed in you today than I ever have." Cammy's eyes widen as he turns towards Flame who has a sobbing Star in his arms. Her and Annalise have been close for a few years, she's been teaching her how to cook and their friendship has grown, she's struggling just as much as Axel.

Cammy looks at me and I scowl at her shaking my head in disappointment before taking a seat, waiting for Axel to return as she storms off, face red with anger and embarrassment. Not even five minutes later Stormy sits next to me, but I don't look at him. I stay in my relaxed position, my back leaning against the chair with my legs stretched out and my arms crossed over my chest when I feel anything but relaxed.

"What did Cammy say to piss you off this badly? You've

always looked up to her."

I snort, of course he's here for them, "called my momma a whore." I look at him with a raised brow, "and we both know that's bullshit, don't we Stormy." He flinches at me calling him his road name. He does every time, but I guess he can thank his wife for that. I look forward again hoping he'd fuck off, but he doesn't,

"Son, when are you going to get over this whole woe is me act you've got going on? Was I hard on you growing up? Fuck yes I was but you made Leslie's life hell and she didn't deserve it son, I mean hell, she took you in when you were only a new born, she's raised you as her own."

I just laugh causing a few brothers to look our way with furrowed brows and I lean towards him and get in his face, "hard on me? you nearly broke my fucking jaw when I was 9 all because Leslie said I broke the tv in anger. Do me a favor Stormy, go ask Ink what really happened to that tv and ask him where I actually was." Then I get up and walk out of the room ignoring his furrowed look of confusion.

I stand outside, taking a deep breath when I hear a sniffle and I sigh, not wanting to deal with an upset woman right now. I go to ignore it, but instincts are telling me to take a look and I'm fucking glad I did. When I get round the corner and see Melanie wiping a tear, something pulls in my gut, and I walk over to her.

She quickly wipes her face when she sees me walking towards her and I lean against the wall, crossing my arms over my chest, "you ok?" I know she's not, why the fuck did I just ask that.

Fuck. What am I a fucking idiot. Shit.

She nods, "sometimes, it gets hard. Your friend seems like a nice guy and this woman, his woman has had her baby kicked out of her. I mean, what evil would do something like that." She shakes her head and wipes some more tears, "it's just hard sometimes." I give her a small smile.

Fuck.

I love how she cares. Not like fake cares but actually cares, it's fucking refreshing.

I clear my throat, "you did good. Despite having several big bikers staring at you. You kept Axel your main focus and when Cammy over fucking stepped, not thinking of her blood son, you did. You put him first." She gives me a small smile and my heart fucking melts. Fuck she's got a beautiful smile.

I stand, feeling bold before I bend and gently kiss her forehead causing her to suck in a breath and I smirk. Good to know I'm not the only one affected. I gently wipe away another tear and fuck, her skin feels so soft. I give her a smile before I turn and leave, "I'll be seeing you Melanie." I hear her gasp when I say her name and I smirk again.

Hook, line, and fucking sinker. She's mine!

As I get round the corner I see Cammy standing by the doors with tears falling down her cheeks and she looks at me, "I didn't put my son first." I just shake my head and keep walking while I say over my shoulder, "you've got a habit of overstepping lately Cammy" before I head into the hospital to see if Axel has been out yet.

Dagger: An MC Romance

Chapter 6

Melanie

I sigh before I scrub my hand down my face. I look around the corner one more time and curse inwardly. I have to go check on Annalise Lawrence but the guy who I caught fucking Cassidy is currently standing near the nurses desk, which is right near her room, talking to Sarah the OB who is supposed to be happily married. I tilt my head and raise a brow while watching her touch his arm, twirl her mousy brown hair, and giggle all while Cassidy stands back with a scowl on her face.

I snort.

Ok, time to pull my big girl panties up and just go see my patient.

Right. My patient who has gone mute.

Fuck.

I take a deep breath and walk out from where I was hiding. I was planning on just walking by hoping they don't notice me because of their deep flirting, but Sarah decides different.

Damn it.

"Oh, Melanie, just the nurse I was looking for." I stop by her and give her a smile, ignoring the man next to her. She side eyes him, her brown eyes sparkling, and I try not to smirk as she slowly moves her ring around like that'll hide the fact she's married, poor Peter he deserves better.

"What can I do for you Sarah?" I ask nicely and she looks back to me clearing her throat, probably hoping I didn't just catch her eyeing someone who isn't her husband.

"I've left all of Ms. Lawrences notes on the desk for you. She's officially discharged from my services."

I nod, "ok I'll make sure to log it all. Did you do the second scan?"

She smiles wide at my question; she loves it when I ask the right questions instead of waiting for the patient to ask me then go and find the doctor in charge who could be busy with another patient. I find out first then relay the message along.

"Yes, I did, and no abnormalities have appeared. I have explained it to her but unfortunately she's still not communicating verbally."

I give her a smile and thank her before I walk around the man and head into my patient's room, completely ignoring him while feeling his eyes on my back making my body tingle, just remembering the feel of his warm lips on my forehead makes my while body set a light. Shit, I really need to stay clear of him. I knock on the door and enter pushing the gorgeous man with beautiful grey eyes out of my mind.

Annalise doesn't look up from her stomach and my heart breaks for her. "Good morning Annalise. I'm just going to do some of your observations." She nods but still doesn't look up and my gut tugs. I start checking her blood pressure then pulse before checking over her injuries incision sights, "your looking good Annalise, a few days and you'll be able to go home." I look at her, but she doesn't react, and I sigh before tilting my head and smile a little, wondering if this would snap her out of it, I mean it's worth a try right? even though it's not professional?

I think fuck it before I start to fill in her notes and talk, "did you know Annalise a few days ago when you were brought in, another nurse who for some strange reason doesn't like me decided she had to tell your family an update about your condition all because one of the men had caught her eye. I ended up walking in on them in a storage room and to make it worse, the man decided to hit on me while still thrusting into the nurse, I mean who does that? And the nurse he was with now blames me as to why he didn't finish. Apparently I interrupted them, and he lost his performance." I shake my head with a chuckle and look at her but nothing. Not a smile or a smirk or even a flinch.

Damn.

I sigh again and squeeze her hand, "I'll come by again in a little while before I head home after hand over."

I turn to leave before looking at her one more time. When I

get to the nurses desk Dr Thomas is there with the man, but I ignore him again and grab Annalise's discharge notes from OB before placing them in her folder, "How's Annie this morning Melanie?" I look up to see both men standing in front of me and in a partial eye I can see Cassidy glaring at me just like she was at Sarah. It's like she thinks he's hers. I sigh,

"Her observations are good. OB has already discharged her; her scan came back normal. A few days and she should be ok to go home."

Dr Thomas smiles a little, "has she spoke?"

I give him a sad smile back, "unfortunately not, I tried telling her a funny story and I didn't even get a flicker from her." He nods while the guy sighs, running a hand through his hair, "Doc how long is this going to go on for? I mean, can't we try and snap her out of it? Axel is falling apart."

Damn, why does his voice have to sound so deep and mysterious for.

"Brother, she's been through a major trauma, it'll take her time. She'll talk when she's ready." The guy shakes his head looking frustrated and I understand he's worried, but he can't rush her, he needs to understand where she's coming from and what guilt she probably feels for not saving her unborn child. If they force her before she's ready they could lose her mentally.

I clear my throat to get his attention and both men look at me. I give him a small smile before stating,

"Annalise doesn't look up from her stomach. She doesn't speak or show any emotions." Dr Thomas looks at me with a raised brow clearly wondering where I'm going with this while the guy looks at me intently, those grey eyes burning into my soul, "she's showing signs of PTSD and survivor's guilt. She unfortunately was clearly awake during her trauma and had to watch her baby leave her body not able to do anything to save it, it's why she keeps staring at her stomach. She feels guilty and most likely blames herself. Her reaction right now is her brain and body's way of helping her through her traumatic experience, but, saying that, when she does speak and she will in time, she'll most likely fall, and she'll need all the help she can get." Dr Thomas nods his head in agreement while pride shines through his eyes as well as determination, but I just shake my head at him. Apparently, I should have gone for my M.D instead of my nursing degree but I prefer being a nurse, I like the connection you have with the patient.

I clear my throat again, looking back at the beautiful man in front of me, "I understand your frustrated and I understand Axel is struggling but if you push her before she's ready then you'll all most likely lose her mentally. She does just need time for her mind to process what's happened to her and what she's lost and when she's discharged we'll ensure she has a counsellor on speed dial for her and I'm sure you'll all rally around her. Just give her the time and space she'll need before she comes back to you all."

He nods his head, his gorgeous eyes showing gratitude and something else that I can't name and goes to speak but I cut him off, I can feel Cassidy glaring at me hard, and I can't be assed with their relationship drama, plus his intense stare is causing all sorts of tingles in my body so I need to get out of here.

"I've got to go finish my rounds before hand over." Then I turn to the Doctor, "I'll see you tomorrow Dr Thomas." He nods and give me a smile before smirking at the guy.

Huh, weird.

I shake my head and go towards another patient's room to finish the rest of my shift.

A few days later, I'm walking into Annalise's room to give her medication to her before she leaves, and I sigh when I see it's empty. I was just in here ten minutes ago and she nodded that she'd wait. Guess I should have known differently. Shaking my head, I walk out of her room and go to the nurse's desk where Meghan's just putting some paperwork down, she looks up with a scowl, "how in the hell do you work alongside Cassidy. I've just left an uncontrollable patient."

My eyes widen, "what she do this time?"

Meghan shakes her head, "hit on her husband right in front of her. My patient has cancer, she no longer has her hair, and she had the nerve to comment on it."

I snort out a laugh, "sounds about right. Did I tell you that I walked into the storage room to see her bent over while a biker was ramming her from behind?"

Her eyes widen in shock, and I nod, "yeah. Dr Thomas asked me to inform the patient's family about her condition and Cassidy snatched my clipboard before shoving hers into my chest. Turns out she noticed the man when he came in and she didn't even give the patients family an update, I had to still go in there to inform them."

"You have got to be shitting me?"

I shake my head, "nope, and then she had the gall to blame me as to why she never got off. Apparently I interrupted them, and he couldn't finish. Yet, if her cart was full like it was supposed to be then she would have gotten off."

Meghan bursts out in laughter while I grin shaking my head. Then I sigh and pick up Annalise's notes, "Annalise Lawrence discharged herself but didn't wait around for her medication."

Meghan sighs and compassion shines through her eyes, "that poor woman. I cannot imagine going through something like that. My girl, she's my whole world," I nod in agreement and give her a sad smile, "I'm going to finish my rounds and try to clear up Cassidy's mess. See you at dinner in the dining hall?"

I smile and nod before she walks away.

I try to call Annalise several times but there's no answer and I sigh before dialing Axel's number, it rings three times before he answers.

"This is Axel."

I clear my throat,

"Hi Axel, its Melanie Wilson, I'm calling because even though Annalise checked herself out this morning, she left her medication. I asked if she'd wait the ten minutes until I had the script ready for her and she nodded but when I got back to her room she was already gone, I tried calling her mobile, but it just rings out."

Guilt builds in my chest because I know he thought he was picking her up this afternoon, but I think she needs to be alone for a little while. She needs to go through this in order to help Axel through it.

Axel clears his throat,

"Her mobile is at her flat, we found it the day she went missing so she hasn't got it on her, one of the brothers will pick her medication up, is that ok Melanie?" The poor man sounds devastated. Then I realize what he just asked. Shit. I really don't want to see that man again. He makes me feel things I haven't before which sucks because he's clearly a man whore. I can feel myself gravitating to him every time I see him, like he knows trauma and pain just like me but again, he's a man whore and he has heart breaker written all over him.

Damn it!

"Yes, that's not a problem but uh, um Axel, can you ensure its not the brother I caught in a storage room please."

He lets out a snort then tries to cover it up by clearing his throat and I roll my eyes, men!

"I'll try, thanks again Melanie."

I hear him chuckle when he hangs up and I slowly close my eyes, shit! When I open them again, I see Cassidy walking towards me and I look at Annalise's medication, then back towards Cassidy and I smile. Wide. A plan forming.

"Cassidy?"

She looks up but sneers at me when she sees its me who called her name, "whatever it is I haven't got time to do it, it's now my break time."

I smile and shrug, acting all innocent, "huh, oh ok. I guess I could ask another nurse to hand Annalise's medication over to one of the brothers that's coming to pick it up." I furrow my brows like I'm trying to remember something, really playing it before I click my fingers and raise my brows and point at her, ", you know him. It's the guy you were with, you know…"

She goes from bored to excited in like 0.2 seconds. Hook, line, and sinker. "Huh, well, I mean, if you have something you need to do then I guess I can hang here for my break." I give her my best relieved expression. Fuck she's gullible.

"Are you sure? I know how busy we've been, and everyone needs a decent break." Even though she's barely done fuck all today except for cause shit for Meghan's patients. She nods and I thank her profusely, handing her the medication all while she looks at me like I'm the idiot and she played me.

Ha. If only she knew!

A few hours later and I'm finally heading home. Cassidy spent the rest of the shift with a permanent scowl so I'm guessing she didn't get her re-do but I did manage to dodge the guy because of course he's the one who showed up.

My heart flutters at the thought of him refusing her and I ignore my reaction to that, I mean, I don't even know his name!

I yawn while walking towards my door after leaving the

stairwell when I feel something hard hit me on the back of my head from behind. I grunt and fall to the floor only for someone to grab a hold of my hair tightly before putting their hand over my mouth. My mother comes into view, eyes full of anger.

Fuck.

She gets in my face, "ever hear the expression 'snitches gets stitches'? Thanks to you Harris is sitting in jail because his name red flagged. I just lost my connection to my drugs you little bitch and I'm now fucking wanted." She punches me hard in my face before whoever is holding my hair shoves my head forward and I end up headbutting the floor. I hear a crunch as immense pain shoots through my face before someone smacks a hard object onto my back then kicks me hard in my side, causing me to roll slightly with a scream before they kick me again. My mom gets down in my face again as my vision blurs, blackness wanting to take over, "don't disappear you little disappointment. I have several men who want you for a night."

She spits in my face before leaving with whoever was with her cackling and I cough. Pain shoots through me making me groan and I try to crawl towards my door before pulling myself up. Dizziness fills me and I struggle to stay on my feet, my eyes wanting to close. I quickly unlock my door and shuffle inside before bolting it shut. I manage to get to my brown fabric sofa before I collapse, and everything goes black.

Chapter 7

Dagger – 2 weeks later

Me – your missed sweetheart, your man needs you, please message him back. The club wants their queen back.

I'm sitting at the bar in the clubhouse tapping my finger on the solid wood looking at the text I've just sent to Annalise feeling fucking frustrated. Two weeks. That's how long it's been since Axel has heard from her and he's struggling and the more he struggles the angrier Cammy becomes. I sigh, two weeks is also the last time I saw Melanie. I've gone to the hospital a few times and apparently she's been on sick leave. I've managed to get her address from Flame much to Doc's dismay, but she hasn't fucking left her apartment or answered her door when I've knocked.

I take the shot of whiskey that the prospect just dropped down for me in one gulp before the clubhouse main doors open and Stormy walks in. As soon as he sees me he makes a beeline towards me and I grunt not in the fucking mood for this, I get up and walk out of the common room,

"TRAVIS."

I ignore him and go to my office, ensuring I lock the fucking door. I hear a bang from the common room, but I just shrug before sitting at my desk starting the inventory for Untamed Girls needing a fucking break from this place.

A few hours pass by when someone tries to open my door, "what the fuck? Dagger open up." I furrow my brows at Axels voice which is laced with fury, and I quickly get up and open it.

He looks pissed as he barges past me,

"brother? Is Annalise ok?"

He just chuckles darkly, "I haven't even had a chance to see her yet. Fuck brother." He breathes deep, linking his fingers behind his head before he rasps, "two weeks ago Flame decided to go off with Ginger on his friend date with Star." I scowl leaning back against my desk. What a fucking idiot, seriously, how many times is he going to hurt that girl. I shake my head as he continues before fury fills me, "She went to the toilet because she started to cry but she didn't make it there, instead she was dragged outside to the alleyway where Hairy, the Devil's VP who also happened to be Killers cousin, anally raped her in front of the camera so Flame could see."

I stand again, my eyes full of terror and pain for our club princess. Fuck no. I rasp as tears fill my eyes, "where is she?"

He shakes his head, his own eyes shining, "she's gone

brother. She gave Flame her virginity last night as a goodbye and a fuck you to him and left early this morning. We've just spent a few hours on the highway trying to find her, but she's gone."

My tears fall and I quickly wipe them, and I question using our club brothers birth name, "Zayne?"

He shakes his head, "Slicer, Dad and Stormy had to restrain him, he's in the basement. When we got back, he started punching the shit out of the wall just as Stormy slammed out of the common room."

I nod, ignoring the shit about Stormy because I just can't with him. Since I returned 5 years ago he's been more persistent to get me to talk to him, yet when I fucking needed him when I was younger, he took her side, still does. I walk out of my office with Axel on my heels knowing I'm the one he'll listen to before Clitter tries to intercept me as we walk through the common room, but I ignore her making her huff before I get to the basement stairs, going down them.

I open the door to see our brother chained to a chair while Dead Shot, Slicer and Stormy are leaning against the wall with pain in their eyes. I ignore them and walk over to Flame. His hairs a mess, knuckles are bleeding, and his face is covered in his tears as guilt shines through his eyes. I kneel in front of him. He doesn't look up, so I grab his cheeks, hard.

"You fucked up. You did. Badly."

He closes his eyes as more tears fall but I just squeeze his cheeks making him look at me, "you love her. You have for as long as I can remember. This whole 'she's too good and deserves better' bullshit needs to stop, and it needs to stop now. Yes, you fucked up, big time. But what you going to do about it Zayne? You going to kick off and hurt yourself or are you going to finally fucking grow a pair and go get your girl?"

He shakes his head before rasping, "she's gone brother."

I nod, "then use your big fucking brain and go find her."

He doesn't break eye contact with me, and I see his determination start to come through and I smile as he starts to nod. I undo his chains before I grip his shoulder, "go find your girl and bring our princess back home even if it takes you months brother." He nods and rushes out of the basement with Slicer on his heals to help where needed, and I look at the other men, "Axel go bring our first lady home and finally fucking show her that house. When you come back to the clubhouse, I expect to see that fucking ring on her finger." He grins and I pat him on the back while Dead Shot and Stormy chuckle before I turn and leave the basement while mumbling, "I've got a fucking nurse to go see."

Twenty minutes later I'm outside of her flat block again sitting astride my Harley. It's not the safest of buildings but at least it's in a safe part of town. I nod to myself determined to get her to open the fucking door and start to get off my bike when the building door opens and what do you know, my soon-to-be old lady walks out, and I grin like a fucking loon before I sit back down on my bike and cross my arms over my chest. Fuck she's beautiful and so goddamn precious. She's in a plain white t-shirt and a pair of jeans that hug her ass nicely while her hair is fucking down. It goes to the middle of her back and is curly as fuck.

Fuck me I want to wrap her brown locks in a fist.

Fuck.

She starts to walk towards her car which I'm parked right next to, and I grin wider. When she notices my figure she tenses but as soon as we make eye contact she relaxes while my whole body tightens and rage flows through me. I jump off my bike and stalk towards her, meeting her half way before I cup her cheek with my right hand while my left moves her hair out if her face which is so fucking soft.

Her nose is a little bit bruised with some swelling which had clearly been broken recently and her lip is cut.

"Who do I need to kill precious?"

Her eyes widen before she clears her throat, "me I guess, seems as I lost my footing on the concrete stairs."

I raise a brow,

She's lying. Her fingers are twitchy, and she won't meet my eyes. I nod like I believe her because at this moment I don't have a leg to stand on with her, but I will be getting Flame on it.

"What are you doing here?"

I grin at her, "I've come to see if you'll go out on date with me this weekend."

Her cheeks blush making me smile which soon drops when she shakes her head, "I'm sorry but I can't, plus I don't share." Then she shrugs stepping back from my touch before walking the rest of her way to her old beetle. I quickly rush after her and grab her door before she can close it making her jump before I kneel.

I sigh, "I know how we met didn't exactly paint me in a good light. I fucked up, I know this but all I'm asking for is one date, that's it and if you don't have a good time then I'll walk away."

She tilts her head a little, assessing me and I give her a small smile, "just one date Melanie."

She looks at war. I can see in her eyes she wants to try this with me, that she feels this, but she's scared, and I get that. She clears her throat and looks forward for a second before looking back at me, "I'm sorry, I just can't. You have heart break written all over you, I'm sorry."

I sigh as she leans forward and places a gentle kiss to my cheek before putting her seatbelt on. I nod and stand before leaning towards her, "I'm not giving up Melanie. I mean it, I know you feel this baby."

She gives me sad eyes before I shut her door and I watch her drive away. It doesn't matter how much she tries to push me away; I'll just pull her harder. I know she feels this between us, so she'll give, sooner or later. I grin before getting back on my bike with determination heading back to the clubhouse.

When I walk through the doors, I see Ink sitting at the bar frowning and I walk over to him. I pat him on the back before taking a seat then nodding to the prospect for a beer before turning back to him, "what's up brother?"

He shakes his head, "when you first saw the nurse, how did, I mean, when did. Fuck." He runs a hand through his hair in frustration before looking at me, "how did you know she was the one." Both my brows shoot high into my hairline, and I bite my bottom lip to stop the laughter from coming out and he growls, about to get up, "fuck it, never mind."

I laugh and quickly grab his arm, pulling him back down, "I'm sorry ok, sorry. I just knew. I felt it in my gut, it was like everything stood still and she was all I could see."

"Fuck" Ink bangs his head on the bar,

"Alright brother. What happened?"

He sighs and sits back up, "I was at the bar hoping to score some new pussy when this beautiful vision walked through the door, fuck brother, I felt like someone punched me in my fucking gut, like instantly I knew she was meant to be mine."

I snort and nod my head, "yep, that sounds about right brother."

He growls in frustration. "I hit on her, but she fucking turned me down, said she wasn't interested but I could see the spark in her eyes when she looked at me." He runs his hands through his hair again, "she's Leah's roommate and apparently kind of seeing someone. A banker or some shit. Damn it." He bangs his head on the bar again and I pat his back chuckling,

"don't give up brother, kind of seeing isn't actually seeing. Persevere and all that fucking shit." He sits up again and nods his head before he looks at me and tilts his head, "why did dad ask me what happened to the tv when I was 8?"

I snort at his conversation change and shrug, "don't know, why what did you tell him?"

"Trav, don't give me that shit. Why in the fuck is he asking me shit from years ago?" his eyes are serious, and I nod knowing he needs to know. As long as he doesn't know everything then it'll be all good. Ink doesn't need to know his momma's an abuser. I clear my throat, "Stormy nearly broke my jaw for it."

His eyes widen in shock, "but I was the one who fucking did it, momma pissed me off and I pushed the tv over, you weren't even fucking home, you were at homework club. What the fuck?" I just shrug before I pat his back again and get up, "don't worry about it brother, it's in the past. I'll see you later." I go to walk towards the door when I hear him call for me again and I turn slightly, "how many other times were you punished for my wrong doings?" his eyes are serious while realization and concern shines through them, but I just give him a smile before continuing down the hallway to my office to start a thorough search of my girl, "like I said brother, it's in the past."

A couple of days later I'm sitting outside of the hospital with Melanie scowling at me from one of the windows when my phone pings from Axel,

Axel- stop stalking the nurse and meet me at the courthouse in an hour, don't tell anyone and call the judge, tell him to expect us.

My brows hit my hairline before I message him back,

Me – ok, it's not fucking stalking when she knows I'm here and I know she knows because of the fucking glares she keeps sending me. I'll see you in an hour.

I sigh, putting my phone away before I look up at the window one more time to see she's still there before starting my bike up. I nod, determined to see her tomorrow and get my fucking date and rev my girl before heading towards the courthouse.

Time's up Melanie.

Chapter 8

Melanie

I walk out of Mr. Samuels room and sigh. Pain echoes through my body for the sweet man. He hasn't gained consciousness in 3 weeks and Dr Thomas has said it's only a matter of time. He's deteriorating every day. This is part of my job I really hate, especially when he treated me like family.

I go to the nurse's desk placing his notes in the locked desk draw when a shadow covers me, and I look up to see a scowling Cassidy. Fuck, I really cannot be bothered with her today, especially after watching Samuel for a little while.

"Why has my man been stalking the hospital asking for you?" Her eyes are full of anger, and she's crossed her arms over her chest trying to intimidate me even though she looks like a plastic barbie, right down to her bright blonde hair. I just raise a brow at her not affected at all, I mean come on, I just had two weeks sick leave after my mother had me beaten up. The police are currently searching for her and apparently the man who was with her turned out to be Harris's cousin Marvin, he's already been arrested and charged but has no idea where abouts mom has disappeared too. Probably hiding in her little hole.

"Ok, one, I have no idea who your man is and two, last time I checked no one's stalking me." ok the last one was a lie, the guy whose name I still don't know, who I'm guessing she thinks is her man, has been to my apartment quite a bit in the past few weeks sitting on his bike and as well as sitting out in the parking lot here too. I should probably report him, but I don't know why whenever he's near I feel safe and the thought of him not around makes me want to be sick which is ridiculous, I still don't know his flipping name, plus I can't go there. No matter how much I would love to.

Like I said to him a few days ago, it's not going to happen. He would chew me up and swallow me fricking hole, I just know it.

I know my body lights up when he's around and I know he makes my heart race and that when our eyes connect it's like the whole world has disappeared and that I can feel his darkness and hidden pain as it connects with mine but he's not a one-woman man and he does have heart break all over him plus he slept with her so he can't exactly have good instincts because Cassidy has psycho written all over her.

I stand while she narrows her eyes at me and I try to distract her, "don't you have a break coming up now?" She looks at her watch and frowns before she nods her head at me and leaves while I let out a breath. Now don't get me wrong I love my job I do, but I hate having to work with her, she thinks she's above her job and if that was the case then maybe she should have gotten her M.D instead of her nursing degree.

I shake my head and start to walk towards a patients room who has colon cancer when I bump into a hard body making me gasp. I nearly fall onto my ass when two strong hands grab a hold of my upper arms, the touch setting my body a light and tingles run through me. I look up to see the gorgeous traumatic filled grey eyes that have filled my brain for weeks now. I clear my throat and step back out of his grip, and he smiles at me, and I suddenly become flustered as a blush coats my cheeks.

"Hi you." Hi you, hi you? Did I seriously just say hi you? Shit. He smirks at me, and I scowl at him making him bite his bottom lip to stop his chuckle coming out loving that he's flustered me.

Fuck, why does he have to look sexy when he bites his lip?

I raise a brow at him, and he clears his throat, "sorry" I nod knowing he's full of shit and he just grins. Damn, that's a nice grin, like really nice. His whole face lights up. Shit, I shake out of my thoughts,

"What can I do for you?" ok, know what he wants but I just, fuck, he's got me flustered.

I just don't think it's a good idea.

"you know what I want Precious."

I bite my bottom lip at his nickname for me just as Cassidy comes round the corner. Crap, so much for her break.

She comes to a halt looking between us before narrowing her

eyes at me then saunters over to the man. She drags her nails down his arm, and he shivers removing her touch instantly. My eyebrows hit my hairline in shock before I tilt my head, that wasn't a shiver of delight, it was one of disgust. He steps away from her and looks at her with a furrowed brow,

"Can I help you?"

My brows shoot high into my hairline again hearing the coldness in his voice and she steps back a bit before she crosses her arms over her chest and juts her hip out, "you owe me an orgasm and a date."

He just snorts while I bit my lip to stop my laughter, "no I really don't. You were never going to get one to begin with. You took over another nurse's job just because you wanted to fuck me and you didn't even update my pres, my best friend on the condition of his woman who had just lost their baby after being attacked. Now we don't hit woman, but I know a whore when I see one and I knew one way to fucking punish you. And a date, keep fucking wishing, now do me a favor and piss off."

My mouth drops open while Cassidy gets redder in the face. Just as she's about to scream Dr Thomas comes into view bringing me out of my shocked state, "problem?" He's looking at Cassidy and I clear my throat trying my hardest not to laugh. She just growls and walks off, shooting daggers at the man, thankfully not looking my way. "Huh, obviously not. Brother, Melanie." He says as he looks at us both then he turns, walking away while whistling. I blink a couple of times before I look towards the man. He's staring at his arm again where Cassidy touched him, and I furrow my brows. I move a bit closer to him and touch where she did making him look at me and his brows furrow, I use my other hand and trace over his eye brows, why, I don't know, it literally just feels natural. His brows relax and a smile shines when I question, "so, you were talking about a date that you so badly want?"

He chuckles, "you finally ready to give in?"

I shake my head and step back a bit, removing my hand from his arm making him look at it again in confusion. Hmm. This man is a mystery.

I sigh, "I don't even know your name."

His head shoots up to look at me in surprise before he lets out a laugh when he realizes he never actually gave it to me, "my road name is Dagger, but you can call me Travis." He holds his hand out for me to shake it and I chuckle, placing mine in his feeling tingles going through my hand. He pulls me towards him so we're almost touching, "one date Melanie, just one, what can you lose? You hate it then we remain friends."

I look deep into those troubled eyes which hold so much hope and I sigh, "Christ, Cassidy is going to make my life hell for this. One date." He grins wide, "but, you even look at another woman and it's bye-bye, got it."

I say it sternly, he needs to know other women won't work with me. He nods before he leans forward and kisses my forehead, staying a little longer than necessary making my heart flutter before he pulls away, "I'll pick you up tomorrow at 8." Then he kisses my forehead one more time before turning and walking away while I stand here stumped, "that's a bit quick don't cha think?" I say dumbfounded and he just chuckles, saying over his shoulder as he walks around the corner,

"Less chance of you pulling out last minute,"

I start to giggle, shaking my head, I have to give it to him, the man's not dumb, I just really hope I haven't made a mistake.

I look at the chart in my hand and take a deep breath before knocking on my next patient's door,

"Mrs. Colne, hi."

She smiles at me, her brown eyes shimmer with amusement, "honey, who was that gorgeous specimen of a man? And is he single?"

I can't help it, I burst out in laughter while her husband shakes his head with a smirk on his face.

Did I mention how much I love my job?

The next night, I'm sweating bullets, geez, I'm nervous.

I barely slept last night and after Mrs. Colne decided to talk none stop Travis yesterday much to her husband's amusement, my nerves just built up. Why does he want me? seriously why me? I'm plain and boring and let's not forget full of baggage with daddy issues. I mean, he could just have Cassidy, she said it enough after he left yesterday not realizing he asked me on a date.

I shake my hands out.

I can't do this, why did I say yes,

Shit.

"Fuck it." I mumble to myself, and I grab my phone, ready to call Travis who I don't know how, managed to get my number yesterday. He said I had to apparently wear something warm. This whole date thing has heart break written all over it and I've had enough of that growing up. My phone rings and I jump out of my skin, nearly dropping it, "Shit" I mumble before I answer without looking at the number,

"Hello?"

"Get your jacket and keys and head to your parking lot."

I frown and look at the caller ID, "Dr Thomas?"

He lets out a chuckle and I hear a female giggle in the background, "I think we're at the stage where you can call me Doc don't you think Mel." I snort, "now if I know you which I do, your about to call Dagger and cancel." Shit, "now don't. Get your jacket, get your keys and head to your parking lot. Trust me Mel, you'll have a good time and he'll treat you right." I sigh and thread my fingers through my hair, shoving my bangs out of the way,

"Doc, it's just, I...urgh."

He chuckles again, "I get it. How you met wasn't under the best circumstances but I'm telling you Mel, never and I mean never has Dagger wanted to take a woman out. Just give him a chance. Walk out the door sweetheart."

I sigh before looking in my mirror. My hairs loose, I have minimal make up on, a plain white v neck t-shirt with my black jacket on and my skinny jeans and high knee boots. I'd admit, I look good.

I nod, "ok, I'll go."

"Good girl. I'll see you tomorrow night at work."

I groan realizing we're on nights for the week commencing tomorrow in the E.R while he hangs up laughing. Damn, I hate nights.

Shaking my head I leave my apartment and start walking down the stairs, shaking. I mean, this is my first fricking date and with a guy I walked in on with another woman in a storage cupboard for Christ sake. Maybe Harris hit my head harder than I thought.

When I get to the door I hear a loud rumble of an engine and my eyes widen. We're going on his bike? His frigging bike?

Shit.

Shaking my head and taking a deep breath I open the door and come to a halt when I see him sitting astride is Harley. I swallow hard, tight black t shirt with his vest thing on and tight jeans, finishing the look off with his biker boots. Double shit. I look up and see he's smirking at me, his grey eyes sparkling with amusement, and I blush, hard and walk over to him while he gets off his bike.

When I'm near he wraps an arm around my waist and kisses my forehead before rasping, "you look beautiful precious." My cheeks heat up some more and I clear my throat before looking up to him, "I, uh, I've never been on a bike before."

He grins wide, "good, I'm glad I'm your first, come on I'll help you on." My face heats even more if that's even possible. Shit. I need to calm down. I wipe my hands down my jeans before I put one in his hand as he helps me on his bike, "alright precious, I want you to keep your feet on the pegs, don't put your legs on the pipes because they'll be hot and when I'm on, wrap your arms tightly around me alright?" I swallow hard again as he puts a helmet on me and nod before he gets on. I do as he says, keeping my feet on the pegs and as soon as he's seated I wrap my arms tightly around him, squeezing him tightly causing him to chuckle before he rev's his bike and it rumbles underneath me, my stomach sinks as fear takes place, I can feel my hands start to shake and I squeeze him even more tightly before laying my head on his back. He tenses for a moment before relaxing making me furrow my brows, but I don't get to question him because he pulls out of the parking lot and I squeal in shock causing him to laugh, geez this man has a great laugh.

We're on the road for about twenty minutes before we arrive. I look around with my arms still squeezing him tightly as his hand rubs along my arm to help calm my shakes and I gasp. We're at Hudson Lake where there's a blanket with picnic food laid out and candles going around it. He definitely did the saying 'go big or go home'.

It's beautiful.

I quickly climb off and take the helmet off while I look at the beautiful view in front of me. Just past our picnic is the lake which has floating candles on with the moon shining bright over it and my heart flutters. I turn to look at this man, who is so different from what I thought. He's leaning against his bike with his arms crossed over his chest and he's looking at me with such intensity that I feel like he's looking into my soul. I want to break away, but I just can't, it's like I'm locked in and in this moment, I know, he would turn into my everything, which is the most terrifying thought going especially with someone who has abandonment issues and more baggage than this man deserves to deal with.

☐

Chapter 9

Dagger

I lean against my bike and just watch her as she takes in everything I've done for the date. I knew I couldn't just take her to a movie and dinner, I knew I had to woo her, so, after talking to Doc and finding out she's a romantic at heart and the help of Annalise, the pres's old lady and Leah, the woman who basically runs our bar and who Gunner is head over heels for but refuses to admit it, we came up with this idea and its fucking worked. She turns around and looks at me with awe and I can't help the smile that comes across my face. I push off my bike and walk towards her where she's frozen on the spot, staring at me with most probably the best look I've seen on her so far.

When I get to her, I gently take her hand before kissing her palm making a small smile appear on her beautiful face and I pull her towards the blanket before helping her sit down, I take a seat opposite her when she finally speaks, voice full of awe, "this is amazing."

I smile wide, "you can thank Leah, one of our staff members and Annalise for that."

She looks at me with wide eyes, "Annie's finally talking?"

I grin and nod, "yeah, she had her fall, it was bad, but Axel helped her. They actually got married a few days ago and I was their witness much to Flames dismay."

Her beautiful eyes light up as she places her hand on her stomach, relief floods her as her whole body relaxes, "gosh, I'm so happy for them." I smile again before handing her a chicken wrap from Sweet Treats and she smiles at me thanking me before taking a bite. Her eyes widen and she groans which goes straight to my cock. Shit. I do not need a fucking hard on right now.

Think of bikes.

Think of the brothers.

Fuck, think of Cammy and Leslie.

Yep, that did it.

"These are amazing."

I clear my throat and nod, "Annalise again. She owns sweet treats."

Her eyes brighten, "I love that bakery."

I chuckle before taking a bit out of my own wrap before I wipe my hands and clear my throat, "ok, so how we met, well, it sucked, I know and I want a do over." she raises a brow at me, amusement shines through her eyes and I smirk at her, "twenty questions."

She giggles and nods her head, "ok, you go first." She takes another bite of her food and I hum,

"age?"

She quirks a brow, "23."

I nod, "30."

She grins at me, "your old Travis."

I grin and lean forward tickling her under her arms and she giggles, "old huh?" she shakes her head laughing, "n-no, sorry-sorry." I chuckle and sit back down again, "alright, any siblings?"

She chuckles before shaking her head, "no, well, not that I'm aware of anyway." I quirk my brow at her wanting more, and she smiles at me. Fuck, I love that smile, "my dad left when I was four and I haven't seen him since. I know where he lives but never went to see him."

I nod as compassion fills my eyes, "his loss precious."

She grins at me, "what about you? Any siblings, well, I mean blood siblings?"

I chuckle, "the brother who spoke to you with Axel at the hospital, you know the day you gave him an update on Annalise, full of tattoos. He's my blood brother and goes by Ink."

She nods, "I did think he looked a lot like you to be honest, a lot of the same facial features and the eyes, you both have a distinct grey. He kind of scared me at first."

I laugh, "he has that effect on people but he's actually a teddy bear." Well, when you don't piss him off anyway, but I'll leave that bit out.

She grins, "are you older or younger than him?"

"older but by only a year, we have different mums, mine passed during child birth."

Her eyes grow soft, "I'm sorry Travis."

I just shrug and grin at her, "I love that about you; how much compassion you show for people."

She chuckles, "yeah but it's also my downside, I have a habit of getting close with my patients. I build a bond with them so when they don't make it, I take it hard. My friend Meghan, she's a resident doctor and she tried to warn me about it, but I didn't listen. I've only been out of school for a year so I'm learning my way."

I smile at her before leaning forward and moving some of her hair out of her eyes, "you have a big heart baby." She smiles at me before looking down shyly. Fuck, this girl, her every move consumes me.

She clears her throat, "ok, so what do you do for the club? I mean have you always wanted to be a part of it?" I smile at her question, "ok, so, you're not allowed to be pissed but I manage the strip club, Untamed Girls with Axel and yes I've slept with some of them, but I won't be any more now that I have you in my life." I give her a pointed look and she bites her bottom lip to stop the laughter that clearly wants to come out, "and no actually, I never did want to become a brother. I never got on with my father growing up and I never liked Leslie, my stepmother; the feeling was definitely mutual, and Ink well, I grew up resenting him, so I had a plan. I left as soon as I hit legal age and joined the Navy seals and went into active duty for 8 years. I only came back 5 years ago because Axel asked me to." Her eyes go soft before she leans forward and rubs a finger along my brows. It's only then I realize I'm frowning. My expression goes softer, and I give her a small smile before I grab hold of her hand and kiss her palm. It's weird and so fucking right. Never have I let anyone touch me, not since Leslie allowed her 'friends' to molest me. Hugging Axel at the hospital was fucking difficult, yet this woman, having her touch doesn't burn and doesn't make me feel dirty, it feels right. So fucking right.

She's mine, I'll make sure she knows it too.

We spend the rest of the date laughing and talking while eating the food Annalise made, who I fucking owe big time for this. A few hours later she's leaning against my chest in between my legs, head against my chest as we look out towards the lake. It's getting colder, it's 11pm and I know I need to take her home, but I just don't fucking want to. I sigh before placing my head in the crook of her neck, breathing her strawberry scent in. Tonight has been fucking perfect, we click. It's like she was made just for me and I her. I just hope she won't be disgusted when she finds out about my past.

"I guess I should take you home." I rasp against her neck holding her tighter, and she giggles, "you're going to have to let me get up Travis." I grin against her neck before gently kissing her there. I help her up and she goes to clean everything up, but I just shake my head at her, pulling her towards my bike, "don't worry precious, I have prospects coming to clear it all up."

She looks at me with furrowed brows, "prospects?"

I grin as I help her on my bike and place my helmet on her head. I really need to get her one of her own, mines too big for her, "men who want to become a brother. They have to show their worth for about a year before being voted in, all brothers go through it except for me because I was away."

She nods, "so like a bitch boy?"

I laugh, "yeah baby like a bitch boy." She nods again, her eyes sparkling, and I climb on in front of her before she wraps her arms around me tight and I sigh, fuck she feels good wrapped around me, her whole-body lighting mine up.

It doesn't take long to get her back to her apartment, and I sigh while I pull up near the building's front door. I help her off and take the helmet off before strapping it back to my bike and I take her in my arms. Her arms go around my waist under my cut but on top of my t-shirt, and I expect to tense as her hands splay over the scars, but I don't, her touch feels warm and oh so right. I smile at her before leaning forward. I kiss her gently on the lips, one, two, three times before placing my forehead against hers, "this thing, it's happening. So get ready precious." She grins at me before going to her tip toes, kissing my lips again while her hands fist the back of my t-shirt. I deepen the kiss, bringing her tightly to me, making her arms go up around my neck as I lift her, making her legs wrap around my waist before I smile into the kiss, making her grin back.

"Head on in precious, I'm being a gentleman today." I rasp against her lips causing her to giggle. She kisses me one more time before dropping her legs and I reluctantly let her go. I bend down and quickly give her one more kiss before she turns and heads inside, the need for my lips to always be infused with hers pulling me deeper. I stand there for five minutes before I climb on my bike with my cock hard as steel and head home with my girl on my mind hoping I don't fuck it up because I've got a feeling, a life without her in it would be damning.

The next evening I'm sitting in my office at the club tapping my fingers against my desk feeling agitated. I haven't heard back from Melanie all day. I've texted several times with no reply, and not even Fisher, one of my men from my squadron could cheer me up and he's our joker, instead he told me to stop being a pussy and just call her.

I sigh and scrub a hand through my hair before mumbling, "fuck it."

I grab my phone and dial her number, she answers on the second ring,

"Hi you, I was just about to message you back."

I instantly relax at her sound of her voice, leaning against my chair, "yeah?"

She chuckles, "yeah, I've literally just woke up."

I furrow my brows and look at the clock, "precious, it's 6pm. Whatcha do, party after I dropped you off last night?"

She laughs and it sounds so fucking sweet, "no, I deep cleaned the flat to keep me awake. I'm on nights this week with Doc."

I wince, "fuck, that's got to suck."

She laughs, "yeah, not the greatest part of my job although we do get some interesting people in the E.R. Last time some woman managed to get a cucumber stuck inside her."

I chuckle just as my office door opens and Sunny saunters in, wearing nothing but nipple pasties and a thong, for fucks sake. I sigh, rubbing a hand down my face,

"what's wrong?" concern laces in her sweet voice. See all heart my girl.

I clear my throat, "one of the staff members just walked into my office."

She snorts before coughing to hide it obviously picking up my frustration, "wearing what exactly?"

Her voice sounds so innocent, yet I can hear the amusement, and I growl at her, "seriously? Your enjoying my predicament right now?"

She laughs, fucking laughs.

"Hi Dagger, I missed you baby, you ready for my tight pussy?"

Her laughter instantly fades, "ok, yeah, I'm not finding this funny anymore."

I laugh this time before I turn to Sunny and state sternly to her, "you don't walk in here without knocking and unless it's about work then you need to leave. I'm no longer available." Her eyes widen as tears fill them and I roll mine, like that would change my mind, she was fucking sucking Slicer off yesterday. I hear my girl snort on the other end as Sunny gives me a pout and huffs off out of my office making me chuckle. "alright precious I'll let you go get ready for work."

She hums, "ok, speak soon Trav."

I smile as she hangs up.

Four hours later I'm deep in paperwork when my door opens again, I look up to see a frustrated Axel and I raise a brow at him, "fucking Hairy was sighted a few towns over. Snake, Ink and Flame went to his last known location and he's fucking vanished again."

I scowl while he sits down, leaning back in the chair.

"Fucks sake. He's got to have help; he can't just disappear this easy. But the question is, fucking who?"

He nods and goes to say something else when my phone rings and I sigh, answering it without looking at the ID,

"yeah?"

I hear a sniffle and instantly sit up while Axel looks at me with a furrowed look also sitting up.

I hear the sniffle again before my girl sobs, "I-I'm sorry if-if your busy."

I tense, "what's wrong precious? What's happened?"

She sniffles again, "Mr-Mr Samuel's passed away ten minutes

ago."

I sigh and relax back into my seat and go to comfort her, loving that she called me, but she beats me to it, "I-I'm sorry for calling, I'll s-speak to you tomorrow." Then she hangs. Fuck.

"Everything alright brother?"

I furrow my brows while looking at my phone before I shake my head and stand, collecting my keys before looking at Axel, "I need to go. That was Melanie, she lost a patient, one she was close to. She needs me." He gives me a sad smile, "go brother, I'll finish up here before I lock the offices up." I nod and pat his back before rushing out of my office while shouting over my shoulder, "TELL FLAME TO CHECK THE TRAFFIC CAMERAS." I hear him chuckle an OK back while I rush past a pissed off Sunny who tries to grab my arm as I run past, I'm going to have to talk to Axel about her if she continues and maybe we need a 'no sleeping with employees' clause in the contracts because fuck have I messed up sleeping with her. I wave to the bouncer as I get to my bike and quickly climb on, revving her up.

Not even fifteen minutes later I'm parked up and heading into the hospital. I head towards the nurses desk when I see Doc before I pat him on the back, "hey Doc, you seen Melanie?"

He turns to look at me and he smiles a sad smile, "she's in the staff room just down the corridor where I sent her. She has such a big heart Dag, and she was close to the patient, played gin with him every day, even on her days off. Take care of her brother, she's a gooden." I give him a smile back, nodding my head before I pat his back and head towards the staff room but when I get near the nurse I fucked, Cassidy I think Melanie said her name was, blocks my entry. She puts a hand on her hip, cocking it while twirling a bit of her ponytail in her finger, trying to be seductive, "well, it's about time you came back."

I just shake my head and go round her, "not here for you, I'm here for my girl."

I hear her gasp, but I ignore her and go into the room, following the sniffles. When I round the corner I see my girl sitting on the bench trying to calm down her tears and a woman with black hair and blue highlights sitting next to her, trying to comfort her. The woman looks up when she hears me and instantly relaxes, her blue eyes showing relief. She stands up walking over to me before she whispers, "thank you." I give her a smile and a nod before going around her to my girl. I kneel in front of Mel and cup her cheeks before wiping them with my thumbs. When our eyes connect more tears fall from her beautiful eyes as a sob comes out.

My eyes soften, "precious."

I pick her up and she wraps her legs around my waist, making her dress ride up as she places her face into my neck, sobbing and my fucking heart breaks. She cares so much.

I look towards the door and see her friend with tears in her eyes while Cassidy stands there glaring at my woman making me narrow my eyes at her. The other woman notices and shoves Cassidy out of the room shutting the door behind them while I take a seat with my girl straddling me. I place one hand at the nape of her neck with the other on her back, holding her close to me tightly.

"I've got you baby, I've got you." I rasp into her ear, meaning every fucking word.

Dagger: An MC Romance

Chapter 10

Melanie- 1 week later

I'm standing at the nurses desk in the E.R waiting for Meghan. I'm finally going to meet her little girl and I can't wait; she sounds like a cracker. I look to my left when I see movement and see Mr. Samuel's son walking out with a box of his father's belongings and I swallow hard as pain hits my chest when last week comes back to me.

I just come out of a cubicle. The patient had somehow and don't ask me how but had lodged a butt plug up his anus. I shiver. Sometimes, my job fricking sucks. Although it's a good story to tell your grandkids when your old and it'll especially be a great story to tell Mr. Samuel's even if he is in a coma.

I've just placed some paperwork on the desk when Dr Thomas comes up to me and I chuckle at him not noticing his sorrow look, "you're not going to believe what I just had to do, I mean seriously I'm scarred. A man and his wife came in and he somehow, managed to lodge a butt plug up his anus." I laugh a little because yeah, it was hilarious and trying to keep a straight face while I dislodged and removed it was not easy.

"Melanie." Doc rasps sorrow lacing his voice.

I look at him quickly with a furrowed look, concern for Travis spins through my head before he grabs my hand squeezing it,

"Mr. Samuel's passed darling."

I freeze looking into his eyes that are full of sorrow and tears begin to well. He squeezes my hand again, "go on for a break, I'll get another nurse to cover the E.R., why don't you head to the staff room, I'll find Meghan ok."

I sniffle and nod my head before heading to the staff room. I take a seat and let out a sob and without thinking I grab my phone and dial a number.

"Yeah?"

Dammit, what did I do. I sniffle instantly regretting ringing him. He sounds distracted and I've probably just disturbed him.

I sniffle again before I let out a sob, "I-I'm sorry if-if your busy."

His voice becomes tight with worry, and I start to feel guilty for worrying him, "what's wrong precious?"

I sniffle again, "Mr-Mr Samuel's passed away ten minutes ago."

I hear him sigh and the regret ringing him intensifies. It's so fricking scary how my first thought was to call him.

Shit.

He's now probably going to think I'm clingy. I let out another sob, "I-I'm sorry for calling, I'll s-speak to you tomorrow."

I hang up as my body wracks with my tears when a pair of arms wrap around me, and I lean my head against Meghan's while she holds me tightly not saying a word. I don't know how long we stay here but when the door opens, Meghan sighs in relief before placing a kiss to my head and gets up. I sniffle trying to calm myself down.

He was such a nice man.

Someone kneels down and two strong hands cup my cheeks and when my eyes connect with his grey ones more tears fall, and I let out another sob. His eyes soften as he rasps "precious" before picking me up. I wrap my legs around his waist and place my face into his neck, sobbing. I hear some commotion near the door, but I ignore it while he takes a seat, making me straddle him as he places one hand at the base of my neck and the other on my back holding me close.

"I've got you baby, I've got you." He rasps into my ear, and I sob some more.

A little while later, once I've finally calmed down I rasp into his neck, "I'm sorry you had to come here, I shouldn't have rang you."

He squeezes me before making me look at him, cupping my cheeks again. He wipes his thumbs under my eyes, "baby, you need me, you call me."

I give him a sad smile, "we've only been on one date."

He shrugs before smirking at me, "yet, your first thought was to call me. I think that's fucking perfect to me." I chuckle a little before placing my head back into his neck, "he was such a nice man." He hums and squeezes me tightly, "maybe I should try Meghan's advice and keep a distance from the patients."

"No precious. You caring is what makes them feel safe with you and it's what makes you, you. And you wouldn't be able too even if you tried baby. You have a big heart."

I sniffle and nod my head feeling so fucking grateful he came while he holds me tighter to him.

I blink. We've been on two more dates since last week, well more like he's shown up at my flat once he knows I'm up so we can have dinner together before he drops me off at work. He's so attentive and kind. He makes my heart flutter and I just know I could fall madly and deeply in love with him. He'll consume me, I know he will.

I'm brought out of my thoughts when someone slams their palms down on the desk and I look into the angry green blue eyes of Cassidy. Great.

I sigh, not wanting to deal with her today. "What can I do for you Cassidy?"

She sneers at me, "what you can fucking do is stay the hell away from MY man!" I raise a brow at her, but she continues, "I saw him first. I had him first. He is MINE!" she shouts the last bit getting some of the patients attention and also our head nurse who comes over, "Cassidy, is there a reason your shouting in my E.R?"

I tilt my head at her, smiling a little, and she pales knowing I could land her in deep shit right about now. When Annalise was admitted she fucked up big time and she knows it. Cassidy shakes her head, "n-no, sorry Mary." Our head nurse nods her head before giving my shoulder a squeeze. Cassidy squints her eyes at me about to say something else but is interrupted when Meghan purposely bumps into her, and I smirk.

"I'm sorry, did I just hear you threaten Melanie to stay away from a man who only fucked you as a punishment to leave you hanging after you decided not to inform his president the condition of his woman who had lost their baby?"

I bite my bottom lip to stop the chuckle as Cassidy's face turns red, but Meghan's not finished, "a little news flash for you love. He wanted her. He chased her. He's now DATING her. Not you. Her! So do me a favor and fucking do one!"

Cassidy looks at me and I just shrug. Her face goes redder, but I ignore her and turn to Meghan, "ready?" she smiles and nods her head and we both walk away from Cassidy who looks ready to blow, I mean, if she was a cartoon character then literal steam would be coming out of her ears right now. Meghan links her arm through mine, and we head to the car park. Travis drove me this morning which I told him he didn't have to, but he was adamant, so I head to Meghan's white Buick with her and climb in before she starts the car and head to Parkville Nursery.

"I can't believe the nerve of that woman. If we weren't in the hospital, then I would have smacked her one. She should be grateful you never reported her after she failed to do her job correctly."

I nod and chuckle, "she's going to become a problem I think

but I know nothing's going to be done about her. Apparently, she's blowing the chairman of the hospital, it's why I never bothered to report her."

She slams on her breaks before leaving the hospital car park making me jolt forward before looking at me wide eyed, "no way?"

I chuckle and nod, "yeah. I've got a feeling my jobs just got harder because no doubt she'll run to him."

Her eyes widen more if that's even possible, "but he's 75."

I snort before laughing hard all while she stares at me in shock.

"Fuck that's gross." She finally says before I burst out in more laughter. She laughs before turning out of the hospital car park heading to the nursery to pick up her little munchkin.

Twenty minutes later I'm waiting in the car as Meghan goes in to get her girl and my phone pings, I roll my eyes at the name that's programmed in my phone that I never entered before shaking my head, fricking Travis.

My man- fancy meeting me at Sweet Treats after your park date? xxx

I grin.

Me- I'd love too. I'll be about an hour and a half before Meghan has to take Lilah to ballet. xxx

I put my phone away when I notice Meghan coming back with a beautiful little girl with bright hazel eyes and long brown hair in her arms. I quickly get out and open the door for

Meghan while Lilah smiles wide at me, "Mel-Mel." I grin back, "hey sweetheart, you have a good day at nursery." She nods her head and I smile. For the past few months whenever Meghan facetimes the nursey or babysitter I've been with her and managed to bond with the little munchkin. She's fricking amazing, Meghan has done so well raising her. She's got sass, cuteness, and boldness all in one., the perfect child really.

Once Meghan gets her strapped in we head off to the park for some fun time where we spend more time than we should of playing. The beauty loves the swings I tell yah and nearly two hours later Meghan's dropping me off outside of the bakery. I smile before turning round to say bye to Lilah, but she's zonked, and I chuckle while Meghan grins.

"I'll see you tomorrow at work." She nods and I kiss her cheek before getting out. As she drives off I walk into the bakery and stop near the doors, my mouth hangs open before I start to silently laugh. Travis and another man who has hazel eyes and a man bun with short back and sides, are stood near the counter as two women who don't even look old enough to drink stand in front of them, boxing them in. Both men look really uncomfortable as the women try to touch them. Now I know I should be pissed and go over to help them out, but this is fricking hilarious.

I look back at Travis and lock eyes with him. He narrows his as mine show amusement and I swear I could hear him growl like a fricking dog from where I'm standing. I can't contain it anymore; my laugh escapes as he moves past the woman who frowns while the other man's eyes widen at being left to defend himself. When he's close enough he grips my waist, pulling me tightly to him and I grin wide. It's only then I realize his hair is down and I instantly fricking melt.

He's every woman's wet dream. I can't help it, I reach up and gently run my fingers through his shoulder length hair and he smirks at me before bending down to place one, two, three gently pecks to my lips making me hum in contentment.

"How was your park date?" he rasps, and I grin, "amazing. I tell you Trav, Lilah is fricking perfect, Meghan's done right by her despite trying to go to school, struggling. And her sass." I shake my head, "she's going to be one little heart breaker."

He grins back before questioning, "where's the kids dad?"

I shrug, "it was a one-night stand, although she's told me several times about how it felt more to her, like he was her soulmate or something but someone she worked with, was friends with knew him and the next morning they bumped into each other when she went to answer a call in the hallway of the motel and they said he doesn't do seconds when she gushed how much of a connection they had, so she left heartbroken but then had found out she was pregnant. Her parents kicked her out because she kept the baby and she's been trying to find him since." He nods and gives me a sad smile about to speak again but the other man interrupts, smacking him on the back, "fucking incoming brother they won't give up." Then he looks at me extending his hand which I shake, "hi there gorgeous, the names Slicer. Do me a favor and act like a possessive girlfriend and not the woman who was ready to piss herself laughing watching her man uncomfortable with jailbait over there." I bite my bottom lip while Travis snorts, shaking his head before smacking Slicer on the back of his head, "don't call my woman gorgeous, only I can." This time I shake my head before really looking at Slicer. He looks really familiar. Hazel eyes, brown hair, even a dimple on his left side of his cheek. Seriously, have I met him before?

I'm brought out my head when some woman tries to touch Travis's chest. He grabs a hold of her hand just before making contact. I've noticed he stiffens when anyone other than me touches him. I know its signs of trauma, but by who?

Slicer raises a brow at me. Shit, right, possessive girlfriend.

I growl, yes me, growl, like a dog, doing as Slicer asks even though I want to laugh again, "do you mind NOT touching my man!" I cock my hip, placing my hands on them and raise a brow, then I turn to the other woman and tilt my head at her, "did you know, my best friend Meghan is trained to shoot a gun and right now, you'll be her target for touching her husband." Then I look at the other woman who's looking at me with skepticism and I narrow my eyes at her, "you have three fucking seconds to move before I smash your face into the wall." Her eyes widen at my cold voice before they both scamper off and I smile wide while the men chuckle before Travis puts his arm around my waist while rasping, "that's my girl" making my smile turn into a grin.

"So, this friend of yours Meghan, was it the woman who just dropped you off? Because the back of her looked fine."

I snort at Slicers question although his eyes show something else, hope maybe? I look at Travis as he shakes his head with a little bit of sorrow in his eyes. Huh? Sorrow? What did I miss?

"No chance brother, that's my girls best friend and she also has a four-year-old." He says the last bit as a matter of fact, and I furrow my brows.

Slicer sighs at Travis' words looking extremely irritated, "damn it," he shakes his head before placing a kiss to my cheek, "it was lovely meeting you darling, thanks for the help. Dag, I'll see you in church later. BYE ANNIE." He shouts the last bit before leaving the bakery while Annalise shouts back, "BYE SLICER." I grin finally hearing her voice before I look at Travis with a raised brow and he sighs, running a hand through his hair, "about five years ago he met a woman whose name was Meghan, he fell for her instantly, but she was gone the next morning. He spiraled after that, turned into the biggest man whore just so he can try to forget her, but it hasn't worked, she's all he sees and wants and hasn't stopped looking for her." My eyes widen and hope fills my chest, it sound so much like Meghan's story. I grip his arm, "maybe she is the same Meghan?"

He gives me a smile at my optimism and shakes his head, "he went back to her workplace as soon as he woke, apparently she was only in town a few days, she left that morning." I sigh damn it, Meghan stayed for a year before leaving, "it was worth mentioning baby." I nod because I know he's right.

I wrap my arms around his waist, placing my head on his chest over his heart and smile as he wraps his arms around me tightly. We stand like this for a few minutes when the doors to the back opens and Annalise walks through them with a tray and I instantly move towards her making Travis chuckle. She looks up when she hears him, but her eyes come to me. She grins while tears fill them. She drops the tray and rushes to me, and I hug her tightly, "you're ok." I rasp, feeling relieved. I was so worried when she left the hospital.

She nods before pulling back, wiping her tears, "you saved me." Her voice is raspy, but I smile and shrug, "I was just doing my job."

She shakes her head, "no, you were doing more than your job. You spent more time in my room than Logan, you went 110% in on my care, and I can't thank you enough." I smile wide as Travis wraps his arm around my waist from behind before leaning his chin on my shoulder. His woodsy scent fills me, "told you precious. Your kindness and willingness to connect with the patient centers them and its who you are."

Annalise nods her head while wiping her face and I smile wide, leaning back against the man who I know will consume me and excitement fills me on the love we could have.

If only I could see the future and the heart ache he will cause me.

Chapter 11

Dagger- 2 months later

Axel's just banged the gavel, ending church and I sigh getting up. We have a run in two weeks to Wincher and it's my turn to go which has come at a bad fucking time. For the past week, Melanie has been off, really fucking off and I don't know why.

Sighing again I head towards the door before Axel nudges me, I look at him and he nods his head towards Ink. I furrow my brows when I see he's still sitting there, lost in his own head. I give Axel a head nod and walk back to the table taking a seat next to him, nudging him as I go. He snaps out of it before looking around the table,

"Shit" he mumbles, and I smirk.

"Alright little brother, what's on your mind?" I can't hide the amusement. He scowls at me, crossing his arms over his chest,

"I don't want to talk about it."

I chuckle and nod my head, "Sophie?"

He scowls harder, "I don't fucking get it. We have a connection; I know she fucking feels it, but she won't give. Leah told me she's a vet and I've fucking taken Princess to the practice she works at several fucking times. I even saw her with her 'kind of boyfriend' and she barely lets him touch her. Why the fuck won't she give me a chance?"

Someone from behind starts laughing and I turn to see Stormy who obviously decided to stay behind with us. Fucking great.

"It's not fucking funny dad, out of all the fucking women I feel a major connection with, and she wants fuck all to do with me."

I can't help it; my laughter joins Stormy's and Ink scowls harder.

Shaking my head, I clear my throat, "ok, so you want her? Then go fucking get her! I never pegged you as a quitter brother. She clearly thinks you're a player so prove to her you're not. Stop fucking sulking and be the badass biker we all know and love." He looks at me with wide eyes causing me to chuckle before he nods his head and slaps my back before running out of our chapel and I chuckle again. I turn to see Stormy smiling at me and I sigh before getting up myself. We're having a BBQ that I normally don't participate in, but everyone wants to meet Mel, so I asked her to join us and now I have a girl to go pick up. He grabs my arm as I walk past, "can we talk son? Please."

I move my arm, his touch burning me, and I shake my head, "you mean just like I wanted to talk to you growing up and instead I got beat for 'lying'. I don't think so Stormy."

He sighs, shaking his head, "you were a troubled child then teen blaming your stepmom for your mother not being here."

I just snort and shake my head before walking out without

looking back. I fucking wish that was my only problem with the bitch but it's not and because of him, I had a traumatic childhood. He didn't even look at me whenever I tried to explain, he literally shoved me aside time and time again.

As soon as I get to my bike in the compound parking lot, I climb on as my phone rings. I furrow my brows when I see it's the special forces commander.

"Sir?"

"Sniper"

I sit up straighter as Axel comes over to me to see what's up after seeing my reaction, shit. I put the phone on speaker because him calling me Sniper only means one thing,

"Your team needs your help Lieutenant."

Axel tenses and I clear my throat,

"Misson?"

"Traffickers in DC, they're due a pick-up in eight weeks, the teams scoping the place out, intel is in deep, too fucking deep to pull out. We need your expertise; I know your retired and you know I wouldn't ask if we didn't need you."

I sigh and scrub a hand through my hair before looking at my pres, my best friend to see he's dropped his chin to his chest. He nods lightly knowing I need to help.

I clear my throat again, "send me the details through budgie."

I hear him sigh in relief, "will do, thank you lieutenant" he says before he hangs up.

I look at Axel and see his head still dropped, his whole-body tense before I notice a shadow near the door. Stormy stands there with panic in his eyes which means he heard the phone call. Great. I sigh before squeezing Axel's shoulder making him look at me, "I'll be good brother, I always am."

He nods but still doesn't say anything, so I start my girl up and give Stormy a head tilt. He may be a prick but he's still my father. His panic is still there but he nods his head and I drive off out of the compound.

Fuck, how am I going to tell Mel?

I get to Melanie's flat about to get off my bike when she walks out the door. I instantly smile. Her hairs down, she's wearing a black tank and jeans with her cowgirl boots and looks fucking beautiful. I quickly readjust myself. I haven't had sex since the nurse incident and my balls are feeling it but Mel's not ready for that yet. I know she's had limited boyfriends so I'm taking it slow for her, but fuck do I miss getting lost in the pleasure when my head starts to fuck up with the memories I'm starting to struggle.

As she gets closer, I grin hoping she doesn't act off with me like she has all week, "hey precious."

She gives me a small smile before placing a quick kiss to my lips. There's no light in her eyes like there normally is. What the fuck did I do? Pretty sure I haven't done anything, but I must have, right? Sighing, I quickly put the helmet on her before she climbs on behind me and I instantly relax as her arms wrap around me tightly. Starting my bike, I try to think back to what I could have fucking done.

We get to the clubhouse about twenty minutes later and I

help her off. She wipes her hands down her jeans, and I grab them, pulling her towards me and I smile. Fuck, I love this girl, so fucking much. I don't know when I fell but I did and hard. She's kind, gentle, has a sense of humor with a heart of gold. I kiss her forehead before rasping, "they'll all love you baby." She looks up at me and her eyes shine with the love I feel for her shining back at me, and I can't help myself, I kiss her lips, hard and passionately making her moan, my tongue massaging hers while my arms wrap tightly around her. I stop the kiss a couple of minutes later, feeling myself become really fucking uncomfortable as my dick strains against my jeans before I rub my nose along hers.

She smiles at me, "I missed you this week."

I grin and hold her close, "not as much as I missed you precious."

She sighs and places her head on my chest, mumbling, "I'm sorry I've been distant, it's been a hard week."

I smile into her hair where I've got my nose, "so I definitely haven't done anything to piss you off?"

She pulls back, her eyes wide, "you thought I was mad at you?" I nod sheepishly while she slowly closes her eyes as a tear falls, shit, "I'm so sorry."

I pull her close again, "Mel? What's happened baby?" she just shakes her head, sniffling, "can we just have a good day then tomorrow I can tell you everything?" I smile and nod, knowing she needs a fun day, we both do, "come on then baby, let's introduce you properly to the motley crew." She smiles wide while I wrap my arm around her waist holding her close to me before we walk towards the door.

When we walk into the clubhouse everyone turns and she slinks behind me a little, making my arm drop while I scowl at the brothers and the women. I told them in church not to fucking openly stare at her because she's so fucking shy. Just when I'm about to shout at them I hear a squeal and turn just as Melanie runs from behind me,

"A PUPPY."

The brothers laugh while the women except for Clitter who is scowling, grin wide. I shake my head as Mel picks the dog up, who's loving the attention from my girl as she coos at her. I grin loving finally having a smile out of her, but my grin slowly fades when she turns to me with pleading in her eyes and I shake my head and point at her, "no" she pouts her bottom lip out, fluttering her eye lashes and the brothers laugh harder, fuck even Flame who's missing his girl like crazy is laughing. I point at her again trying to keep stern, "Melanie." She walks over to me with the dog in her arms, all the way so she can lean against my chest with the dog between us and she looks up from under her lashes, her bottom lip out while Princess tries to lick my stubbled chin.

I scrub my hand through my hair, wavering. The look she's giving me is hard to say no to, it's a look I'd do pretty much anything for.

"Don't do it son, stay strong, fight your ground." I hear Tank say while even the sweet butts start to laugh. I fist my hands down my side as she leans against me some more, her eyes shining with some unshed tears.

Aw come on, now that's just not fair.

But her whisper is my undoing, "please."

I slowly close my eyes and drop my chin to my chest, fuck. I nod my head slowly and she squeals while the men shout at me for being whipped while the women laugh. I look at Axel and he grins, "I'll give you my guy's number." Sighing, I nod my head before looking at my girl and I smile at the look of awe on her face as she looks at me. But then suddenly and very fucking slowly she blinks at me lovingly and I furrow my brows as she starts to walk backwards towards Annalise, "thank you Trav, just make sure when we get one you feed it when I can't because you know, I can't have any pets in my apartment." And with that she turns and dashes to Annie who has tears running down her cheeks while holding her stomach laughing. My brothers laugh at me while my mouth drops. Fucks sake. I drop my chin again shaking my head. I've just been played and lumbered with a bloody dog. Hmm, maybe this would convince her to move in with me? I smirk, a plan forming in place, and I side eye Axel who grins wide when he sees the determination in my eyes as I lift my head.

I feel a slap on my back, and I turn to see my blood brother grinning at me and I shove him making him laugh while I shake my head and go to my girl. He seems happier, so hopefully that means it went well with Sophie because a brooding Ink is fucking hard to deal with.

As I get to my girl, I wrap my arm around her waist from behind, she looks up at me and I smile before gently kissing her lips then petting the bloody dog that's still in her arms. She leans back against me, sighing making me melt right along with her. As she talks to Annalise I look up when I feel intense eyes on us to see Gunners parents, Butch and Hazel, staring at my girl with shock and I furrow my brows. I look towards Gunner to see if he's noticed but he hasn't, he's talking to Ink who's sitting right next to the bitch from hell, Leslie. She's the reason why I don't come to these events, but Axel wanted Mel to be brought into the family especially after I asked him to order her a cut, so I gave in after some coaxing from Annie's baked goods. Now I'm regretting coming here because the bitch has determination in her eyes to talk to me. Well, more like to ensure I keep my fucking mouth shut about what she did to me for years. I scowl at her before turning back to my girl who's talking to Annalise about dog names. Fuck.

I look towards Gunners parents again and I tense, they're still staring at my woman and now Hazel has tears in her eyes. I turn back to my girl and kiss her neck before I whisper in her ear, "I'll be right back precious." She smiles, nodding her head before reaching around to kiss me. I smile into the kiss while the bloody dog licks my chin making her giggle. I squeeze her waist and head to the Coopers. I pat Axels back as I walk past and nod my head towards the table, and he follows. I have a feeling my pres is needed for this conversation.

I take a seat at the table with Axel and they both finally break their stare from my girl. Gunner comes to take a seat next, and I look at him to see he's looking at his parents weirdly too. I clear my throat, "want to tell me what's going on?" Hazel looks down while Butch clears his throat, "it's nothing to do with you Dag." I nod, "sure, you staring at the woman I'm going to marry and make my old lady, whose cut is on the way is nothing to do with me. This isn't some kind of fling Butch. She's the only one to touch me." That gets his attention, and his eyes widen. Everyone in the club knows I have a no touching rule and only Leslie knows why.

"Dad?" I can hear the hesitation in Gunner's voice, he's

worried too.

Butch rubs a hand through his blonde hair while his blue eyes shine and I stiffen noticing the familiarities,

"No fucking way."

He looks at me with shock and his blue eyes that resemble my woman's, have fear shining through them,

"you're her fucking biological father?"

Gunner stands up, hands fisted, and I look around, some brothers look on with a furrowed brow, but my woman is too busy with the puppy and Annalise to notice the tension.

Hazel sniffles making me look back towards the couple, "we had split up at the time, you were only small Lucas." He shakes his head before looking at Mel with anger and I pull him down making him scowl at me, but I just shake my head at him and look at Butch who too is looking at my girl. Gunner hasn't clicked, he obviously thinks she's using me but she's not.

"She doesn't know, does she." I question him making Gunner stiffen again looking at his father with shock and disappointment.

I know the answer because she would have told me, but I want to know why he never claimed her. He clears his throat, "no, she does not. She was better off with her mother and father, and I didn't want to put a strain on my marriage." Hazel lets out a sob while I snort making him narrow his eyes at me.

I lean forward, "her father left when she was four years old. She hasn't seen him since." His eyes widen in shock while Hazel gasps, "oh no." We look at her with furrowed brows and when she whispers, "I offered him £100,000 if he gave us custody of her when she was four" Gunner looks ready to blow while Butch stares at her in shock and I growl, "so you're the reason he left his family?" she sniffles as guilt shines through her eyes while Axel whispers, "what the fuck."

I shake my head and stand before Gunner grabs my arm, "where are you going?"

I look him in the eyes, "to tell my woman the truth, she deserves to know." He nods looking relieved while Butch goes to protest but Axel just puts his hand up being what I need him to be, our pres, "you can't expect him to lie to his woman, he's ordered her cut Butch." Butch squeezes his eyes shut tightly, and I turn ignoring Hazels sobs going back to Mel where I'm about to tear her world apart.

Chapter 12

Melanie

I look up to see Travis walking back to me and I grin. I told Annalise I don't really expect him to get me a puppy, although I would love one but we've only been together a few months and I just wanted to play with him a bit. This week's been hard and being around my man and seeing this fluff ball has finally brought me back out of my shell and messing with him was just the icing on the cake for me.

I sigh as my mom comes to mind again.

Last week, while I was on shift trying to dodge a still pissed off Cassidy, an emergency overdose rushed into the E.R with Dr Shell shouting for me to meet in him triage. When I walked into the room, I instantly froze while the doctor screamed at me to not stand like a 'fucking statute'. As soon as I told him she was my mother he paled because he's one of the few doctors who are aware of what she did to me because he treated me after her drug dealer's cousin beat me up. I tried to call Doc, but he was out of town, so I called Mary and she brought Dr Shell with her.

When he snapped out of his shock, he told me to leave and get Cassidy which I did, and she bitched about it until I said she was my mother. I think that was the first time I saw compassion in her eyes, not that I needed it. I'd spent most of the week with police after I called them to let them know she'd been admitted and they're now holding her hand cuffed to a bed ready to escort her to a cell once she's recovered. It did drive me insane a little and I did pull back from Travis. Not because I wanted to but because I didn't want to burden him, you see, I love him, so much. He's become my center and I can't lose him because of my baggage. He's become the reason I breathe; I need him.

When he gets closer, I notice how tense he is around his eyes, and I furrow my brows at him. He takes the dog and I instantly start to whine, "Trav not the puppy, I want the puppy." A few people around chuckle while Travis gives me a fake smile before passing the dog over to Axel whose eyes are full of concern. I drop my playful whining and look at them both,

"What's wrong? What's happened?"

Axel leans forward and presses a kiss to my head before going to Annalise while Travis takes my hand, "come walk with me precious."

I nod with my brows furrowed but he just smiles at me before kissing my lips, once, twice, three times then wraps his arm around my waist. He walks me out the back door which leads to a large open field with picnic benches and a climbing frame set with swings and I smile seeing it. These big bad bikers are all heart really.

Travis walks me over to the bench and we sit down before he looks at me with sad eyes. He moves my hair out of my face, and I smile at him, "just spit it out Trav, whatever it is." I can tell he's struggling so whatever he needs to say then he needs to say it and hopefully not break my heart because right now my minds going to the worst-case scenario, which is him ending things, I mean he just agreed to get me a puppy even though I was only joking, so he wouldn't leave me would he, right?

"Shit baby, I don't know how to say this but a club brother who goes by the name Butch has just admitted to being your biological father after I confronted him for openly staring at you." I instantly freeze. Out of everything to come out of his mouth, I wasn't expecting that. He carries on while I slowly die inside when I realize, mom is the reason why my dad left, shit my dad? No not my dad? He must be wrong right? He's wrong? Please. "Baby, his wife Hazel admitted to offering your dad $100,000 to sign his rights over to Butch when you were four."

When I was four? When my father, Callum, left us and I became my mother's punching bag!

"He said. Shit. He said he didn't want to put a strain on his marriage. It's why he didn't claim you precious."

I blink, not saying a word,

"You uh, you also have a half-brother, Lucas but goes by Gunner in the club, he's our enforcer, he, uh, keeps us safe."

I finally look at him and I clear my throat when a door opens and we turn to see a man, the same age as Travis I think, with blonde hair and grey eyes looking at me intently and my heart races in my chest. I can't deal with this right now because I'm pretty sure that's my half-brother, I mean, we don't even look alike but he's looking at me like he wants to wrap me up in cotton wool. I look back at Travis again and clear my throat, "I uh, I need to leave but um, I'll call you." I stand off the bench, and he stands too, his face full of panic and I hate that I've put that look on his face.

"Baby, I drove you. Look why don't you come to my house that I have here, you said you wanted to see it today."

I just shake my head, "I just need some time and a walk will do me good, I'll call, I promise." I lean on my tip toes and kiss his cheek before walking round him towards the gate that leads to the parking lot. I don't look at the man near the door. I keep my head down and walk away, my mind reeling.

I walk for over an hour when I find myself standing outside of the hospital staring at the doors. I don't know how long I stand here for but the longer I do, the angrier I get. She blamed me, she punished me for her own wrong doings. She lied, she cheated, she kept someone else's baby and passed it as her husband's. She's the problem, not me.

With that thought I storm into the hospital. How dare she, how fucking dare she.

I get to her floor and see a policeman standing outside it and I walk over to him, he looks at me with wide eyes, "I'd like a moment with my mother please, your welcome to join." He clears his throat before nodding and we both enter. My mother looks at me with a furrowed brow before she snorts, "here to ruin my life some more."

I just tilt my head at her, she's a mess. She's lost even more weight which I didn't think was possible and her arms are full of track marks. "I ruined your life?"

She sneers at me, "I lost my husband because of you."

I nod, "oh and here I thought it was because you were a whore who couldn't keep her legs closed." The policeman coughs while my mother's eyes widen. I continue feeling pissed, "I mean, you did fuck a biker and get pregnant with his child." She stiffens, "and the only reason your husband had found out about your cheating ways was because the bikers wife wanted me and offered him money."

Tears fall from her eyes as she rasps, "I only slept with him once. Your father and I had an argument, and I was drunk, it was a mistake."

I nod, "and yet you punished me for your misgivings. You beat me, broke my bones, let old men leer at me then tried to sell me for your habit. You blamed me when all along YOU were the problem. You were the reason he left, not me and yet you had me beaten up."

She lets out a sob, "h-he was all-all I h-had."

I snort at her, "wrong MOTHER. You had me, a four-year-old who only wanted a mommy's cuddle to make things better." She sobs some more before I sneer, "I hope you rot in prison. Don't try to contact me because your dead to me." Then I turn and thank the policeman before walking out while hearing my mother's sobs. As I get to the ground floor my body vibrates with anger as I bump into Cassidy. She glares at me, back to being a bitch, "well look who it is, the boyfriend stealing bitch."

I keep walking, making sure to ram into her shoulder as I state, "oh look who it is, the whore who likes to fuck family members in storage closets instead of giving them the news of their loved ones before sucking off the chairman."

She gasps while a few nurses and doctors look at her with wide eyes while the head nurse crosses her arms over her chest looking at Cassidy. I don't stop though, I keep walking. They have no proof, only my word, so she'll most likely just get a written warning, a lot less than she actually deserves.

Forty minutes later I end up walking back to my flat and start to pack a bag before I book a ticket to Mexico with my emergency fund that's supposed to be used on a house. It's only an hour and a half flight and I can find a motel when I'm there.

It's time to put my past to bed so I can finally move on with the man I've fallen head of heels in love with.

Chapter 13

Dagger – 2 weeks later

I sigh and drop my phone onto my desk before leaning back in my chair. I'm in my office at the clubhouse and I'm fucking frustrated. Two weeks. That's how long it's been since I've heard from Melanie. After I told her about Butch and Hazel and she walked out looking calm as fucking anything, she messaged me that she just needed some time and would call me when she was ready.

But she hasn't fucking called.

I slam my laptop shut before grabbing my phone again and I dial her number. It rings several times before I give up and hang up, throwing my phone back onto my desk. Why the fuck won't she answer. I know I dropped a bomb on her, but I knew I had to tell her, if I hadn't told her straight away then it would have bitten me in the ass.

I run a frustrated hand through my hair wondering if I made the right decision when my office door opens and a pissed off Ink walks in. I raise a brow at him, "what? Sophie turn you down again." He just narrows his eyes at me before taking a seat opposite me on the other side of my desk, "look, I know this is going to piss you off and I know you don't want to talk about it, but it has to stop brother."

I tilt my head at him fucking confused as fuck, "what are you talking about Ink?"

He clears his throat, "I just left our distraught mother because you refused to even look at her at the BBQ. Stormy's pissed and is ready to come over here and kick the shit out of you and to be honest brother, I'm having to restrain from punching you. She wanted to meet Mel but couldn't because she left, she said you purposely got your girl to leave."

Fucking Leslie again.

I slowly stand before placing my palms on my desk, leaning on them and sneer at my blood brother. I've already told him to stay out of this shit and yet again he's decided to get involved because mommy dearest has decided to bullshit. Leslie is playing them like a fucking fiddle. "I never fucking told Melanie to leave the fucking BBQ twenty minutes into the event Jackson. I had just told her that Butch was her biological father and Hazel had offered the man who she thought was her dad $100,000 for custody of her. It's how her dad had found out she wasn't his and coincidentally he left that same year. She needed time and I don't fucking blame her one bit."

I lean forward while his eyes are wide with shock. Yeah that's how we felt too, "and tell me something brother, why is she inconsolable two weeks fucking later? I don't know what her fucking problem is or what her game is but she's playing you both like fucking fiddles and if Stormy wants to kick the shit out of me then let him fucking try because I'm not a little boy anymore, I'll fight back and I'll make sure to fucking kill him." He looks at me with furrowed brows before I sit back down, "do me a favor Jackson and fuck off out of my office."

He runs a hand through his hair and sighs before getting up heading to my door, "she's our mom Trav, you can't keep treating her this way. Would it really be that hard to just have a dinner with her and introduce her to the woman you want?"

I just snort, that's twice he's said it now. "Nah, she's your mom, my momma's dead and my mom, I see her every Sunday for dinner."

With that he growls before he carries on leaving my office, slamming my door on his way.

I shake my head, my frustration growing, memories from my past flittering through my mind. Their touch burning through me making my body itch and I grab my phone again, trying to ring my girl but she doesn't answer, and I growl, slamming my phone down before there's a knock on my door,

"WHAT."

The door opens and in walks a dressed up clitter or well in her case, dressed down. She smirks at me as I admire her outfit. The dress is tied with three bows on either side barely covering her bare pussy and my cock grows in my jeans. I can't fucking help it. I haven't had sex in months, and I need a distraction, I need these memories gone, I need their touches off of my skin and there's only one way I know how to rid myself of them,

"Hey baby, I heard your quite frustrated, so I thought I'd come and relieve you."

I sit back down and tilt my head to the side as her brown eyes sparkle with lust making my own heighten. I know I shouldn't, this is the one condition my girl gave me, no other women. I know I should tell her to fuck off, but Melanie isn't answering her phone, Inks pissed me off and inadvertently brought back my past horrors and my dick is hard as fuck since she walked in here dressed like that. I need to forget, I need to be in control, so instead of telling her where to go and try to find my girl, I make the biggest fucking mistake of my life and open my legs wide for her to kneel in front of me while she grins wide doing as I want. She goes to run her palms along my jean covered thighs before reaching my zipper where my rock-hard cock is, but I stop her. She knows the rule, no fucking touching. Instead, I grab her hand and place it on my cock through my jeans making her rub it causing me to groan out loud. Fuck that feels good.

I lean back relaxing as she removes my cock through the zipper hole, cold air hitting it before she circles the head with her tongue then sucking it gently into her mouth before deep throating me while swallowing at the same time, I grab her bright blonde hair tightly,

"Fuck, that's it my little whore, fucking suck me hard." I grunt while she moans around my cock.

She sucks me hard, moving her head up and down and I slowly close my eyes, tilting my head back, loving the sensation of her warm fucking mouth. I open my eyes when I hear a soft click of the door after hearing a gasp but no one's there. I look down at Clitter to see she's looking back at me with triumph, which is fucking odd, but I ignore it and grip her hair tighter before I start to fuck her mouth.

I moan while she rubs her legs together, "fucking finger yourself, make yourself cum while I paint your fucking throat." She closes her eyes and groans while doing as I ask, starting slowly first before speeding up her movements and I grunt as she comes, her moans vibrating around my cock.

One, two, three more thrusts down her throat and I cum on a groan, closing my eyes while keeping her head still so she can swallow it all. Fuck me. I needed that.

I pull out of her mouth and put myself away while she smirks at me. She stands before going to touch me again, but I stop her and raise a brow. She pouts but nods her head before standing. Its then I notice her cum dripping down her leg and I smirk before leaning forward. I rub my fingers through it then place them at her mouth. She opens and sucks my fingers clean of her juices,

She moans then rasps, "thanks baby" before turning around and leaving and I furrow my brows, my brain now catching up.

Fuck. Fuck, fuck, fuck, fuck, fuck.

What the fuck did I just do?

My breathing picks up realizing I just fucking cheated on my girl.

Fuck, fuck, fuck.

I quickly grab my phone, a picture of us together smiling at the lake pops up and I swallow hard before I try calling her again but again, she doesn't answer. My guilt increases. She's struggling with her parents' betrayal and instead of understanding I fucking used her distance as an excuse to fucking cheat. Oh fuck, fuck, fuck, no, what did I just fucking do. I stand up from my chair, pushing it away as I start to feel sick, sweat building on my forehead.

I'm mid freak out feeling like a heavy weight is sitting on my chest when there's a knock to my door and Axel walks in. He looks at me and furrows his brows, "what's up brother? You look like your about to pass out."

I clear my throat and shake my head before I rasp,

"I just fucking let Clitter suck me off."

He stills, his eyes widen, "what the fuck."

I start to pace, running my fingers through my hair feeling guilty as fuck as panic sets in, "fuck, I don't even know what the fuck I was thinking."

He scoffs, "well, obviously you fucking weren't were you. She'll leave you Dagger. She told you no other women or she's out, that was her only rule for your relationship."

I shake my head, "no, no, she won't find out. I'll fucking make sure of it; she can't fucking find out. I can't fucking lose her brother, I need her. FUCK, WHAT THE FUCK DID I JUST DO."

Just as I said the words my office door slams open and Amy, aka 'bubbles', a sweet butt who didn't actually want to be a sweet butt but thought it was the only way to have our protection and tried ruining the pres' relationship with Annalise, walks in and she looks pissed. I raise my eye brows when she points at me,

"Did you seriously just fucking cheat on that sweet nurse?"

My eyes widen while Axel sucks in a breath, fuck. I go to talk but she's not done reaming my ass yet,

"Are you some kind of fucking idiot. That woman looks at you like you hang the fucking moon, she's in love with you! and you go cheat on her with Clitter. Why, because she needed some time after the big bomb you dropped on her about her father. I hope your fucking dick rots off!!"

Then she storms back out of my office slamming the door while Axel and I look at it in shock. Just as Axel is about to speak the door opens again and Amy points at me, "you should be fucking grateful I like Melanie. I told Clitter the next time she opens her fucking mouth about what happened in here then I'll skin her alive" then she slams the door again while we look at it with raised brows fucking shocked.

"I think I preferred it when she wanted to keep us happy."

I nod in agreement because fuck bubbles was a lot less scary than Amy.

My phone pings and I quickly grab it but sigh when I see it's only Flame.

Flame – let's roll Brother.

I look up to Axel, "I gotta go, Flame's become impatient since losing Star and he's ready to roll out. I'll see you in two days."

He nods and pats my back, "it'll be ok brother." I just snort and shake my head. I don't see how, if someone doesn't tell Mel what I just fucking did, my guilt will every time I look into her beautiful eyes.

I get to my bike and fist bump Flame before starting her up

and we all get into formation ready to roll out. I quickly text my girl before placing my phone in my cut and we leave the clubhouse grounds to Wincher.

My Heart – gone out of town for two days on a club run. Call if you need me precious. I know your struggling with everything, let me help you through it, I miss you xxx

Chapter 14

Melanie

I'm pacing the driveway of the clubhouse. The prospect Shane is sat back in his little hut, arms crossed over his chest watching me with a raised brow. I've been doing this for the past twenty minutes and Travis has already called me in that time. Two weeks, that's how long I've stupidly ignored him to try and sort my head out. I huff feeling frustrated with myself. I just need to get this over with. I return to work tomorrow after taking a vacation, so I need to pull up my big girl panties and tell Travis about my mom and my past.

"Just pull the band aid off Melly."

I scowl at Shane. I may have ranted about my mother and the shit with Callum and Butch and how I'm now on ramen noodles for the foreseeable because I spent part of my savings on that stupid flight to Mexico and the rental car when I arrived after he questioned why I just don't go in. I think he may have regretted speaking to me.

I raise a brow at him, "Melly?"

He shrugs, "think it suits you."

I chuckle and shake my head before I start pacing again with Callum coming to mind. I shake my head again at the nerve of him and his selfishness, I may not have been his blood, but he was still there when I was born up until I was four years old, I was still his little girl.

I wipe my hands down my jeans. I'm scared and nervous being here and a little shocked that this is where he lives. I look down the street and see more run-down houses and trailers and I swallow hard, patting my pockets to ensure the pepper spray is still there, I don't feel safe here. I should have spoken to Travis first, asked him to come with me. Damn me and my stupid pride. I take a deep breath then knock on his trailer door. There's no answer so I knock louder before I hear a grunt and some swearing.

The door opens and a man with black shaggy hair and red rimmed eyes answers and I nod my head. He's on drugs, of course, so now that's both parents that has chosen them over me while my biological father chose his other family, awesome, way to make someone feel loved.

He looks at me up and down and leers at me, this man, who was supposed to love me unconditionally until he was told I wasn't his.

Such a disappointment.

"Well, what can I do for you sweetheart? If you're looking to be paid for a good time then come on in."

My eyes turn wet. He doesn't even recognize me, the man who called me his princess, his Mel's. I take another deep breath, "I guess it's not classed as incest seems though you're not my biological father, right dad?"

His eyes widen and he stumbles a little, "Princess?"

I snort, "I haven't been your princess since you left me with my mother who proceeded to blame me every single day as to why her husband left and I don't mean with nasty words, I mean with physical abuse."

His eyes widen with each word I say, and I let my tears fall, "I always wondered why you never took me with you until yesterday when I was told you weren't even my father. But still, if you loved me like I was your daughter then you still would have found a way to take me but I'm guessing by the track marks in your arms and your red rimmed eyes, my mom's not the only one who chose drugs over their child,"

He swallows hard, "I did want to take you Mel's, I really did but I had no legal rights over you and I-I.." I finish his sentence, "and you were too busy wanting to get high to even care." He squeezes his eyes shut and I nod. This is my closure. I turn to leave but he grabs my arm, "wait, please. Why did you come? Your 23 now right? so why?" I turn to look at him with glossy eyes, "my mother tried to get her druggie boyfriend to pimp me out a few months ago and when I went to the police and he got put away she got his cousin to beat me up," his eyes widen before dropping his hand on my arm in shock, "she was finally found last week after she overdosed and is now currently in the hospital, handcuffed after overdosing before being transferred to the state prison for what she did to me. I'm here to get the closure I desperately needed from the man who was supposed to protect me. I get it you had found out I wasn't biologically yours, but I was still yours. I was still your daughter. And I needed you. So this is me finally letting go of my past so I can be all in with the man I've fallen desperately in love with.

Goodbye dad."

I turn and wipe my tears as I walk over to the rental. I get in and drive away while he watches me leave with tears running down his cheeks. He made his bed; this is what he wanted so I won't feel guilty for getting my closure that I desperately needed in order to let Travis in my heart fully.

My phone rings again, bringing me back and I look to see Travis calling again. I look at Shane and he gives me a small smile, "he'll understand."

I sigh and nod my head because he will. That's what I love most about Travis, he understands me and knows I needed to wrap my head around everything, and I know he has demons too, so he won't judge my past. With that thought in mind I start walking towards the doors when they open, and two men walk out chatting and smiling and I swallow hard. I recognize one of them from the BBQ; Gunner and the man next to him could be his twin, shit, Butch.

Double shit.

I look towards Shane, and he gives me a nod to keep going in and I take a deep breath and continue walking forward. They both look up when they hear me and freeze but I ignore them and head towards the door.

"Melanie"

I turn my head slightly when I'm near the door to see Butch looking at me, but I just shake my head at him and continue to walk inside the clubhouse, refusing to deal with him right now, the man who actually fathered me but chose his marriage over his innocent child! Don't get me wrong, I understand he loves his wife and son but if she loved him just as much then she would have been there and stood by him no matter what but instead he took the easy way out and I was abused until I left for college.

I get to the big room but don't see anyone and I frown looking around. Travis hadn't shown me around at the BBQ, I left before he could, so I have no idea where to go. I look towards the back door thinking about checking out there when a woman with ginger hair comes out of a door near the bar, she raises both her brows at me before an evil gleam enters her eyes making me step back a little,

"Your Daggers woman right?"

I do not like the amusement in her voice right now. She has the same bitch attitude like Cassidy. I nod anyway to her question; we've been together for three months now and I won't let her make me feel crappy because this woman has evil written all over her.

She grins wide, "well, it's nice to meet you. He's in his office, just down the hallway here, 3rd door on the right, it should be unlocked," she points to behind her and I nod again and thank her with suspicion lacing my voice before going down the hallway, all whilst she smiles.

Something sour sits in my mouth, and I feel like she just set me up to hurt me on purpose. In my gut I know. I do know, it doesn't matter how much I try to convince myself that he knows me and knew I needed time, I know. I haven't spoken to him for two weeks and we haven't had sex yet because I'm not ready, so I know what's waiting for me behind that door, I can feel it in my gut. It's going to kill me, but I need to see it in order to believe it. I need to see the man I'm in love with cheating on me because let's face it, that would just be the cherry on top of the cake with everything else that's going on. I take a deep breath and walk to the 3rd door on the right. I hear a females muffled moan and a males groan, and a few tears spill down my cheeks and I quickly wipe them.

Like I said I knew.

I take another deep breath and slowly open the door, being as quiet as I can. When I open it enough to fit my head in I take a look and see my man, the man I love, sitting back in his desk chair, head back and eyes closed as pleasure washes over him while some woman who is dressed for a street corner is rubbing her thighs together while she sucks him off. We make eye contact, and a satisfied gleam enters her eyes. She's happy I saw this and she's making it perfectly clear, he'll always stray and go to her, which is probably true. I nod my head before I quietly shut the door and head back out, not willing to fall apart just yet, no, I'll do that at home.

I rush back through the clubhouse the way I came while the bitch smirks at me as I run past her. When I get back to the gate Shane frowns, standing up from his seat while I quickly wipe away a tear. I turn to him and rasp, "I was never here, please."

He furrows his brows in confusion before realization comes across his face and pain for me shines through his eyes. He nods his head as anger takes over his body, anger for me and I kiss his cheek before I leave without looking back.

It doesn't take me long before I arrive back at my apartment and as soon as the door is shut, my tears fall, hard and fast. My sobs wrack my body while I slide down my front door as images of his pleasured filled face enters my mind while she's on her knees for him.

Pain like no other fills me and I can't breathe. I knew I shouldn't have given him a chance, he had heartbreak written all over him and I still went there knowing this. I thought we had a connection, I thought he'd be the one.

I sob even harder feeling like an idiot for not keeping my walls up.

I don't know how long I sob for but by the time I finally manage to get up off the floor its dark outside and my head is killing me. I go to my tiny bathroom and quickly wash my face before going to bed with a heavy feeling in my gut, like my happiness just died.

I lay here for a little while before I reach for my phone and see a missed text from a few hours ago.

I open it and my anger takes place,

My Man – gone out of town for two days on a club run. Call if you need me precious. I know your struggling with everything, let me help you through it, I miss you xxx

Yeah, he missed me so much, he went and got a blowy from some whore who knew I was there. I click on his contacts as my rage flows through me and I block his number. As far as I'm concerned,

We're done.

Chapter 15

Dagger

We've just pulled up to the clubhouse and I sigh feeling fucking exhausted. Normally the run is done in roughly 8 hours but because of the thunderstorms we had to schedule it for two fucking days. I can't wait to sleep in my own fucking bed tonight and preferably next to my girl but that'll have to wait until tomorrow.

I get off my bike and give a nod to Shane, but he turns his head towards the road, ignoring me and I furrow my brows about to head his way to find out what his problem is when Ink slaps my back, "come on brother, I'm fucking starving, I need food before I go find my fucking woman." I just raise a brow at him, and he scowls at me, "she is my fucking woman, she knows it, she just has to get on board."

I laugh as we walk into the clubhouse, forgetting about Shane's weird behavior. Ink said some stupid shit apparently before we left, and she's ignored his calls since. I honestly don't know who was worse, Flame or Ink. I shake my head as we enter the clubhouse. Just when I'm about to follow Ink to the kitchen I notice Stormy and Leslie who both intercept him, yeah, fuck that shit. I pat Ink on the back and continue walking down to my room here at the clubhouse ignoring his call.

I can't be assed going all the way to my

house I have here, I need a fucking shower. I got Axel to build it while I was away. Apparently, Leslie was trying to convince our then president Dead Shot that I gave permission for Ink to have my plot of land so he can have a bigger house built. When Axel rang and asked why I didn't want the plot I told him to get my house built but don't give my keys to anyone and to this day only I and Axel have a key. I barely stay in it to be honest though, it's next door to Inks who started building a year after mine was built and Leslie's always round his house trying to interfere. The less I have to see her the fucking better.

I get to my room and unlock my door, ignoring Clitter whose leaning against Axel's door waiting for me. I walk in and quickly shut it before she can even move. Like fuck is she getting in my room. I hear a screech and I roll my eyes. I fucked up I know, I shouldn't have let her fucking touch me, and if Melanie finds out then I can kiss my relationship goodbye. Fuck, why the fuck did I do it? I sigh and shake my head before heading to my shower. Melanie won't find out because I won't fucking lose her. I messed up, I clearly wasn't thinking. I know I was trying to forget my demons which is no excuse, and I was trying to punish Mel for not leaning on me, making me a fucking dickhead for it. I fucked up, big time but I cannot lose her, I won't.

I turn the water on before undressing and climb under the spray. I drop my head against the tiles while closing my eyes. Melanie's beautiful blue eyes come to mind, and I sigh again. Fuck do I miss my girl. I've called her several times in the past two days, but it rings out like she blocked my number, but I know she hasn't. She may not have said the words, but I know she loves me, she just needs time to process everything. My cock starts to get hard, and I picture her slowly going down onto her knees in front of me, her big blue eyes looking at me with innocence. Fuck, I palm my cock while picturing her running her hands up my thighs before wrapping her hand around my rock-hard cock. I moan as I squeeze my dick hard from base to tip. She slowly licks the tip of my cock that oozes with pre-cum, moaning at my taste before taking the head into her mouth, sucking it gently. My hand moves quicker as I picture her deep throating me while moaning around my cock, my spine tingles before cum spurts from my tip hitting the shower wall.

"Melanie..." I groan out before I open my eyes and see it's just me in the shower and I sigh, wiping my hand over my face, fuck. I grab my shower wash and pour a healthy amount in the palm of my hand before scrubbing it in my hair with my head under the water. I wash my body before getting out and dry myself before wrapping a towel around my waist before heading back into my bedroom. I come to a halt when I find a naked fucking Clitter lying on my bed fingering herself and yes, my cock takes notice, but I ignore it as my rage takes over. I know I lead to this like a fucking idiot by letting her touch me and an even bigger idiot for not locking my fucking door but she's taking the fucking piss.

Her eyes lock mine and she smirks, "come on baby, join me."

I flare my nostril, "you've got exactly one minute to get the fuck out of my room before you realize exactly what I'm like."

She just smirks, thrusting her fingers faster, moaning, "that's not what you were saying two days ago baby, come on, you know you want me. Your cock is standing to attention."

I walk over to her, and she grins wide which soon turns into a screech when I grip her arm and drag her towards my door. I quickly open it and shove her out of it just as Axel and Annalise walk down to his room. Their eyes widen while I point at Clitter but looking at my best friend and president, "she decided it was a good idea to come into my room while I was in the shower. I want a club fucking meeting about this." He nods while his eyes narrow on Clitter who is trying to hide her body. When she looks at a pissed off Annalise, she swallows hard.

Annalise gets in her face, "you do realize he has a girlfriend, right?" fuck her face is red and she's angry but it gets worse when Clitter smirks before looking at me,

"didn't stop him from having my mouth around his cock two days ago."

I stiffen while Axel drops his head. Annalise looks at me, she whips her head my way so fast I'm surprised she hasn't gotten whiplash. Her eyes flash with rage while I grind my jaw. Fuck.

"Clitter you're on fucking toilet cleaning for the rest of week, touch a brother then you're out."

She whips her head towards Axel, her eyes wide at his cold tone while I haven't taken my eyes off Annalise's angry violet ones. I don't think she's ever looked at me with this much disappointment before and my heart fucking hurts. Clitter quickly rushes away from us while Annalise gets in my face, "please tell me she was fucking lying, please tell me you did not let that woman touch you when you're still with Mel? Mel who happens to have a heart of gold?"

I swallow hard and look down. I look back up just in time for a loud slap to echo in the room and my cheek stings like a fucking bitch. She points at me in my face and sneers "you disgust me" before turning around, going into hers and Axel's room, slamming the door and I slowly close my eyes as pain shoots through me because I know I'm about to lose my girl. Annalise won't keep this from her, I know she won't.

Axel pats me on my back, "I'll talk to her, I'll make sure she doesn't say anything."

I just shake my head at him planting my hands on my hips, "I won't let you get involved, it'll put a strain on your relationship."

He nods, "I can still try, you won't lose your girl brother because I know if you lose her then we lose you." I look at him with a furrowed brow and he just shrugs, "I know you have one foot out of the door and Mel is the only thing keeping you here, fuck, you've been asked back on a mission which I know you won't come back from if you lose her. I heard the rumors growing up Trav, about what you were accusing Leslie of and how they were all lies yet years later you still won't go to functions or family events, I mean the BBQ was a one off because the brothers wanted to meet Mel but otherwise you stay away. You even fucking left, I was the only reason why you came back. She is the only reason why you've stayed.

They weren't lies were they Trav." I swallow and look down before managing a small head shake.

"I won't let Annalise ruin this for you. I love her, I do, she's my wife but your my brother and Mel is your anchor. You fucked up but I'll help anyway I can. I won't lose you again."

He pats my back before he goes into his room and I sigh again, rubbing my hand through my hair before I head back into my room. I lock the door before grabbing my phone and I try ringing Mel again. It rings out and I sigh again before dropping my phone back on my black bedside table. I look towards my bed and see my black bed sheets wet and I scowl before I rip the sheets off, throwing them in my laundry basket and quickly grab some new ones before climbing in looking at the ceiling.

A sinking feeling forms in my gut and I swallow hard, I need to see my girl. I look at the clock; 10:30 in the evening. Tomorrow, I'll go to her work tomorrow. Sighing, I close my eyes to try and get some sleep.

The next morning I'm in the kitchen at the clubhouse finishing my breakfast when Butch and Gunner come in. Butch goes straight to his wife and old lady Hazel who was already sitting at the small table in here while Gunner comes over to me where I'm leaning against the counter near the coffee pot. He grabs himself a cup before sighing, looking back at his parents who are looking all loved up. I turn to look at him,

"You alright brother?"

He just snorts, "look at them, they're acting like dad never fathered another child then deny paternity and Momma's sitting there all smiling like she didn't offer a man $100,000 for my little sister." He turns to look at me his eyes full of pain, "don't you think it's strange that when she was four years old Momma offered the money and that same year her father leaves?"

I look at them, they're in their own little world all loved up not realizing the torment their son's going through, "no brother, I don't think it's strange and its defiantly not a coincidence either."

He nods, "that's what I thought." He sighs, running a hand through his hair, "it's a piss take, two days ago she came here to see you and dad called out to her like it was normal, like he didn't deny her paternity, I mean, who fucking does that."

I frown, "Melanie came here two days ago?"

He nods, "yeah but I think you were already getting ready to roll out."

Fuck, I sigh, placing my cup in the sink before I pat him on his back, "alright brother, I'm going to go see my girl then. All this shit must be a head case for her."

He nods, "it is for me, so god knows how she feels." He shakes his head, "I'll see you later brother." I nod and walk out of the kitchen leaving a confused Gunner with his parents. He'll soon perk up when he gets to the bar and he sees Leah, our bartender. I've noticed for a while now that they have a thing for each other, so it's only a matter of time until they give into their feelings.

When I walk through the common room, I see Annalise and go to walk over to her, but she just huffs and walks the opposite way to me, and I sigh. I ignore Clitters eyes that track me as I walk to the door and fucking pray Annie girl won't tell Mel about my fuck up because Axel's right, if I lose her then I'm gone.

I get to the hospital about twenty minutes later and I grin at the prospect of finally seeing my girl. The guilts still there and I know it probably always will be, but I can't lose her, she made it perfectly clear, no other women, it's the only fucking rule she gave me, and I broke it and probably her trust too. She can't find out.

I get to the reception desk and I grin wide, "hey Cilia, how's George doing?"

She smiles at me her brown eyes sparking, "he's doing better thanks Dagger. Mel's working in the E.R today darling." I grin at her and thank her before heading to find my woman. Cilia is a lovely woman in her 70's and always puts a smile on your face, Mel loves her, and I can't say I blame her, the woman's an angel. When I get to the E.R Cassidy intercepts me, grabbing my arm and I instantly tense before ripping my arm out of her clutch and she scowls,

"Seriously?" she sneers, and I scowl back before going round her and looking around the E.R. It's flittered with patients but not my woman. I turn to go to the desk to ask the receptionist where she is, but I find my woman standing there doing paperwork instead. Her backs to me and she's writing something down. I grin before I sneak up behind her and I wrap my arms around her waist, smelling her strawberry scent, finally feeling at home. She tenses and I smile before rasping in her ear,

"I've missed you precious."

She tenses even more, and I furrow my brows as she gets out of my hold. Cassidy has now taken a seat at the desk and is scowling at my woman while Meghan, Mel's friend walks up beside her and narrows her eyes at me and I start to feel pissed at her reaction to me before my words escape my mouth without realizing the consequences.

"What's going on Mel? I haven't heard from you in nearly three weeks and your acting off with me? shouldn't it be me pissed that you ignored me, not the other way round." Ok that came out completely wrong because I fucking cheated, but it doesn't make sense for her reaction unless she knows and there's no way she does because Axel would of pre warned me,

right?

Chapter 16

Melanie

I'm literally looking at the man I've fallen in love within shock. Seriously, he cannot be this fucking thick. He cheated on me, and he thinks he has a right to be pissed at me? Rage overtakes my body, my phone burning in my pocket. A text from an unknown number warning me to stay away from 'her' man with a picture of the same woman he let touch him with her mouth sprawled naked on his bed then another picture of him walking into the room in nothing, but a fucking towel and he has the fucking balls to stand there looking pissed at me for ignoring him.

I scoff and shake my head before going around him to head for my break. He can go fuck himself, or better yet, he can go fuck that bitch. Shit. A lump forms in my throat and my eyes start to sting. Damn him! I clear my throat and keep walking but just as I get past the storage closet he grabs my arm and pulls me inside it slamming the door behind us. I look around and snort before raising a brow at him, "really?"

He narrows his eyes at me then looks around too before mumbling, "shit" realizing it's the same closet I walked in on him and Cassidy fucking in. He looks back at me, but I just cross my arms over my chest making him sigh, placing his hands on his hips, "baby, you ignored me. You basically pushed me away and for some strange fucking reason your pissed at me. What is it I've done so fucking bad for this reaction?"

I tilt my head him and raise a brow, he really is clueless, he seems to think I wouldn't have found out about his dirty deed. My heart hurts just looking at him, I have a lump in my throat, and I want to really fucking cry. I clear my throat, "we're over, don't come to the hospital looking for me and don't come to my flat. We are done." His eyes widen in shock, mouth hangs open a little while his head goes back like I slapped him which lucky for him that I haven't done because trust me I really want to. He walks over to me and goes to touch me, but I take a step back and he furrows his brows, "is this because I told you about Butch? I thought you had a right to know precious." I flinch at his nickname before my eyes turn sorrow and pain shoots through me. Trying to keep my exterior cold towards him is fading. He's hurt me, broke my heart, just like I knew he would. I look him in the eyes so he can see my pain causing him to take a step back in confusion, "no Dagger," he flinches, "it's because of the woman you had in your office."

His eyes widen in shock before he rasps, "Annalise told you?"

I huff out a laugh and shake my head, of course she knew and didn't mention it, not even this morning when we had a coffee date at her bakery before work. I guess he is her family. I look back at him, "no, I saw you doing the dirty deep three days ago then your lovely lady decided to text me a picture of her fully naked in your bed with you just in a towel this morning. So, we are done Dagger. I told you no other women and you decided otherwise." He shakes his head as pain flashes in his eyes, but I ignore it and go to walk around him. He grabs my arm, "Mel please. It was a mistake, I love..." I don't let him finish because like hell is he saying those words to me, "goodbye Dagger." He flinches again before I remove my arm from his grip and open the storage door, both Cassidy and Meghan are standing there, I go straight to my friend who links arms with me, pulling me towards the staff room while I say over my shoulder, "he's all yours Cassidy." I hear a bang, but I ignore it and continue walking with Meghan as tears fill my eyes. She notices and pulls me quicker.

When we enter the room, she quickly shuts the door as my sob comes out and my tears start to fall. Meghan grabs a hold of me, wrapping her arms around me, "I'm so sorry Mel." I nod against her shoulder as another sob comes out, "I-I love-love him." She squeezes me tighter at my admission and I sob some more for the pain I feel right now.

Why wasn't I enough? Why did he have to betray my trust in him?

A little while later we were sitting on the bench in the staff room, and I've finally stopped crying, I just feel numb now.

    Meghan smiles at me, "you don't have to do it today." I just give her a sad smile back, "I kind of do though. She's being moved to the prison's medical facility in the morning so it's now or never. I got my closure with Callum, and I know I need it with her too then I can finally put my past behind me." She gives my hand a squeeze and we both stand.

When we get out of the staff room, she kisses my cheek before going off to do her rounds while I head to my mother's room. I only have twenty more minutes of my break so it's now or never. When I get to her room, I furrow my brows when I hear voices while the police officer is sat outside her door. I give the officer a nod and he gets up, opening the door for me and I freeze when I notice Butch and Gunner standing there with concerned looks on their faces. What the fuck.

I don't let myself be known wanting to hear what they're saying first,

"She's always been out of control and now this." My mother sniffles, "after she told her father I was cheating on him which I wasn't she turned so spiteful. She told the school I was hurting her when she was hurting herself, and now she's telling the police I attacked her. Why would she do this." She sniffles again while Butch looks pissed on her behalf. I look towards Gunner who's looking at me and I just raise an amused brow at him making him bite his bottom lip to stop from laughing. Unlike Butch, he's not falling for her bullshit, and you know what, I really can't be assed with explaining myself so instead I grab my phone and get my door cam up and smile as I get to the conversation between her and Harris.

I start it just as she speaks making both her and Butch turn to look at me, her eyes widen while Butches narrow, *"I know you're in there Mel's, open the door now."*

"She's obviously not fucking there Beth. Let's just go and try again later before the neighbors call the fucking pigs." Harris snaps

"No, I refuse to fucking leave, if she won't give me the money, we need then you'll pimp her fucking out like you should have done when she grew fucking tits." My mother's face has gone paler, and I just smile.

He sighs, "we'll try again later and bring some guys to grab

her, come on. I've already seen three people looking out of their fucking doors."

Butch snaps his head towards my mother with hate in his eyes while I get the next folder up and play it too. Gunner's face goes red while Butch is ready to throttle my mother. You can hear a bang as I fall to the floor before my mother speaks,

"Ever hear the expression 'snitches gets stitches'? thanks to you Harris is sitting in jail because his name red flagged. I just lost my connection to my drugs you little bitch and I'm now wanted." You can hear the punch echo in the room and the crunch of my nose as it breaks on the floor making Gunner flinch. You can hear my grunt and my sob as they hit me before my mother talks again, "***don't disappear you little disappointment. I have several men who want you for a night."*** I end the recording on my cough before I look at my mother with a raised brow and she swallows hard.

Both men look at my mother while she stares at me. Fear shines through her eyes, "I told Callum you cheated did I mother, at the age of four? that's funny because Butches wife offered him $100,000 for full custody of me when he had no idea I wasn't his. That's why he left because you're a whore. And yet from the age of four until the time I could finally leave, you abused me. You told teachers I was hurting myself after I went to one for help at the grand old age of 8. You broke my wrist that night didn't you mother and after every other mark I had or broken bone I endured, it got ignored because of your lies." Her fear oozes from her and she swallows hard while Gunner has to be held back by his dad who looks ready to explode. "and let's not forget the men you'd bring round and allow them to leer at me. I had to lock myself in my room in the trailer for days when you had your druggie parties because some of them tried to touch me. I had no food or water and had to use my trash can as a toilet and yet your trying to get sympathy off a man who couldn't be assed to claim me because his marriage was more important to him." I see Butch flinch but it's the truth. "Do you want to know who I saw two weeks ago mother." I raise a brow at her while tears fill her eyes, "the man who was supposed to bring me up. The man I thought was my father and abandoned me. You two are a match made in heaven, both druggies. Heck, before he even realized who I was, he offered to pay me for a night." Both men growl while her eyes widen in shock, "this here mother is my closure, just like how I got the closure from him too. I don't want to see your face again and I don't want you contacting me from prison, as far as I'm concerned you died during your overdose and I'm now an orphan. Goodbye Beth." Her tears fall as I turn around and leave. I can hear Butch shouting at her, but I keep walking until someone grabs my arm and I turn to see Gunner. He gives me a sad smile, "I'm sorry Mellie."

I can't help the smile that takes over my face, "that's what Shane calls me too, he said it suits me." Gunner grins and nods his head, "I want to get to know my sister, what do you say?"

I tilt my head and see in his eyes how sincere he is, and I nod making him smile wide before he takes me into a hug. I hug him back tightly before letting go. We hear a bang, and he sighs, "I better go sort that out. This weekend come to our bar in town, Untamed Fire, please, I can introduce you to Leah and Sophie." I give him a smile and nod my head before we hear another bang from my mother's room. The police man just shrugs, continuing to read his paper making me tilt my head at him.

"Shit." Gunner mumbles before looking back at me, he kisses my head and quickly heads to the room, "I'll see you at the weekend sis." I smile at his endearment. I always wanted a big brother. Shaking my head, I go back to work. I have a few patients in need of a catheter change.

I look at my watch a few hours later and sigh. Finally home time. I quickly head to my locker in the staff room and grab my stuff before heading to my car. When I get to it I see Travis leaning against his bike. He tilts his head at me as pain flashes through his eyes, but I just shake my head ignoring him. I unlock my car about to get in when he grabs my hand, pulling me towards him. I squeeze my eyes tight as my tears start to fall causing him to slowly place his forehead against mine before rasping, "it was a mistake Mel, I fucked up, I can't take it back, but I can promise it won't happen again, please precious, I can't lose you." I sniffle and squeeze my eyes tighter before looking at him while my tears stain my cheeks, "you lost me the minute you allowed her to touch you with her mouth." He slowly closes his eyes as a tear falls down his cheek and I let out a sob, causing him to hold me tighter to him, "please baby."

I take a deep breath, breathing in his musky scent one more time before I slowly pull out of his grip making his arms fall down his sides as I wipe my cheeks with the back of my hands, "I can't, y-you broke my trust." I climb into my car, about to shut the door when he rasps, "I won't give up baby. Your mine, just like I'm yours. I love you." I let out another sob before rasping back, "just not enough to stay faithful."

I close the car door and start her up before driving out of the hospital car park ensuring I don't look back. He broke my trust and that's just something I don't think he can gain back again.

Chapter 17

Dagger

I'm sitting at Untamed Fire with a bottle of water in front of me. Leah has refused to serve me, something about the way I look broken and not cleaning up after my ass in her bar, her words not mine. I look up and see she's watching me closely and I shake my head. I swear you'd think she was older than me the way she's being a mothering hen right now. I take a sip of the water trying to forget the look of heart break in Mel's eyes. I know I should leave her be now, I cheated, fucked up big time but I can't, I fucking need her like I need air, she's mine just like I'm hers. I just need to make her realize that.

I take a another sip when someone sits next to me, and I turn to see Gunner. I raise a brow at him, he looks like a fucking wreck. He nods to Leah clearly wanting liquor but Leah being Leah decides to drop him a water too and I snort. He frowns then looks up at her with intensity making her clear her throat before she shrugs then turns around going to another customer all while Gunner watches after her and I smirk. I swear we're all dropping like flies. Axel with Annie, me with Mel even if she hates me right now, Ink with Sophie who also hates him right now and is adamant she's giving this other guy a go much to my brothers frustration then Gunner with Leah. I shake my head before he speaks,

"how much did Melanie tell you about her past?"

I frown at his question before looking at him, "not a lot, only that the man she thought was her father left why?"

He clears his throat again, "turns out her mom had been abusing her for years, blaming her for why her dad left when in reality he had found out she wasn't even his. She tried selling a sob story to dad when she contacted him out of the blue about how Mel was out of control and got her arrested, put her in hospital and shit, but Mel showed proof of her own fucking mother having her beat up a few months ago and admitting to trying to sell her body to men for a fix." My eyes widen. That explains why we clicked so quickly, same tortured soul, fuck. "the two weeks she didn't call you, she was getting closure, apparently she went to see the man she thought was her dad, turns out he's a druggie too."

"Fuck."

He nods in agreement. "yeah, so not only did my dad choose his marriage over his daughter but both her parents chose drugs. Everyone who was supposed to love and care for her hurt her and left." He shakes his head and I freeze. Shit. I just fucking cheated on her hoping she wouldn't find out. Gunner looks at me and frowns when he sees my frozen expression.

I clear my throat, "I fucked up and she found out, walked in on it actually."

Gunner frowns before looking at me,

"I let Clitter suck me off in anger."

Gunner slowly closes his eyes on sigh, and I brace, I deserve it and it's something a big brother requires to do. He punches me square in my jaw and I barely manage to stay on my stool while Leah rushes over to us with wide eyes, she goes to say something, but Gunner moves her hair out of her face gently before rasping, "it's what big brothers do for their sisters." Her brows shoot high while he looks at me, "fix it brother. You love her and its plain as day that she loves you, so fucking fix it."

He leans over the bar and places a kiss to Leah's head before turning and leaving and I look at Leah with a raised brow. She clears her throat but shakes her head, "we kind of slept together last week." I start to grin ignoring the pain in my jaw fucking happy for them, but she just scowls at me, "no, it's not happening. He's not interested. Some guy asked me out, wouldn't take no for an answer and he intervened and took me back to his house at the compound, we drank too much, and it happened. He doesn't really want me, if he did then he wouldn't have let Cara sit on his lap yesterday, he wouldn't had taken her to his office." I sigh at my club brothers stupidity, "and he would have remembered that we slept together in the first place." My eyes widen at her confession before she shrugs, "it doesn't matter. Look, you fucked up, I don't know what but clearly it's bad enough for Gunner to hit you. But if you love her like you say you do then don't give up. Prove to her that she can trust you." She gives me a sad smile before going off to serve customers. She's right, like always, fuck, Gunners an idiot. With that thought in mind and determination in my gut, I knock the bar counter twice, giving Leah a head nod who smiles wide at me, happy I'm taking her advice, and I leave with a plan forming to get my girl back and the first stop is to Axels guy.

I have a puppy to buy!

4 weeks later

I throw my phone on my black glass top coffee table in frustration. Fuck I miss my girl. Four fucking weeks and she still won't talk to me. I've shown up at her place more times than I can fucking count and called every single day groveling, but it's like I don't exist to her. I stopped going to the hospital when that Cassidy bitch tried to proposition me right as Mel was walking out of the doors and the hurt that crossed her face nearly brought me to my knees, so I learnt my lesson there. I sigh before scrubbing a hand down my face before a wet nose nudges my hands and I smile. I look at the chocolate lab that's only 6months old and nod, "yeah Bella, I think it's time I use you too." Bella barks and I smile before rubbing her head. I go to grab my phone again, hoping sending her pictures of Bella would make her talk to me when my front door opens, and I furrow my brows wondering who the fuck that could be until Stormy comes into view from the archway and I roll my eyes regretting not locking the door. We've barely spoken the past few weeks, not for his lack of trying.

"Ever hear of a doorbell Stormy." I don't look at him as I speak, instead I just stroke the dog in front of me.

He sighs, "I'm your father Travis, I shouldn't need to knock."

I just snort before standing with Bella in my arms and I face my so-called father, "what can I do for you Stormy?" he shakes his head at my tone, "dinner, this Sunday at home. Be there." I just laugh, "I fucking mean it Travis. I spoke with Jewels, so I know she's away for a few months travelling with her husband, so fucking be there."

"Yeah, no thanks, I'd rather drink acid."

He tilts his head, his eyes cold, "you either fucking be there, or I'll tell Ink the time you gave his mom a black fucking eye." I just smirk, not taking the bait. One of the men she allowed to molest me actually gave her the black eye at her request. Stormy broke my arm the next day. I just shrug making his jaw go tight, "if you're not there Travis then I'll make sure the whole clubhouse knows what you did to my wife, my old lady over the years. The abuse and hurt you put her through, and you'll lose your fucking VP patch, this house, and your place in the club. I've had enough of your fucking behavior over the years so fucking be there or kiss goodbye to your family." With that nice little speech he walks back out, ensuring to slam my front door while I grind my teeth, trying my hardest not to grab my fucking knife.

Rage boils over. For years he's treated me like shit all because his woman didn't like the fact he got someone else pregnant and had to take the fucking child in and he comes into my fucking home and threatens me.

"Fuck."

Don't get me wrong, I'd fucking leave now if I could, but I want Mel. She's worth seeing his face every day. Sighing I place the dog on her bed before ensuring to lock up. I can't face him and his wife over dinner alone. I've managed to stay the fuck away from the bitch for years, but I think it's time the fucking truth comes out. I know the brothers love Leslie, but I've got years of scars on my body as proof to what she did as well as Ink who can confirm the shit I was punished for was supposed to be for him and she lied for her own amusement. It's bullshit that they've believed every fucking word she's said over the years. Makes you wonder why I gave fucking in to Axel when he asked me home in the first place. If

I didn't want Mel so fucking bad then I would have left 4 months ago when I thought about returning to my team.

I quickly get on my bike and speed off towards the gates of the compound. Shane is on the gate, and I stop by him. He furrows his brows in confusion, and I clear my throat, "I understand your loyalty, you looked at her like a brother, but you should have told me she knew what I did. You're going to be a patched brother soon. Loyalty Shane even when an old lady asks you to keep quiet, you need to talk so we can fix our fuck ups and what I did was the biggest fuck up of all." He smirks at me, and nods and I nod back, "thanks for having her back though." That makes him grin and I rev my bike before heading out of the clubhouse grateful to have him become part of our family. I looked through the camera's a few days ago and saw he was on duty when she came round. He knew I was in but didn't know what a fucking idiot I was being while she spent a good hour pacing the front gate before entering and when she left, her tears were coating her cheeks which explained his reaction to me when we got back from our club run. He spent most of the time convincing her to come talk to me only to leave devastated and heartbroken.

Twenty minutes later I park up outside of the hospital, and I take a deep breath, really fucking hoping she'll talk to me. I get off my bike and head into the hospital to the desk where the receptionist smiles seductively at me, and I inwardly roll my eyes, the woman looks fifteen years older than me with all the make-up she has on and the fake tan. Jesus.

I give her a fake smile, "I'm looking for my fiancé, Melanie Wilson. She's a nurse who works on different wards each week." The receptionist scowls before looking on her computer before snapping, "E.R" I nod and give her another fake smile before heading that way to find Melanie. I know I did wrong, but I fucking need her. I find her coming out of a cubicle and I quickly intercept her before Cassidy sees me. They seem to be always on the same fucking shift. I grab her arm surprising her, "what the…" I don't let her finish as I drag her to an empty cubicle before shutting the curtain. I turn back round to her and see she's glaring at me, and I swallow hard.

"Dagger, I'm working you can't come in here and do this." Her voice is low when she hisses at me, and I clear my throat trying to hide my flinch at her using my road name before I slowly remove my cut making her furrow her brows at me. Fuck, I hope she doesn't run scared when she sees. I gently lay my cut on the bed before I take a deep breath and ring out my hands, she takes a step forward seeing the panic in my eyes,

"Trav?"

My heart flutters when she uses my given name and I gently take the hem of my white shirt before I slowly rise it up and above my head, taking it off. She gasps, her eyes widening as tears fill them before she comes the rest of her way to me, dropping the clipboard on the bed with my cut while I grip my shirt in my hands, shaking. I stand completely still, not moving while she gently lays her hand on the scare on my right side that my molester did when I was 12. She slowly moves her hand towards my back, and I tense, worried she'll be disgusted. She walks around and I can hear her breathing, its picked up but I don't move as she inspects every scar on my body. When she gets back in front of me, her tears coat her cheeks and pain flashes through her eyes for what I have endured. I relax when I don't see disgust before I rasp,

"For as long as I can remember Leslie, my stepmom, has abused me. Physically and verbally. If my brother Ink had done something wrong, she'd placate him then tell my so-called father I was the problem that day which earned me a beating before being starved." She tenses at each word, and I swallow hard, "When I was 10, she would allow her 'friends' to tie me up naked then touch my body anyway they wanted while they got off. If I fought, I got stabbed."

Her eyes widen in shock while I feel fucking physically sick. Worried this may push her away even further.

Chapter 18

Melanie

I stand here in shock at his revelations. Not only was he abused, but he was also molested, and it was all caused because of his stepmother's jealousy!!

Where the fuck was his father?

I wipe away my tears with anger before taking a deep breath. "wh-why? Why are you showing me now?"

He swallows hard, fear etches in his eyes and my heart tugs. If I could just switch off the love I feel for this man then I would in a heartbeat. He broke me. Hurt me. But my love still holds tight to him.

"My father has decided I need to attend Sunday dinner after threatening to tell my club brothers, my family that I hit his wife growing up if I don't show, he's threatening my patch, my home and my family all for his wife, my abuser."

My anger intensifies and his wrong doings pushed aside. He threatened his own son with his family, are you fucking kidding me? He clears his throat, "I think it's about time I told them some home truths and I know I fucked up, believe me I know, I'm paying for my mistake every day because I fucking miss you more than life itself but I fucking need you Precious, I really need you at this dinner. I've spent years purposely locking myself in the storage cupboard that she graced me with as my room to stay away from them. I've never really had a family meal there unless a brother came round, she ensured I was hardly ever fed but this dinner, I need you, your my anchor Mel." My anger consumes me for what he had to go through. For what his own family allowed him to go through.

I look into his eyes; they're pleading me to do this.

Can I do this for the man I love? Can I have a dinner with his family and him after he cheated? After he tore my heart out? I know he fucked up, but what's stopping him from doing it again and again? My mind is spinning. Questions running wild as my heart tugs to him, wanting to shield him from the pain he's fought all his life.

Fuck.

"Please Precious, I can't do this without you." He rasps. He opens his arms out wide, his abs tightening, "this is me. The scars and all. You're the only one I've ever allowed to see me like this, to touch me. You're the only one whose touch doesn't burn. I know I fucked up baby, I know but I'm not giving up on us. Me and you, we're meant to be, and I'll spend the rest of my fucking life making up for the pain I caused." My heart skips a beat and I want to believe him, I do, so much but what's stopping him from doing it again. I know he's tried to show me how much he wants me; how sorry he is; he came to the hospital a lot before Cassidy decided to try and come on to him so instead he'd sit outside of my flat every single day after leaving a rose on my doorstep. I know he wants us but seeing that woman on her knees for this man whose become my everything, it broke me. He says he loves me, yet he let someone else touch him.

That's not love. He steps the last little bit towards me and grips my cheeks with both his hands when he sees me struggling, "I know you're not ready yet Mel and I won't rush you, I know I need to earn your trust again, but I need you baby. I can't do this without you. She'll deny everything and my father will follow her. Please Precious." I swallow as some tears fall and he quickly wipes them away with his thumbs. The pain in his eyes are killing me and the scars on his body. I shake my head and he sighs dropping his head, his hands falling limp at his side before I squeeze my eyes shut making more tears fall, hoping I'm not making a mistake.

"Okay."

It's all I can say in a rasp, my gut is telling me to do it, but my heart wants to protect itself from the pain he tore through me. I understand he has needs but to do that to me? He should have just ended things if he couldn't wait until I was ready and if he was having a bad day then he should have gone to the gym. I know he doesn't know I have zero experience with men, but he didn't respect me and that's something I'm struggling to deal with. After what my mother put me through growing up, trust is hard for me, and he broke it.

His head shoots up and relief instantly takes place over his face before he takes me into his arms. I wrap my arms around his waist, feeling all of his scars making some more tears fall. I take a second, just one second to hold him because God do I miss him, so much, before I pull back and wipe my tears,

"this doesn't mean anything though Dagger." I think I say it more for myself, to remind myself what he did. I can't go there with him again. I won't be made a fool. I just won't.

He drops his head again but nods, "I'm not giving up on us Mel, I won't. I need you like I need air; I'll gain your trust again and I won't take it for granted; your mine. I'll pick you up on Sunday before the dinner at 6." He kisses my head, lingering before putting his shirt and vest back on before kissing my head one more time then leaves but not before rasping on his way out, "I love you baby," and my tears fall again while I whisper back when the curtain shuts, "not as much as I love you". I don't know how long I just stand here for before the curtain opens and Meghan rushes in. She sees my face and instantly wraps her arms around me, and I sob.

She pulls back and wipes my cheeks, "what did he want?"

I sniffle, "He won't give up on us, he wants what we had back, but I just don't know how to trust him again. He says he loves me but how can you cheat on someone you love?" I sniffle again, "he wants my help on Sunday, the pain in his eyes." I shake my head, "what he was put through, I said yes, I couldn't turn him away."

She nods her eyes showing concern but also understanding, I wouldn't say yes to going unless it was serious. She knows how much I love him, how I'm bonded to him, but she also knows how much he freaking hurt me. How do you get over the person you want to spend your life with cheating on you? Haven't I had enough bad karma growing up?

"Maybe, maybe take it one day at a time? He hasn't been with anyone else, we both know he spends most of his time trying to get you to talk to him, and I know he deserves a swift kick in the balls for what he did, but he hasn't given up Mel. And I know how much you miss him. One day at a time and maybe your trust might return in him." I nod as Meghan brings me back out of my head and the questions that continue to go round, and I hug her tightly. She's right, I know she is, but does that make me a push over? and would he do it again? I'm brought back out of my head again when Cassidy walks in and I try, I really freaking do but my eye roll comes, the woman's a fucking menace and the only reason why she still has a job is because of who she sleeps with on the board. She's staring at me with a scowl, but I just shake my head and go to walk past her with Meghan following before she grabs my arm making me stop. I look at her hand on my arm before looking back at her with a raised brow, "can I help you?"

She narrows her eyes, "stay the hell away from my man! Dagger has finally decided to give us a shot." I snort while Meghan coughs to hide her laughter. I rip my arm from her bruising grip and shake my head before I start to walk out while saying over my shoulder, "last time I checked, it's me he's been trying to contact, not you and it's also me he's picking up on Sunday. Grow up Cassidy!" I hear her screech as I walk out of the cubicle while laughing with Meghan and I must admit, that really did cheer me up.

After a relatively normal week dodging Cassidy and her unneeded drama of constantly reporting me for crap I wasn't even in the vicinity for, (thank god for CCTV), I'm standing in my small living room in a black knee length dress. My hair is down, full of curls and I've placed on minimal make up. I take a deep breath, my nerves kicking in. I have a bad feeling, it could be because of what Dagger did to me, the trust he broke after ensuring I fell deeply for him, or it could be that I'll probably for the first time want to go against my beliefs in helping people and kill his stepmom. Probably the latter. Shit. I take another deep breath when I hear a motorcycle. My stomach flutters full of butterflies that I always get as well as the sinking feeling when I remember that woman on her knees in front of him. Shit, right. I'm doing this because he needs me, and I care too fricking much.

I quickly lock up before heading out front of my building to find him sitting astride his Harley looking too fucking good for his own good. His hair is in its usual man bun and he's wearing his shades while his black tee hugs his muscles tightly with his vest over the top of it. He looks at me up and down before he smiles while I walk over to him.

"Hey Precious."

I give him a small smile back before grabbing the helmet from the back of his bike, but he quickly grabs it off of me and places it on my head himself before he helps me on. I take a deep breath then place my arms around his waist. His hand automatically comes to mine, and he holds them for a few minutes before starting his bike. He revs it then drives off down the road, all while I hold him tight, allowing myself this closeness with the man that had consumed me before he broke me. Could we have it back again? Or will my trust be forever broken? I sigh, holding him tighter before laying my head on his back, my emotions all over the place.

We arrive back at the clubhouse a little while later and Shane lets us in. He waves at me, and I wave back while Dagger drives past the club and into a little estate. He drives past several homes before we come to a big, grey Victorian house and I swallow hard, trying to control my anger. They live in a massive home, yet they gave him a fucking cupboard to live in, what kind of father allows his wife to treat his son this way.

As Dagger turns off his bike bringing be out of my rage filled head, a tall man opens the door before we even get off. He looks like Dagger right down to the black hair and grey eyes. He crosses his arms over his chest before smiling gently when he sees his son help me off of his bike. Dagger removes the helmet and gives me a sad smile while I take his hand as soon as he puts the helmet on his bike and squeeze it tight in reassurance making his eyes soften towards me, showing me the love I want to believe is there before we head up the porch steps.

"I didn't think you'd make it son."

I narrow my eyes at the man's sarcastic statement but don't make a scene when Trav...Dagger, shit, squeezes my hand. I have a feeling it's going to be a long freaking evening. The man looks at me and grins, "you must be Melanie. I'm Stormy, Daggers dad." I give him a weak smile, wanting to scream at him while moving closer to Dagger. This man is no freaking father, he's a coward.

Stormy furrows his brows at me, but Dagger deviates the attention from me to him when he wraps his arm around my shoulders. My body instantly heats up making me want to scowl. Traitorous body.

"Let's just get this over with shall we Stormy."

His dad flinches and pain enters his eyes, but he soon tries to hide it with a look of disappointment making me shake my head. He doesn't deserve Dagger as a son. To me his only fault was not being able to keep it in his pants. Shame she didn't bite his dick, maybe that would have taught him a valuable lesson, 'Don't cheat on the woman you say you love'.

Stormy steps aside letting us pass before we go into the most blinding living room that's full of whites, Jesus. I look at Dagger with a raised brow and he smirks at me before his brother Ink grabs me into a hug. I hug him back with a smile,

"hey sweets."

I pull back from the hug and give him a smile while Dagger growls like a dog wrapping his arm around my waist making Ink shake his head while I snort before a woman comes into view. She has a massive frown on her face, and I instantly know who it is. Short brown hair that's in a bob styled to perfection while her brown eyes hold disgust at Dagger, and I go to take a step forward only to be held back. I look towards Dagger, and he raises a brow at me, causing me to huff while Ink looks at me with a furrowed brow. Shit. Dagger mentioned Ink wasn't aware of his up bringing. He's now only started to question things. I clear my throat as she comes closer. She looks at me before dismissing me and goes to hug Dagger. He tenses but I intercept her and stand in front of him making her take a step back while furrowing her brows, she has another thing coming if she can touch my fucking man.

Fuck, I mean, crap!

"Mom, I don't think you've met but this is Daggers woman Melanie. Mel this is my mother Leslie."

I give Ink a smile but refuse to look at his mother. This woman is a disgrace to our gender and what I would give to scratch her eyes out right now. Dagger squeezes my waist and I look at him, giving him a reassuring smile and he visibly melts before my eyes. God, why did I have to love this man so much, maybe if I didn't, I would be able to let him go but instead I'm tethered to him. Daggers dad comes in and moves past us towards the dining area which again is full of whites, seriously, does this woman not like color? I look towards the she bitch herself when she speaks,

"come on in and take a seat, the foods all been served."

Her voice is tight, but we all listen and take a seat. Stormy sits at the head of the table while his wife sits to his right and Ink to his left. Both Dagger and I sit on Inks side. The food is already on the plates, but I don't pick up my utensils. I don't trust this woman. I look at Dagger and see he's about to pick his fork up, but I grab his hand and he looks at me in confusion, I subtly shake my head at him when I see Leslie look at him with a slight smirk. She's done something to his food, and I'm fucking pissed. She's playing a game, but she doesn't realize, there's a new player around!

Let the night begin bitch.

Chapter 19

Dagger

I look at Mel in confusion but all she does is smile at me before grabbing my plate and swapping it with hers. I hear Leslie suck in a breath, and I try really fucking hard not to smirk her way. I knew she messed with my food; I was going to just play with it, but I guess my girl has another idea. And yes I said my girl because she fucking is mine, I will win her back and I'll never fuck up that badly again because let's face it I'll probably do something fucking stupid at some point to make her pissed at me, just not like this. I'll never let another woman touch me a-fucking-gain.

Leslie clears her throat while Ink sits back in his chair in confusion. Stormy tilts his head, "Mel darling, what are you doing?" I bite my lip, fucking hating him talking to Mel, he may be my father but he's also a fucking prick.

Mel shrugs, "it's our thing, right Trav?" she looks at me with the sweetest smile, but I can see the anger in her eyes. She's struggling, fuck. An idea comes to mind, a fucking bad one at that, but one I know will temporally divert her anger; I sigh, hoping she doesn't head butt me, which face it, I would deserve. I lean forward and gently kiss her lips making her narrow her eyes at me while I smile at her, glad she didn't nut me one before nodding to her question, "yeah precious we do." Her eyes never leave mine and she smiles gently at me before picking up her fork. She stabs it into the bland chicken, and I swallow, hard. I give her a subtle warning with my eyes not to take a fucking bite out of that food, knowing she'll be ill for weeks. I can see how pink it is from here, the fucking bitch wanted me hospitalized by the looks of things.

Just as she's about to put it in her mouth, I go to grab the fork but Ink leans over me and beats me to it, "what the fuck? Mom, why is this chicken still pink? It looks fucking raw!"

Leslie's eyes widen while she gasps making both Mel and I roll our eyes, "oh my, I'm so sorry Mel, I had no idea."

Mel snorts, shaking her head, "you are aware that my chicken, on MY plate is cooked perfectly."

Both Stormy and Ink look at her plate with a furrowed brow before looking at theirs then Leslie's and I just sit back, crossing my arms over my chest, staring at my childhood abuser. I think she's gotten a bit rusty in her old age. Leslie clears her throat, "I, uh, had no idea it wasn't cooked like the others." I just shake my head while Mel narrows her eyes. I place my hand on her leg and give it a gentle squeeze making her relax a tad. I bite my lip to stop my grin. Now is not the time to feel fucking proud that she relaxes at me touch still. Mel side eyes me with a raised brow but I just shrug not wanting to piss her off any more than she already is. I've never seen Mel lose control and I don't fancy it happening here.

       Just when I thought he would question his wife, Stormy sits up straighter making us all look at him before he grabs his fork and starts eating like his wife didn't try to fucking poison me. Ink furrows his brows while Leslie smirks at me and starts to eat and I just shake my head while Mel speaks up with anger lacing her voice making me grab her leg again to keep her seated.

"Are you seriously just eating like your wife didn't try to poison your son?"

Everyone at the table shoots their head in her direction but she doesn't back down the stare with my so-called father, "your literally just sitting there, ignoring what she tried to do to your own child? Have you got any idea what that meat could have done to him? how ill he would have gotten? She literally just seared it to make it looked cooked!" her voice gets louder while Stormy's face goes red, "now listen here little miss, I understand you have a crush on my son and I know he thinks he's in love with you when in reality he'll move on next week, but this is nothing to do with you. Leslie didn't do it on purpose, it's an honest mistake."

Leslie's smirk widens while Ink watches his mother in new eyes. I just snort before looking at my father, "first of all, I am in love with her, I fucked up and yet she still came here for me, she's mine so this has everything to do with her." He scowls at me, but I'm not done, "this also wouldn't be the first time she gave me food poisoning would it Stormy. Or ensured I starved for two days as a punishment for something I didn't even do."

Stormy sighs before shaking his head, "when are you going to grow up Travis, your acting like child."

I just smirk, "hey Ink, who broke Leslie's crystal vase."

Ink sits back in his chair, not looking away from his mother's death stare towards me, he tilts his head, watching her reactions. "I did. I kicked my football into by accident, mom told me not to worry." Stormy's eye brows furrow while I nod, "yeah, you gave me a split lip for that Stormy while banishing me to my 'room' with no food for the whole day. I wonder what our club brothers would think if they knew their old VP did that to his own son." Stormy looks at me with narrow eyes, "so what, she mistook one bad thing Ink did. We both know the rest were you Travis, we had evidence." Ink snorts, realizing our father thinks he was saint. Yep, some fucking saint who decided to bring a girl back at the age of 13. Yet it was me who got my head slammed into the wall as punishment because Leslie said I forced her.

Mel bangs her hands on the table making us all look at her in shock, but her eyes stay on Stormy, "are you fucking kidding me? Have you even seen your son's body? The scars YOUR wife had caused? How dare you sit there acting all high and mighty when I can guarantee several instances he was punished for was probably Ink that had caused them and not just small punishments like being grounded or sent to his room, I mean YOU kicking the shit out a child for something he never fucking did. You're a blinded fool who shouldn't be allowed to have children and your wife needs to be locked up in a loony bin. Maybe you can get matching cells." Stormy's face goes brighter while Ink bites his bottom lip to stop his laughter at the shock on his mother's face. I just sit here staring at the woman who has become my person, my whole world, my heart standing up for me, showing me the love she feels without realizing it. I may have fucked up badly, but her love still shines through. I'll get her back, this proves it, it'll just take time.

"I've seen his body. I've seen the trauma you let your wife doll out on him. You let her lie and manipulate you and why? Because she was jealous you had a baby with someone else." Stormy slowly stands, trying to intimidate my woman and I stand quicker, staring him down but Mel isn't finished, she pushes me behind her and leans forward but I quickly wrap my arm around her waist. She might be small but she's fucking mighty, ready to jump across the table to him. "I heard a funny story from Ink last month. Apparently when he was 11, he set off a bunch of fireworks in school when they told him he wasn't allowed to draw during class hours. I thought it was hilarious but then I got a little confused because apparently your wife knew about the incident, yet he wasn't punished? Seems odd doesn't it?" I continue my stare with Stormy when his eyes widen. I was 12 and spent most my time in the library. I thought if I worked hard then my father would love me. Fucking idiot is what I was. Leslie told him I set the fireworks off, and Stormy had broken my wrist that day. He told me I was liar like my Mom when I pleaded my innocence then proceeded to tell Doc what I apparently had done. Doc believed him.

Ink stands and looks between us while my father looks at me with guilt, "wait, wait. Wasn't that the same time you broke your wrist Trav?"

Mel snorts, "he didn't break it Ink. Can't you see the guilt in your fathers eyes while your mother smiles happily at the memory."

Stormy quickly looks at his wife who has quickly wiped the smile off of her face and now has fake tears in her eyes causing him to glare at my woman. He points at her, "your lies are not welcome here, you've upset my woman and I want you fucking out now. You can stay the hell away from my son too. Devious little cunts like you are not welcome near my family."

My anger takes place while Ink grabs my arm before I jump the table and attack our father. Mel just laughs, "oh don't worry, I was just leaving." She turns to me and places a little kiss to my lips making her all I see. She gives me a gentle smile and I can see the conflict in her eyes, she loves me, it shines through, calling for me but she also doesn't know if she can trust me again, but she will, I'll make sure of it. She places her hand on my cheek, her thumb rubbing against my stubble,

"I'm going to get Shane to take me home. If I stay here any longer then I'm going to end up going against my beliefs and stab the two people who should have cared for you, call me later alright." I grip her waist tighter, not wanting her to leave, needing her with me, but she just shakes her head and kisses me one more time and I squeeze her hips even tighter, not wanting to let go. She turns to look at a grey looking Leslie and smirks at her knowing she's planted the seed in Stormy's head before walking out of my grip then the dining room before out of the house. Ink lets go of my arm, knowing I need to release this rage. I swipe my arm across the table, everything falling to the floor making Leslie scream out like someone had just fucking died.

"Are you fucking kidding me Travis. You can pay for this shit once you've cleaned it up."

I glare at him. As fucking usual his wife is right and I'm just a liar to a whore that trapped him, yet my mother wasn't what he's accused her off and he knows it. She was willing to bring me up without him. He knows that too but doesn't want to believe she was going to keep his son away from him.

"Mom."

Leslie looks at Ink whose staring at her with suspicion, "what else did you tell dad Travis was at fault with when I did it? because growing up I was a fucking shit, loving that you treated me like I could do no wrong, I took advantage of that as we got older. So what fucking else did he have to suffer from?" anger laces his voice when he realizes some of my trauma, "I broke the TV, yet dad thought it was Trav even though he was in the library where he spent most of his evenings trying to make dad proud, I mean shit; He got valedictorian, and I was the only one who fucking showed up to celebrate." Stormy furrows his brows before looking at Leslie, "you told me he failed all his classes, its why he joined the Navy Seals."

Ink laughs sarcastically while I continue my glare at Stormy for how he spoke to my girl, the fuckers lucky I haven't stabbed him yet with my Dagger in my boot, no one speaks to her that way, fucking no one. "Dad you have to go through extensive training to become a seal. If he failed school then how in the hell would he have the concentration to become one?"

Stormy looks at Leslie again who swallows hard as doubt comes into his eyes, but I can't enjoy it because it's too little too fucking late.

I look at Ink about to tell him to forget about it because I have a girl to go after, but he's not done, "I ripped the wallpaper when I was 5. I stole out of Moms purse to get my favorite candy when I was 7. I broke the crystal vase at 8 then decided to try and carve our family name in the patio glass doors, causing them to shatter when I was 10." I snort because despite getting a bruised rib for that one, it was fucking funny. Stormy starts to look green when he sees the panic in his wife's eyes.

"I brought a girl home at 12, fucked her in the pool. I smoked weed in my room at 13 then had a major banger of a party when you two went away for a few days at age 14 and let's not forget about crashing the club's truck at 15 when I was drunk off of your scotch that I stole with a few buddies. How about when I got arrested at 16 for public indecency. I fucked some girl in the bowling alley, but it was mom who picked me up, yet the next day Trav had a black eye. At 17 just as Trav decided to leave I trashed the clubhouse just to see if you'd punish me, but you didn't, the next day as Trav caught the bus out of here, you gave me my bike."

Stormy's face goes red, "alright Jackson, I fucking get it, Travis took your punishments but that didn't stop him from hitting your mom and making her life hell all because his mom had died of an overdose."

I laugh, like really fucking laugh while they all look at me in confusion, "a-an overdose? That's what the bitch told you mom died of? Seriously?" Stormy growls but I continue, "I think you need to gain access to her medical records Stormy. My mother died during childbirth, preeclampsia. Jewels was also at my birth, she made sure I knew of the life my mother was creating without you in it. It's just a shame my mother thought ending up with a man who told her to get an abortion would be better than care, but she was fucking wrong, nothing could be worse than under your fucking roof."

He face gets redder as realization hits him and goes to say something but is cut off when my phone rings and he points at me, "don't you fucking dare answer that phone Travis, this conversation is not finished." I ignore him and check to make sure it's not Mel, but I tense when I see the name on my screen. I clear my throat and decide to put it on loudspeaker, Ink deserves to know what's about to happen. They wouldn't be ringing me now if it wasn't urgent.

"Sniper here."

Both Stormy and Ink tense while Leslie's eyes widen. Gone the VP and in place the Navy Seal.

"Sniper its budgie. Our intel is exposed, the time frame has been moved up."

Fuck, I haven't managed to explain to Mel yet, "ETA?"

"2hours"

I see Ink shake his head while Stormy's eyes start to mist, and I swallow hard,

"text me the coordinates, I'll be there."

Stormy sits down in a lump as tears start to fall down his cheeks knowing how dangerous my mission now is that our intel has been exposed while Ink bends over, placing his hands on the table.

"You're not going Travis. Please, you can't go, you nearly died 5 years ago before you came home, please."

There's panic in his voice and guilt builds, fuck.

"I'm sorry brother, they need me." I rasp before hugging him around his neck before whispering, "I'll be safe and try to stay in touch, I promise." I kiss his head then I run out of their house to my bike. I have roughly an hour to get packed and get Bella over to Mel's somehow. I'll have to ring her to let her know. Fuck.

I start my girl up as Ink and Stormy rush out of the house, shouting my name but I ignore them. I need to go see Axel and Gunner quickly before I pack, I need them to watch over my girl while I'm gone.

Fuck, I hope Mel will be ok.

Chapter 20

Melanie

I sigh and scrub a hand over my face. I'm sitting on my old sofa with my legs up under my ass feeling guilty for leaving Trav…Dag…Trav. Shit, I sigh again, my head all confused. I missed his call about an hour ago, but I just couldn't answer it, I promised I'd be there for him, and I left, I know I did the right thing walking out and I know leaving him in his family home was hard, but I knew if I stayed, I would have stabbed his father. He just sat there while his wife had tried to poison his own son, I mean, come on who fricking does that? I shake my head; our lives are so similar in a way. Shitty fucking parents. I think that's maybe why we connected so well to begin with, it's just a shame he thought to get pleasure from someone else. I know he wants to try again and work on forgiveness, but I just don't know if it's possible. Does it make me stupid and gullible to give him a second chance? Will I regret not seeing if we can be us again? Or am I better off on my own?

I'm brought out of my head and all the questions when there's a knock at my door and my breathing stops with only one person coming to mind, Travis. I quickly get up and open it but frown when I see Axel and Gunner standing there with worried faces, but I soon ignore them when I see a gorgeous chocolate lab and I squeal, yes I freaking squeal before taking her from Axels arms making both men chuckle while she licks at my chin, "hey beautiful girl, oh your just so gorgeous aren't you, yes you are."

I hear both men laugh at my baby voice, but I ignore them and sit on my sofa with the dog in my lap whose still licking my chin making me giggle. Both men come in and take a seat on the old chairs I have,

"Her names Bella."

I look up and grin at Axel, but it soon fades with his next words and panic takes a hold`,

"Dagger bought her for you and him. He wants you to take care of her until he comes back. He's hopeful he'll convince you to move in with him with this girl here."

My breathing picks up and I ignore the moving in part and go to the comes back part. He's gone away? Where? I've literally not long left him at his dads house. Axel sees the question in my eyes and gives me a sad smile before Gunner takes a seat next to me and panic sets in. They're both here to give me the news that he's gone, so it's dangerous what he's gone to do, right?

Gunner puts his arm around me before rasping, "he's been called back into action with the Navy Seals, they need they're sniper. He had two hours to get to his meet up location which is why we're here. We don't know how long he'll be gone for, just that its dangerous."

My breathing picks up as my tears fall hard and fast and panic sets in. He's gone and he may not come back. His line of work in the Navy is dangerous, I know this, but I haven't had the chance to try and forgive him yet because I kept pushing him away, I wasn't willing to even try to talk it out and now I could lose him. A sob climbs from my throat as reality sets in. Axel quickly takes the dog as Gunner hugs me to him tightly, "he will be back sis, I promise. He'll be safe because he has you to come back too. I know he fucked up; trust me, I punched him for it, but he loves you, he won't ever hurt you like that again. Will he fuck up? yes, we male species don't tend to do things right, but he won't do THAT again. You just have to learn to believe that." I grip him tightly as I sob into his chest, worried for the man I love, the man who hurt me while feeling grateful for this man, accepting me straight away as his sister. His parents have tried to get in contact with me but I'm just not ready. His dad didn't claim me while his mom decided to try and buy me which caused my life pain and suffering. I just don't think I'm ready for that can of worms to be opened just yet.

I feel Gunner grip me tighter as my sobs grow harder.

What if I was too late thinking things through?

What if he doesn't come back home, back to me?

One month later

I smile at Meghan and Lilah one more time before heading into my flat. They've spent the day trying to get me out of my own head and I must admit, it worked for a little while. Between my mother's trail where she got sent down for 15 years without bail and Travis being gone, I've struggled. It helps that Lilah is the funniest kid going and she's not scared to tell you what's on her mind. We were at the zoo when some man walked up to her and asks what she loved most about the animals and her answer, 'well, not your breath that's for sure.' Meghan apologized profusely to the man whose face had gone bright red with anger and humiliation while I was trying not to pee myself from the laughter that wanted to escape. Once he'd stormed off basically calling Meghan out for not teaching her daughter some manners my laughter came out because Meghan was trying to be stern with Lilah, but you could see her trying not to smile herself while all Lilah did was shrug. And when she then decided to point out stranger danger with the man not even Meghan could hide her laughter, or the few parents that were around us. I shake my head, that girl is awesome.

                    I smile a little as I open my door feeling grateful for having such a great friend. Bella greets me and I grin wide picking her up as she whines and yips, "hey beautiful girl, you missed me today did you?" She nips at my chin then licks me causing me to grin wider before I head to my bed on the other side of the room. I plop her on the bed and quickly get into one of Travis's shirts and my sweat pants before joining her. She lays her head on my lap as I check my phone for the hundredth time today. Since he had left, Travis has tried to leave me voicemails. Every time he rings, I'm asleep or on shift. I know he's not purposely missing me. Every time he gets my voicemail you can hear the devastation in his voice. I haven't rang back, I don't want to distract him anymore than he probably is but also I think these voicemails help me feel close to him, and they help me hear the longing in his voice making me believe we can have what we did back, maybe something even stronger because shit, do I miss that man and so does Bella. I feel like I'm missing a part of my soul which helped my decision in hoping to try again, although, if he ever touches another woman intimately again, I'll chop his dick off! Sighing, I sit back against my black rail headboard that I found at a car boot sale for a steal before grabbing my phone from beside me and call my voicemail up. I put the phone on speaker so Bella can hear his voice. We do this every day. We listen to all his voicemails just so we can get a bit of him here with us and so far we have at least 14, some days he can't ring, he explains it as radio silence and tells me not to worry but I still do, I think I always will.

My voicemail beeps and his voice comes through, and I smile instantly.

"Hey precious. Fuck, I wish I was with you right now, then you wouldn't have to find out through someone else." Bella's ears twitch and she sits up, looking at my phone while I smile a sad smile as worry enters me because he hasn't rang today. He sighs and I picture him running his fingers through his hair, ***"I've been called back to duty baby, they need me, and I promised to always be there for my team. It's a promise I can't break, even though I wanted to because the thought of leaving you, it tears me apart Mel. I'll hopefully only be gone for a couple of weeks, but I'll keep you updated.***

I love you Melanie."

I wipe away a tear as my phone beeps and the next message starts,

"hey baby. I've finally landed, I know your probably asleep right now, but I just wanted to let you know I'm at my

destination. I'll call again tomorrow when I can. I miss you precious. I love you."

The phone beeps again and I look at Bella and smile. I rub her head as Travis's voice comes over the phone again.

He sighs, *"hey Precious, I caught your voicemail again, fuck. Things are a lot more difficult here than I first thought so I may be longer than I thought. I'm sorry baby, I'll keep you updated."* I hear someone shout 'Sniper' in the background, *"I've got to go precious; I love you."*

I sigh as the phone beeps again while Bella whines. My tears start to well in my eyes again with his next message, guilt at not trying to work things out beforehand hits me hard. I know what he did was wrong but maybe I should have just kneed him in the balls instead of putting us both through this misery.

"Fuck Mel. I need to hear your voice." He sniffles, and my tears fall, *"we lost our informant today, he was killed. He was like a brother to me, took me under his wing. Marshal would have kicked my ass for what I did to you and now he won't get the chance. Fuck baby, I need you."* The phone cuts of and I sniffle, feeling his pain and loss. Fear for what may happen to him intensifies. I want him home, safe.

My front door opens and Gunner walks in. I give him a sad smile as the phone beeps again and Travis's voice comes over the speakers. Gunner takes a seat next to me, so I can lean my head on his shoulder. He's been staying with me since Travis left much to his parents disappointment. He told me they wanted me to stay with him so we could get to know each other but I'm still not there yet.

"Damn. Voicemail again precious. I was hoping to get you today. I want to hear your voice, badly." He sighs while Gunner frowns. He knows he's been leaving me voicemails, he's just never heard them, ***"I've got to go radio silent for a few days baby, I don't want you to worry so if you don't hear from me that's the reason why."*** Gunner tenses, ***"I promise to call as soon as I can. I love you Mel, don't forget that."***

Gunner presses the red button and I scowl at him, but he just shakes his head, "how many voicemails has he left that were like that, that he was going radio silent?" he sounds concerned and tense and I instantly sit up straight with worry,

"about eight why?"

Gunner stands and starts to pace, "what's the longest you've gone from not hearing from him?"

I swallow, "four days."

He nods before looking at me, "when was the last time you heard from him?"

My tears start to fall when I see the panic in his eyes and I rasp out, "four."

"FUCK" he screams before grabbing his phone out of his cut. Apparently calling it a vest is forbidden, his words not mine.

He runs a hand through his blonde hair before he speaks into his phone, "pres we have a problem. He hasn't been in touch for four days."

I sniffle and wipe my cheeks as worry churns at my gut.

"I'm with her now. alright talk to you later."

He looks at me as he hangs up. His eyes soften before he walks over to me and takes a seat. He wraps his arm around my shoulders while I sniffle, laying my head back on his shoulder. "Axel's going to call his people alright. We'll find out something." He picks up my phone and plays the voicemails again and I close my eyes.

"Hey Precious, we need to talk about changing your automated voicemail because this fucking sucks."

Chapter 21

Dagger

I sigh before leaning my head on the small plane window.

The mission was a success but not without some loses. Budgie squeezes my shoulder as Marshall comes to mind. Finding his body. I squeeze my eyes shut as images of his mangled body flashes into my mind as the memories of finding him come back tenfold.

I look through my scope of my rifle into the old, abandoned warehouse that we know the traffickers use to move they're 'products' which consist of children, men and women who have no family before selling them to sick bastards. We lost contact with Marshal, a man who is more family to me than my own father before I arrived. It's why I was called in so quickly.

The warehouse is two stories. After a thorough check through the rifle scope I determine the top floor clear, and I ensure to let my team know before looking on the bottom. My heart stops when I see a few figures laying on the floor.

Fuck.

I check around and see its all clear.

"This is Sniper, all men stay clear, I'm going in." I state in my earpiece before I hear Budgie reply.

"Copy Sniper."

I quickly clear up before making my way down the hill, keeping my rifle pointing in front of me before moving it around with my eyes, watching my surroundings. When I make it to the side door I slowly open it before pointing my rifle inside from side to side before entering. I soon come to a stop at the site in front of me.

Fuck. No, fuck.

My eyes start to water when I see Marshal and what was supposed to be Marshals body. His fingers are sawed off, eyes missing, and his body cut up to pieces. Fuck no. I look around and see the massacre.

I take a deep breath before getting back on the radio, "Nine bodies. Four children, three women, two men and, fuck, and Hawk all deceased, send a crew."

I hear several fucks in my ear before I make my way over to Marshal. I kneel down and drop my head when I see his Navy Seal emblem tattoo on the shoulder just like we all have. Fuck, fuck, fuck. The door slams open and my team enters rushing over to me. They all start cursing when they see our brother while I slowly stand.

"We need to clear the place and search it, find any information you can. MOVE." I shout the last bit as every member taps my shoulder before Budgie squeezes it,

"we'll get them brother."

I nod and we go in search for any information while the rest of our team clear out the bodies. Our delta team will try to identify the bodies while Marshal will be taken back to base before our commander contacts his family.

I'm brought back when Budgie speaks, "I spoke to Axel, he should be at the landing bay when we arrive." I nod, "we couldn't have done this without you Travis. Marshal will be proud of you stepping up as leader the way you did. You single handedly found and destroyed the traffickers operation."

I give him a half smile, "we did good as a team Shaun. You ever need me, I'll be there."

He grins at me, and I chuckle a little before looking back out the window.

An hour later we land back in Dallas, and I stand before giving Budgie a hug, "you need me, you call." He nods before gently patting my back, "always brother. Now go win your girl round yeah." I chuckle and nod before heading to the doorway of the plane. When I get to the bottom of the stairs Axel climb out of the clubs truck, "fuck Travis, it's good to see you and I know a certain beauty who will be relieved your home." I grin at his words before I walk over to him. He grins back but it soon vanishes, and panic etches over his face before he rushes over to me.

"I'm alright brother, I promise."

He just raises a brow while looking at my shoulder that's all bandaged up. I only have a vest on because of the fucking bandage but I did manage to get my cut on as well, so that's a fucking bonus I guess. Some fucker came out of nowhere when we finally got intel on where they were hiding out in. Budgie had to dig the fucking bullet out. I ensured all the fuckers where dead before I saw medical attention though, no one was getting passed me.

"I promise it's good brother."

He sighs while running a hand through his hair, "alright but I want Doc to have a look when we get home." I nod knowing its useless arguing with him, "right, let's get going then. We captured one of Hairy's guys last night, he's tough so I thought your expertise would come into handy."

I grin at his words and nod, "alright but we need to make a pit stop first."

He chuckles, "yeah, your woman has been worried sick, if I don't take you to the hospital first she'd have my fucking balls."

I grin wider at his words. Maybe me being gone is what she needed to see we're meant to be.

An hour later we arrive at the hospital and head inside to search for my girl. We go to reception before being directed to the E.R where I find my woman being flirted with by a soon to be fucking dead man who thinks he can go near her. I growl when I see his fingers run down her arm and she raises a brow at him, looking extremely unimpressed. Axel chuckles as I walk up behind her and glare at the pretty boy fucker. He has the boy next door look with his perfect fucking trimmed brown hair. He swallows hard at my glare, and I growl, "want to tell me why the fuck your touching my woman?" his eyes widen before he puts both his hands up and rushes away. I hear Mel gasp before she quickly spins round. Her eyes instantly water before she throws herself at me. I manage to catch her with my good arm and squeeze her tight to me before she rasps,

"Your home. You're ok."

I sigh and hold her tighter feeling fucking guilty for not being able to contact her in six days, "I'm ok precious, I'm ok."

She sniffles and holds me tighter making me grunt with the shooting pain going through my shoulder making her pull back in confusion and just like Axel, panic etches over her face seeing my wound. I barely get a word out before she grabs a hold of my good arm and shoves me into a cubicle while Axel laughs, following us.

She places her hands on her hips while nodding to my top,

"Off now."

I try not to smirk at her stern voice and do as she says knowing how worried she is so I slowly and carefully pull my cut and vest off while wincing a little. Fucking shoulder gunshot wounds kill, especially when your teammate has to dig the fucking bullet out.

She carefully unwraps my shoulder while Axel smirks, "well, looks like I don't need to get Doc to have a look at it after all."

I just chuckle while Mel ignores us both as she takes off the dressing. Her tears fall when she notices the bruising and redness around the wound.

Fuck.

I look towards Axel and sympathy shows in his eyes, "I'll wait outside brother." He kisses Mel on her head before leaving us alone and I cup her cheek with my right arm and wipe away her tears, "Precious?" I rasp and she lets out a sob, "I-I could ha-have lost you."

Shit.

I wrap my arm around her and hold her to me tightly, "I wouldn't have let that happen baby, we have a lifetime of happiness together. I told you I'm not giving up on us."

She sobs harder, holding me tightly on my right side ensuring not to hurt me and my grip on her back tightens. The curtain opens minutes later, and Meghan enters while Axel just shakes his head with amusement. She instantly sags in relief seeing me but quickly goes tight when she sees my bullet wound and rushes over while Mel pulls back to inspect the wound.

She sniffles, "they had to dig the bullet out didn't they?"

I nod and she sobs some more. Damn I hate her tears. I grip her cheek while Mel grabs some more bandages, "I promise you I'm ok." She sniffles and nods.

"Alright Dag I'm going to rebandage this while you keep a hold of our girl here. Not hearing from you has been hard." I kiss Mel's forehead as she leans against my right side, putting her face into my neck. I smile at Meghan, and she gets to work.

Five minutes later Mel is helping me put my things back on. "I'll give you two a few minutes. Mel you have a patient in cubicle four." Mel nods as Meghan kisses her forehead before squeezing my arm, giving me a relieved smile. She walks out while I pull my girl to me, kissing her lips gently, hoping she doesn't push me away. She doesn't, instead she kisses me back making me grip her hip with my left hand which is not easy with my shoulder all wrapped up while my right goes to the back of her neck. After a few minutes I slow the kiss and peck her, one, two, three more times before rubbing my nose against hers. She smiles at me with tears in her eyes before rasping,

"I still haven't forgiven you and I owe you a knee to the balls."

I grin at her words before kissing her one more time, "I'll earn your forgiveness and trust baby." I rub my nose against hers again, "I've got to get going and catch up on club business, but I'll be back here to pick you up when you finish."

She narrows her eyes at me and I chuckle, "I'll get a prospect to bring me, and we'll go back to yours in your car. I want to see our girl."

She grins wide, "she's missed you, we both have."

I smile before kissing her again, fuck, I can't get enough of her.

"Alright precious, off to work you go. If I don't leave now then I never will. I'll see you later."

She smiles before kissing me one more time then leaves as Axel enters, he shakes his head, "Gunner had practically moved in with her this past month, I think he's going to struggle without her."

I chuckle as we both leave the cubicle before heading towards the main entrance of the hospital. We pass Cassidy on the way out and she smiles wide seeing me, "Dag baby your finally back." I ignore her and continue walking out while Axel chuckles. We hear her growl in frustration but don't stop our stride. You'd think she'd give up by now, my dick was only inside her for five fucking minutes.

Dagger: An MC Romance

Chapter 22

Dagger

We get back to the clubhouse not long later. Shane is on the gate, and when he sees me, he grins wide, relief etching his features. I do a one finger wave as we drive through towards the clubhouse where I notice pretty much everyone is here. Axel looks at me after he parks, and mischief enters his eyes. I raise a brow at him, "I may not have told anyone about you being home."

I chuckle and nod my head.

Fuck yeah.

We both get out while still chuckling and head towards the door while he rubs his hands together making me shake my head. He opens the door, and I can see the clubhouse is packed. I snort when Axel shouts out,

"WELL, WELL, FUCKERS, LOOK WHO I FOUND."

They all turn and look. Half the brothers and old ladies sag in relief while the other half cheer loudly. Annalise rushes over to me and I hug her tightly to my right side. She lifts her head slightly off my chest before frowning when she sees my arm, but I just squeeze her tighter to me, "I'm good, I promise." She swallows hard, she doesn't believe me as tears well into her eyes, but she shakes her head then nods and kisses my cheek before rasping, "I'm going to go make your favorite beef burger." She rushes off with tears going down her face and I go to go after her, but Axel grips my good shoulder and squeezes it, before smiling at me, "I'll go brother." I nod with guilt building in my gut before he goes after his woman who is all heart.

That woman is an angel.

I go to take a step forward towards the bar when my blood brother grabs a hold of me, hugging me tight causing a sharp shooting pain to rush down my arm, fuck. I grunt making him pull back quickly. His eyes widen with panic when he sees my shoulder before he shouts, "FUCK DOC, HE'S INJURED" making everyone in the clubhouse stop as Doc rushes over to me. They all look in horror when they notice the bandage while the women gasp. Fuck me, you'd think a bunch of bikers have never seen a bullet wound before. I sigh when I notice Stormy. He's got his hands on his hips and is bent forward slightly; pain etches on his face as his eyes stay on my shoulder.

Doc starts checking my movement in my shoulder making me grunt.

"Alright fuckers. I'm ok, I promise. Mel looked at it, she made her doctor friend look at it and my units doctor who is fully trained by the way had stitched it up. I'm ok."

The whole room is quiet, all you can hear is Stormy's footsteps as he walks over to me, fuck sake these men. I shake my head before Doc gets my attention when he speaks, "it's not a through and through. How'd they get the bullet out? Surgery?"

I clear my throat knowing they're going to be pissed, "no, uh, one of my men had to pull it out on scene during a shootout."

The brothers' eyes widen while Doc scowls at me making me chuckle. I give him a side hug, "I'm good Doc I promise I am. There was no way I was leaving my girl." He nods but his scowl is still in place as Stormy stands in front of me, his eyes still on my shoulder.

"I'm ok Stormy."

He swallows hard before nodding then looking back at me, he clears his throat but doesn't get to speak before Axel walks in, "alright brothers, now that our man is home, basement now."

Stormy nods while Ink, Gunner, Butch, Flame and Tank grin, heading down to the basement. I grin at Doc who shakes his head with amusement at me as I follow them. I notice Leslie smirking on my way to the door out of my side eye and I sigh. Clearly Stormy believed whatever fucking shit she spewed after that disastrous dinner where her treatment of me started coming out. Years later she's still trying to make my life hell all because her husband and old man had a kid with someone else when she was barely with him. What's it going to take for my so-called father to see her true colours?

When I get into the basement I freeze on the spot, my question answered. Fuck. The brothers look at me in confusion when I don't move from the doorway while the man chained to the ceiling by his arms in nothing but his boxers grins at me, his brown eyes lighting up, not giving a fuck what kind of situation he's gotten himself in, "well, if it isn't my favorite subject. How are you Travvy? You missed me like I missed you?"

Everyone looks at me with shock while I just stare at my

nightmare. Axel snaps out of it first and punches the man in the face before looking at me when I rasp,

"Shacks."

It's all I can say before Ink comes into my view; his eyebrows furrowed.

Fuck.

"How do you know him Dag?"

I swallow hard before looking at Stormy who looks confused then back at Ink, fully aware of the brothers in the room, knowing my past is about to be in the open. I take a deep breath before I rasp out,

"he's the man who molested me from the time I was 10 years old until I finally left for the Navy."

Ink's eyes widen in shock, while the brothers all suck in a breath but I ignore them and look at Stormy whose body has gone tense, "you can thank your wife for that."

He takes a step back like he was punched while I look back to the man who destroyed my childhood. Shack grins wide, blood dripping from his lip, "aww come on Travvy, we both know how much you loved being chained to your bed, I have plenty of foot…" he doesn't get to finish, Tank rushes up to him and starts to pummel on his face and body. It takes Gunner and Flame to pull him back but not before we all hear a crunch somewhere on Shacks' face, most likely his nose. I look towards Stormy again, refusing to meet my brothers' eyes before I take a deep breath. His eyes show disbelief, he doesn't believe me yet again. It's now I decide to make the biggest decision. To show him my truth. Slowly I remove my cut, barely managing with my shoulder before I hand it to Axel who furrows his brows in confusion. I look back towards Stormy and start to lift my tank. Axel helps me take it off and I slowly turn around to show the brothers, my family, the trauma I was dealt with growing up all while Shacks chuckles with pride in the background despite the wheezing that comes out with it.

"What the fuck?" I hear Flame growl before I turn back around to look at my father. I did tattoo over the ugliest ones but unfortunately, you can still see them.

"Your wife Stormy was never happy about my existence. My body here is the proof of that." I point to Shacks, "that man is proof of that, and you let it happen, to your own child. You shoved me into a cupboard and tried classing it as a bedroom, you hit me whenever she said I did something wrong when I hadn't, you fucking neglected me. That man is the one who hit your wife, and do you want to know why Stormy?" His face is red, and disbelief still shines through his eyes, but I point towards Tank, "because Tank put a lock on my door after I lied and said Ink kept pranking me. She got that piece of shit to hit her and say it was me all so you could kick the shit out of me." The men are looking at me with shock while Tank glares at his long-time friend, but I continue to ignore them and I tilt my head towards the man who was supposed to care for me, "did you even wonder why I stopped calling you dad?" He furrows his brows and I smirk at him before turning around and pointing at my lower back where the skin is raised before turning back to the men, I point at Stormy, "your wife burnt me at only three years old with a hot poker and told me never to call you dad again. As you can fucking imagen, it stuck."

I hear coughing making me look at Ink who's throwing up and guilt eats away at me for him having to find out about his mother this way before Stormy rasps out, getting my attention, "your lying." The brothers look skeptical, my fucking family don't believe me. Mother fuckers. My anger rises and Tank speaks up, "why'd you keep him in a cupboard of a room in that big house Storm? Ink always had brand new shit, yet Dagger was in your brothers hand me downs. Are you seriously going to fucking stand there and say he's lying. For years he said she was hitting him, for years he said she let someone touch him inappropriately. How in the fuck is he lying when he's showing you the scars on his body and that fucker basically admitting it."

Stormy turns to him while pointing at me, "he was a little fucking shit always playing up, he was disciplined how I saw fit and he's a fucking liar, my woman wouldn't do such a thing." I cut in ready to punch him, "why because my mother was a sweet butt?" he turns to look at me, his eyes showing disappointment in me and anger. I shake my head at him, "she wasn't even going to tell you about me when I was born. She was only here to earn money. She fucked Dead Shot once on a drunken mistake; she fucked you twice. TWICE." I shout the last bit and he furrows his brows at me, "why don't you go ask your wife Stormy how Ink was really conceived."

He shakes his head, placing his hands on his hips, "the condom didn't work that was it Travis, don't try and play with my fucking marriage, these lies your spewing about a beloved woman by all are enough to vote you out of the club." I scoff at him while Shacks laughs before stuttering out in pain, "you-your fucking marriage was a jo-joke. She fuck-fucking sucked me o-off more times than I-I can count as pay-payment when that-that shit wouldn't un-unlock his door." Stormy rushes over and punches him not liking what he's hearing before Butch pulls him back. He struggles until I speak, "my mother never played with your condoms Stormy, your wife did. She was hoping to fall pregnant but didn't count on you wanting a woman who had turned you down several times before hand. When my mother finally decided to show you some interest you didn't give a fuck that you'd met up with the bitch a few times. You wanted my mother. Maybe you need to go have a chat with a woman she saw as a best friend, a woman who tried to convince my mother I was better off in her care while she was dying on the OR table. Go speak to Jewels because I can guaran-fucking-tee she'll tell you everything you were blissfully unaware about where your 'wife' is concerned."

He looks at me with anger before Ink speaks, "pres, permission to bring Leslie down. If Travis is lying then she wouldn't react to seeing the fucker over there seems as she's already seen a man tied up in here." I look at my brother and his face etches with pain and guilt. He called his mom by her given name and my heart sinks for him. I nod my head in agreement while Axel speaks, "Flame, go get her but don't tell her why."

Face full of anger towards Stormy, Flame nods before going past me. He squeezes my good shoulder making me flinch, still not good with personal touches except for my girl. He nods in realization as well as the other men standing around while Shacks smirks enjoying my discomfort that he created. I walk over to him, grabbing my dagger off the table on the way and he grins wide, "w-well, about time you came c-closer. Y-you still picturing me stan-standing over you wanking o-off over your body? Do you still feel me-me Travvy?"

The room becomes more tense with each word he says. I grip my dagger tightly in my hand while looking into his disgusting predatory eyes before I pull my fist back and stab the dagger into his cock. His eyes widen before he looks down and screams out in horror all while I smirk.

Paybacks a fucking bitch.

I turn when footsteps can be heard coming down the stairs when Flame walks in first and smirks noticing where my dagger is before Leslie comes into view. Her eyes go wide, and panic enters her eyes when she recognizes Shacks, her eyes flittering between him and me causing all the men to stand straighter while Stormy looks like he's about to be sick.

Ink walks over to his mom, making her eyes flicker to his and she clears her throat putting on an act but it's too late, everyone saw her reaction, "baby, what's going on?"

His jaw ticks, "do you know this man?" he asks pointing at a shocked Shacks who can't stop staring at what used to be his dick. She clears her throat again,

"No sweetheart, why what's going on? Who is he?"

Shacks coughs before looking up at me and I smirk before removing my dagger from his dick causing him to scream. I stick the dagger into his stomach while looking into his eyes which finally show remorse, but I just give him a cold glare back. This fucker ruined my fucking childhood along with the bitch behind me.

I pull the dagger back out and re-enter it into his side where Leslie stabbed me when I was only 6 years old. She told Stormy I fell onto something sharp, and he believed her. I hear her breathing pick up when she realizes I'm giving him all the injuries she gave me. By the time I'm done, Shacks is barely conscious, and I get into his face, the main target not far from my mind,

"Where the fuck is Hairy?"

He coughs, blood drops out of his mouth before he rasps, "A-Arlington."

I nod before taking my dagger and stabbing it into his neck, letting him choke on his own blood. This fucking pervert doesn't deserve an easy death.

I turn back to Leslie whose gone white as a sheet while the brothers all look at Stormy whose eyes are on his wife, anger shines through.

But it's a little too late in my book though for all of them.

Chapter 23

Melanie

I stretch my arms above my head before closing my locker. It's been a long emotional day. Not only did I lose a patient who coded, and another was diagnosed with a brain tumor, but Travis is finally home but injured, by a bullet wound.

I sigh as I quickly grab my bag before heading for the door wanting to get to the parking lot when it opens and Cassidy walks in making me roll my eyes. Everywhere I've been today since Travis came in she's shown up even though she's not on my team today. She's acting desperate and its starting to piss me off. He didn't even spend five fucking minutes with her in that storage room which was months ago and she's acting like he's her long-lost love despite sleeping with several doctors and the chairman since then. The woman's bat shit crazy.

She scowls at me and goes to open her mouth but I'm not having it today, my brain has checked out, I only have one person on my mind, so I shake my head and put my hand up,

"I haven't got the energy to deal with your jealousies today Cassidy, go do your fucking job before I report you to the one faculty member you're not sleeping with."

Her mouth hangs open as I walk past her, refusing to even entertain her crazy ways, I've hit my limit with her. I wave at Meghan who pulls her tongue out at me because she's got a double shift before heading to the doors for the parking lot feeling anxious and jittery. After Travis left my emotions went sky high. He'd been shot and could have been killed, I could have lost him. I know he messed up, but I also know I need him like I need air to breathe.

My heart rate picks up again remembering the bruising all over his shoulder and I rub my chest to help ease the pain. I shake my head and continue walking towards my car hoping he's waiting like he promised. I rush my steps, anxious to see if he's there and when I look up, I see a figure leaning against my car and I smile instantly seeing him. My speed picks up before I walk straight into his open arms, mindful of his shoulder and I place my face into his neck as he picks me up with his good arm, making my legs dangle. I take a deep breath, smelling his wooden cologne.

My how I missed it.

He chuckles before placing my feet back on the ground and I look up into his beautiful grey eyes and mine fill with unshed tears making him give me a gentle smile. He cups my cheek, his thumb wiping away the lone tear that has fallen, "I'm ok precious I promise."

I sniffle and nod before going onto my tip toes, kissing him gently making him smile against my lips. He pecks me a couple of times before holding his hand out making me raise a brow at him,

"Keys baby."

I just snort and shake my head at him before walking over to the driver's side making him chuckle while we both climb in. Like hell is he driving with that shoulder.

As soon as we're buckled in he places his hand on my thigh making me smile before I start my car up and drive out of the hospital, all while feeling eyes on us making my stomach churn. A bad feeling settles over me, but Travis brings me back, squeezing my thigh and I smile at him. It doesn't take us long to arrive back at my flat before he opens my door, helping me out of the car while grabbing my bag before pulling me over to him, wrapping his arm around my waist, guiding us to the door. I lean my head against his chest and sigh, finally feeling at home.

He opens my door placing my bag on the little table I have once we enter my flat before cupping my cheeks with both his hands. I smile at him before he bends down, kissing my lips lightly all while Bella yips at our feet, happy to see her daddy. He gently rubs my hair that's fallen out of its pony tail away from my face before placing his forehead against mine. My emotions are going haywire. I'm still so mad at him for what he did but the thought of losing him, I sigh, closing my eyes as a few tears fall. How can I love him so much but also hurt this much.

"I'm sorry precious, for everything. I love you, so fucking much and I know I screwed up big time, but I can't be without you anymore, I need you like I need air." He rasps and I grip his sides before I rasp back, "I love you too" making his whole body physically sag. He kisses me hard and passionately before licking the seam of my lips and I open willingly, letting his tongue tangle with mine.

After a few minutes he slows the kiss before rubbing his nose against mine, "I promise I won't hurt you like that again. I know it takes action to prove my words and I will prove them. Your everything to me." I nod, my eyes glistening when we both hear a small bark, and he chuckles while I grin wide. He looks down with a wide grin on his face before bending down to pick our girl up who instantly licks at his chin making me giggle. Travis looks at me with all the love he has for me making my grin go wider before he leans forward, gently placing a kiss to my lips while rasping against them, "how'd you feel about burgers from the bar?" I smile wider and nod making him chuckle, "alright baby, go for a shower and get comfy, I'll call Leah then feed little miss." He places another kiss on my lips before going off to do what he said and I smile, my heart full of love but also hope. Hoping I'm not making a mistake giving him another go. Hope we can make a future together.

A few hours later we're cuddled up on my bed watching my small tv with my head on his bare chest, his hand playing with my hair while he explains what happened after he went home. He's told me all about his time away and the pain of losing Marshall. He thankfully skipped the part about being shot and having someone dig the bullet out, I don't think I can bare hearing about it and now he's finally, fucking finally, getting his peace,

"So basically, after Stormy had realized everything, she put me through wasn't a lie or a rotten kid trying cause shit, he ended up dragging her into the common room which was full. Everyone was at the clubhouse tonight. She was screaming that I was lying, Shacks was lying all while everyone looked at her in confusion. It fucking sucks though because Stormy didn't believe a word I was saying until Axel had found Shack's phone which had several insurance footages of Leslie helping him get off, of her tying me up and stripping me before they needed a few people to hold me down, he had everything saved which Stormy decided to shout at her in front of everyone."

My heart stills while my eyes widen, "he told your whole family your trauma?"

He nods, "unintentionally. He didn't want to believe it until the proof was shown. I honestly don't know how I can forgive him Mel or any of them really. For years growing up I had told him and the brothers what she was doing, and they didn't believe me. I showed him my body tonight and he still didn't believe me while the others were skeptical. Shacks was bragging about it but still, nothing. It wasn't until he saw the actual evidence did he finally kick off. He put her before me every single time, yet when Ink heard my story, saw my body, he instantly felt guilt for what I went through and decided to confront her while the brothers were keeping an open mind"

I gently lean my hand up and smooth his hair out of his face, "what happened to Leslie?"

I'm not stupid, I know this Shacks guy is gone. They're not completely innocent these men but they only hurt who hurt their family. Does it make it ok? No, but I wouldn't change my man for nothing, well, except for when he strayed but otherwise, I wouldn't change him.

He sighs bringing me back to him, "Stormy said he couldn't kill her. Ink wanted to even though she's his mother, but Stormy refused. Tank had to be held back from beating his best friend." He sighs, his hand gently running down my back, "Knowing what she did to me it was decided for her to be booted out of the clubhouse and off club property, she's no longer welcome and if Ink decides he wants to see her it'll be in town. Stormy's also taken away her cards too. Cammy attacked her when she came out of her stupor before Butch escorted her off of club property. Cammy tried trying to talk to me after words, but I just walked away from her and all the eyes of my so-called brothers who listened to Leslie's lies growing up. I know I spoke to you about forgiveness but I just.."

I smile gently at him, "she was like a surrogate mother to you, but she took your abusers side before saying crap about your mom and the brothers are your family, they weren't there for you when you needed them like your there for them." He nods and I put my nose into the crook of his neck, understanding. Parents screw up but sometimes they can go too far and when you have such a big family like he does, for them not to believe him or even look into it is just plain wrong and heartbreaking.

He runs his hand through my hair again, "have you heard anything from your dad?"

I nod, knowing he means Callum, "he showed up at my job last week, but not because he wanted to talk to me, he wanted money. I had security escort him out." He tenses but I continue, "I contacted Gunner who made sure he left town with his dad's help." I feel him nod, "and what about your relationship with Butch?" I shrug, "he's been trying to contact me but I'm not ready to speak to him. I understand his love for his wife but not claiming me for her? It's wrong and then for her to try and buy me? most of my childhood was destroyed because of her."

He nods, "I understand baby. When you're ready to speak to them, I'll be there for you like your always there for me."

I nod before taking a deep breath, breathing him in while one of his hands stay in my hair, playing with it and the other tracing his fingers up and down my spine while I trace the tip of my finger over his Navy seal tattoo on his chest. As I trace it I furrow my brows noticing writing just above the anchor. I start tracing the writing before I hear him suck in a breath while his fingers on my spine never stop tracing up and down.

Melanie

My heart skips a beat while my breathing picks up before I sit up a little to look at him, my eyes watering and he smiles gently at me while brushing my hair out of my face before rasping, "I told you precious, I love you." I sniffle and lean forward, kissing him gently on the lips, once, twice, three times before he takes over the kiss, his tongue tangling with mine while his arm tightens on my back, his other hand gripping my cheek.

He rolls us on my bed, making Bella jump off before leaning over me between my legs. Our kiss heats up as he rubs his dick against my pantie covered pussy. My hands grip his back while he leans on his right arm, keeping his weight off of me before using his left hand to gently glide up my side, pushing the t-shirt that happens to be his that I stole before everything happened up and I tense. Fuck.

He breaks the kiss and furrows his brows at me before rasping, "if you're not ready, I'd understand baby, I'll wait however long you need."

I clear my throat and nod before looking at my name above his Navy tattoo not willing to meet his eyes, "I-I uh, I want to, I really do, it's uh, just, uh, I'veneverdonethisbefore." I say the last bit all together before chewing on my bottom lip, worried it may be a turn off before he gently pries my lip from my teeth. He places two fingers under my chin, making me look into his eyes and I roll mine when I notice the pride in them making him chuckle.

"You just made my fucking year precious."

I laugh when he waggles his eyebrows before he kisses me again turning my laugh into a moan. He leans his body further into mine, molding us together before kissing down my chin to my neck, sucking a little in between my neck and shoulder. He grabs a hold of the t-shirt, lifting his body a little so he can take it off me and I bite my lip, lifting my arms up making him smile. As soon as the shirt is off my bare breasts come into view, my nipples pebbling and he groans before leaning down, taking one into his mouth. I gasp at the sensation while his right hand starts to play with my other nipple, twisting it before gently rubbing over it with his thumb. I'm moaning and groaning underneath him as my hands keep a hold of his head, ensuring his mouth stays on my nipple.

He looks up at me, making eye contact before he moves down, his fingers hooking the edges of my panties and I swallow hard before nodding at him. Without breaking eye contact he slowly inches the panties down my legs, ensuring his fingertips graze them, keeping me in suspense. As soon as he throws them on the floor, he glides his hands on the inside of my legs while pushing them open. He keeps eye contact as his tongue pokes out and licks me from entrance to clit making me gasp while he groans. His eyes close as his dips his tongue inside me while his hand moves across my pubic bone, down to find my clit. He flicks it before rubbing tight circles on it while his tongue moves in and out of my entrance. I'm rifling underneath him, not able to stay still causing him to place his right arm over my stomach, keeping me in place. He moves his tongue from my entrance to my clit, circling it before gently sucking it into his mouth and I moan. My stomach flutters before tightening, my heart rate picking up. He continues teasing my clit before gently rubbing a finger around my entrance. He pokes it in gently, a little at a time before pushing his digit in. I gasp, feeling a little full before he pulls his finger out again all while still sucking and teasing my clit. My breathing picks up as he enters two fingers into my entrance, rubbing my walls before curling them, hitting my g-spot. He sucks my clit hard at the same time rubbing his fingers and I cum, hard. I see stars, my eyes blacking out as I scream. I feel myself gush over his face making him groan as he drinks my release.

After my aftershocks has subsided, he gives me one last lick before gently removing his fingers. He stands up with a smirk on his face, his lips shining from my juices. "Holy shit," I rasp, and he grins wide before licking his lips. He undoes his buckle and unbuttons his jeans, "that's just the pre-show baby," he rasps as he pulls his jeans down with his boxers and I swallow hard. He's defiantly all man, shit.

"uh, Trav, I, uh, I don't think it's going to, uh, fit."

He chuckles, "precious, he'll fit, trust me."

He climbs over me, aligning his dick at my entrance as his mouth comes down to mine. He kisses me, letting me taste myself on his lips before rasping against mine, "I want you raw baby, nothing between us."

I look into his eyes and nod, "I'm on the pill." I got on it when we started dating. Subconsciously I think I knew I was always going to give him another chance because I kept taking them, even after I broke up with him. He nods before leaning down to kiss me again and his finger start to strum against my sensitive clit, causing me to gasp. His tongue tangles with mine while the head of his dick pushes into me, stretching me. Gently he pushes halfway in before feeling my barrier causing him to groan against my mouth, our kiss heats up as his finger goes faster before he pulls out a little then thrusts in, hard, breaking my barrier, pushing all the way in. I gasp breaking the kiss as my body tenses while a few tears fall. It's painful and uncomfortable but not so painful I want him to stop. He leans down, kissing away my tears while staying perfectly still. His finger still gently strumming my clit causing me to tighten around him.

He groans before leaning down, kissing my lips once, twice, three times before rasping, "I need to move baby, you ready?"

I wiggle my hips a little to test out the pain before looking into his eyes and nod. He smiles before kissing me again. Our kiss heats up as he gently pulls out before slamming back into me causing me to gasp. Our bodies move together like we've been doing this for years, while our lips stay infused. His thrusts start to quicken while his finger on my clit goes quicker causing me to moan into his mouth.

He angles his hips, hitting my g-spot and my stomach tightens again before I feel like I wet myself, my whole body tensing as my orgasm takes over, my pussy tightening hard around his member making him groan as he comes inside me. He pushes in hard, making sure his seed goes in me deep until he's completely empty causing me to experience aftershocks. He places his face into my neck as he pulls his hips back before thrusting into me one more time, staying there while my breathing tries to slow down, "fuck precious I'm a lucky bastard. Not only am I the only one who gets to taste you but your also a squirter, fuck me I'm never letting you go."

I roll my eyes at his words while giggling causing him to groan as I flutter around him. He gently pulls out of me causing me to wince and he looks down, pride shines through his eyes, and I shake my head.

"stay there baby, I'll be back in a sec."

I nod watching him walk to my bathroom completely naked. That is one nice ass. I grin to myself until I notice some blood between my legs, and I bite my bottom lip, hoping he's not put off by it. I hear running water before he comes back with a flannel and I smile at him as he gently wipes the warm flannel over me, cleaning me up before chucking it back into my bathroom. He leans back over me, placing his member right against my entrance again before pushing into me, making me gasp while he groans out, "that's better." I chuckle before running my fingers through his hair while he runs his nose over mine,

"I love you precious."

I grin at him,

"I love you too."

He smiles back before leaning back down to kiss me again before he spends the rest of the night worshipping my body and I his.

Finally things feel right.

Chapter 24

Dagger

I blink my eyes open to see a lot of brown and I smile sleepily, waking up with my face in my girl's neck, my right arm holding Mel tightly to me over her stomach while my left is under her head with my hand laying on her tit that's just more than a handful not giving a shit about the pain shooting through my shoulder. Its fucking worth it, waking up with her in my arms like this. My sleepy smile widens as memories from last night return before holding her closer to me.

Fuck, a virgin, she was a fucking virgin.

Does it make me a huge dick for feeling pride over that?

I chuckle silently to myself before gently kissing the back of her neck while my thumb gently rubs over her pebbled nipple. Without trying to grunt in pain from my shoulder that's taking both our weights, I move my right arm down her body finding her bare pussy wet before gently rubbing my finger over her engorged clit. She moans, moving her ass over my hardened cock making me groan before I lift her right leg, still ignoring the pain in my shoulder as I put more pressure on my left side. I poke my cock at her entrance before slowly gliding in causing both of us to moan as her hand comes up behind her moving it to the back of my head before running her fingers through my hair, gripping it at the base of my neck.

I kiss the crook of her neck as my hips move back then slam hard forward over and over in a slow painful pace, teasing her. She gasps and moans, begging me to go faster as she squeezes my dick, driving me wild. I strum my fingers faster against her clit while my other hand squeezes and pinches her nipple driving her crazy as she turns her head towards me. I lean down taking her lips with mine, my tongue tangling with hers while my hips go faster with my orgasm fast approaching, I can feel the base of my spine start to tingle and my breathing has picked up, but I refuse to go before her, so I pinch her clit hard at the same time as pinching her nipple, tugging on it, and she detonates around me, her cunt squeezing my cock hard while she screams into my mouth. I swallow it down before groaning into her mouth as my cum spurts from my tip, painting her walls with my seed.

Fuck me, she feels good around me.

I slow my rhythm but don't stop until her aftershocks subside before I place my cock deep inside her, staying right there refusing to lose her warmth. I slow the kiss before placing a peck on her mouth before rasping, "morning precious." She smiles against my mouth, her cheeks reddening as her shyness kicks in making me smile back at her as she rasps back, "morning."

I move back a bit before rubbing my nose against hers while moving my hips back and forth slowly, "how'd you feel about spending the day with me then staying at mine tonight?" she smiles wider, "I'd think that would be great, but I do have an early tomorrow."

I nod, "that's fine baby, I can take you."

She just raises a brow at me, and I roll my eyes, "fine, I'll get a prospect to take you and pick you up then."

She just shakes her head at me, amusement shines through her eyes with a hint of lust as my hips continue moving, teasing her with my now re-hardened cock, "I can take myself Trav, it'd be easy anyway for when I come home."

I just grin, she's cute that she thinks she's returning here. I'm taking a leaf out of Axel's book, while she's working tomorrow all of her stuff will be at mine. She'll be pissed, no doubt about it but I don't give a shit, I am not losing her again. This evening will solidify that when I give the cut I had made for her, stating 'property of Dagger' on the back. I know she's not ready for the ring I have, moving her in will push her as it is but the cut, it means we're married in the eyes of the club and until I know she's ready for the next step then that'll have to do for now, I need her tethered to me in every way, this is just the start.

I look into her gorgeous eyes and nod, "yeah it'd probably be easier, but it'll give me piece of mind, plus then I get to see you so it's a win for me baby."

She grins wide, "alright, you twisted my arm."

I chuckle but soon pout when she moves, making my cock fall out of her heat. She climbs out of bed, and I go to grab her arm, but she quickly rushes away from me, making my pout go deeper making her giggle as her eyes shine with amusement and love making my stomach tighten and heart rate quicken.

Fuck me, I love this woman. I'm one lucky son of bitch.

As she gets to the bathroom door she turns sideways to look at me. A blush coats her cheeks, neck, and chest when she sees me taking in her beautiful, sexy body, that she forgot was completely exposed all over before she clears her throat,

"you coming?"

My grin stretches across my face, and I rasp, "in about ten minutes I will be," before moving quick. I jump out of the bed not giving a shit that I'm naked before chasing after her making her squeal and giggle running into the small bathroom where I catch her, wrapping my arms around her from behind. I use one hand to turn on the water while my other goes down to her pussy. I find her clit and rub it a couple of times making her arch her back, leaning against me before I move my hand further down. I place two fingers at her entrance and slowly slide them into her while she moans.

Fuck she's wet.

I move her towards the shower before placing us both under the spray. It's a tight fit but we both just fit inside it together. I tease her for a little while with my fingers before I let her climb high and send her flying as my fingers move in and out of her entrance fast with my thumb pressing down her clit, rubbing it in tight circles while my other hand teases her nipples. She groans as her orgasm takes place, her ass rubbing against my cock. Once her orgasm subsides I remove my fingers and suck them into my mouth groaning at her taste. Salty but sweet and so fucking perfect. We spend some time in the shower together, washing each other's body in the most intimate way before I pleasure her again while her hand teases my hard cock, then I take her against her shower wall while staring into her eyes, falling deeper for her by the second.

A few hours later after spending most of our time in her bed together, getting to know each other's bodies, we're heading to the clubhouse. We have church that I can't miss, especially because its mainly about my fucked-up childhood. I ensured Mel packed a bag for at least a few days, I don't need her to be suspicious of what I have planned with Axel, Shane, Flame, Slicer, and Gunner later while she's asleep in my club room then again at work tomorrow. I played on it thick, mentioning not being able to see her for so long and she fell for it instantly, not arguing about spending a few days at mine, well, now ours

Does it make me a prick to be excited about how angry she'll be and how hot the sex will be when she finds out I gave her flat up? I grin, looking out of the window with Bella in my lap while she drives us.

When we walk into the clubhouse together, hand in hand with Bella at our feet the brothers all cheer while Gunner shouts out, "ABOUT TIME YOU FORGAVE HIS STUPID ASS" making me chuckle while my girl blushes and places her face into my arm. The brothers all chuckle along with me as I wrap my arm around her shoulders, pulling her to me before kissing her forehead, taking in her strawberry scent.

We walk further into the clubhouse and I instantly tense when I see Sunny behind the bar. Shit. I look towards Axel wondering what the fuck she's doing here when she works at the club, and he winces, realizing he forgot to tell me she's here today. She's the one woman other than Clitter who thinks she owns me. He goes to walk over to us to explain before she gets closer but is too late when Sunny beats him.

She goes to hug me, making me tense further before my pixie of a woman steps in front of me. The clubhouse quietens when she growls,

"touch my man and you'll lose some teeth."

Sunny just smirks before continuing her path to me but is shoved back and my mouth opens in shock when she falls on her ass. I look at Mel with wide eyes. She may be small but fuck she's definitely mighty and now my dick is hard again, fuck, I can't get enough of her.

Sunny scowls getting up, "what the fuck is your problem bitch." I instantly tense and go to take I step forward, but Mel stops me by stepping back into my body, making me relax a little, her touch calming, "my problem, 'bitch' is women like you thinking its ok to try and seduce a taken fucking man, it's bad enough you all do it behind our backs but to do it right in front of me? are you stupid?"

The brothers all bite their lips to try and hide their smirks and chuckle while I wrap my arm around my girls waist as she leans into me. Sunny chuckles darkly and I swallow hard at her next words wondering if this will set my goal back further.

"Didn't stop him a few months ago when he allowed Clitter to suck him off when you two were supposed to be 'dating'." She says dating sarcastically and I look at Axel and Gunner with panic while they step up next to us, scowling at Sunny. I go to speak before Sunny can ruin my plans this evening, but Mel just chuckles while her thumb rubs along my arm trying to calm my nerves, letting me know that we're good.

She shrugs, "he made a mistake, I mean, he had gone over three months without sex and somehow I doubt he'll want used up goods like you and that bitch or whatever disease your riddle cunts have any longer."

The brothers struggle to keep in control wanting to laugh while I clear my throat, squeezing my arm around Mel's waist, needing her closer to me, I know she's acting tough right now, but I can't lose her, I fucking can't. This could all be an act before she tells me to do one. Sunny's face goes red, and she takes a step towards my woman making me growl before out of nowhere Cammy and Annalise step between them making Sunny narrow her eyes. I look at Mel but she's relaxed, still rubbing her fingers along my arm, not one bit bothered by Sunny's drama, making my body loosen up a little while hoping Sunny will now take the hint with the pres's mother and old lady in front of her and fuck off, but she doesn't, instead she opens her big fucking mouth again.

"Yeah like you were some fucking innocent virgin. How many men have you slept with Melanie? I heard your mom was selling you off over the years."

I tense again wondering how the fuck she knew about Mel's mother as Axel and Gunner growl while Hazel looks down guiltily, clearly the one who opened her mouth. Butch slams his hand down on the table near us making Sunny wince and swallow hard when he speaks coldly, "watch how you fucking talk to my daughter!" then he looks at his wife, "you and I will be talking about this later." Hazel swallows hard, nodding but not looking up.

I hear my girl gasp in shock by Butches claim for her and sticking up for her to his wife who over stepped while I tighten my arms around her waist. He's showing how much he wants the title of dad; this is what she needed to hear in order to try and have a relationship with him, even if its just as friends for now.

Needing to end this fucking show, I bend down a little and whisper in my girls ear, "please don't hate me for this baby." She tenses and furrows her brows before I look back at one of my worst fucking mistakes and say with pride that I can't keep out of my fucking voice even if I tried, "that's funny because it was defiantly blood on my cock last night."

Mel tenses further while her face reddens and she turns her head towards me before narrowing her eyes, "I knew you grew a bigger ego finding out I was a virgin. Maybe I should make you wait another three months to bring you back down to earth a little." The brothers struggle to hide their laughter while I narrow my eyes at her, "like you could go that long without my cock."

She smirks at me, "you have fingers and a mouth which your pretty good with, so I don't need your cock."

I bite my cheek to stop my laughter, but my lips still twitch. Her whole face is bright red, but her eyes show amusement. I bend down and kiss her on her lips, once, twice, three times before rasping, "I love you." She grins wide, her eyes lighting up, "I love you too."

I don't take my eyes off my girl as Axel speaks, "Sunny, you volunteered pretty quick to cover for Amy today after refusing before you had found out Dagger was home, now I'm wondering if this was your plan all along. Causing problems with a brother and his old lady is forbidden. It's in your contract and you've broken it. Get your things, your sacked."

I look up in time to see her eyes widen in shock, "b-b-but she's not his old lady, he's just dating her, you can't sack me." I see Clitter and several other sweet butts in the corner of my eye, their eyes wide as they slink back. Good. This was something that had to happen to put these ladies in their place. They were getting too fucking comfortable.

Axel smirks as Stormy stands and walks over to us. He passes me the box, guilt still shining in his eyes, but I don't say anything to him, I haven't since he realized I wasn't a fucking liar. I take the box from him with a nod, and he sighs, shame shining through, but I ignore it as I let go of my girl, making her turn to me and I grin at her as she looks at me confused before I open the box and take out the cut. Axel takes the box while I keep my gaze on my woman's. I hear several intake of breaths from the brothers and the women in the room while Annalise and Cammy look ecstatic, bouncing on their feet making me chuckle.

I lean forward and kiss Mel gently before rasping, "I love you Melanie and I want you to be my old lady." I hold up the cut while her eyes widen as tears pool in them, "what do you say precious?" she sniffles as her tears fall before she nods and the whole clubhouse erupt in cheers while I take her into my arms ignoring the pain in my shoulder and kiss her hard before I help her put the cut on. I rub my nose along hers while gently wiping away her tears before I rasp, "I love you."

She sniffles, clutching my cut on my sides, "not as much as I love you."

I grin before looking up, catching Cammy's eyes and decide to give her an olive branch, "can you sit with her while we're in church." Her eyes water and she nods frantically before rushing over to me. She places a kiss to my cheek, and I smile trying not to tense before I kiss my girl one more time, "I won't be long, then you and I, we're celebrating." Her eyes dilate and I smirk before turning back to a shocked Sunny, "you heard my pres, get the fuck off our property."

Tears fall from her eyes as a couple of prospects come either side of her, grabbing her arms. She starts to plead but I ignore her before heading into church as several brothers pat my back and congratulate me on my way past. I'm tense by the time I take a seat, my skin burning from all the touches. I need my woman and I've only just fucking left her.

Shit.

Everyone takes a seat while I try to loosen up a little and Axel bangs his gavel,

"Alright fuckers, church in session."

Everyone looks at me and I tense up again realizing we're getting straight to it, fuck.

Axel clears his throat, "I know you don't want to talk about it brother, I know most of us ignored your cry for help growing up and your angry at us for that, but we need to know. We all heard the rumors and the stories but now we need to know what was true and what was not."

The brothers all tense, guilt pouring from them while Stormy looks ready to pass out. I ignore them all as I stare a head while the memories start to build up before the words spill out of me.

"The first memory I have was when I was three which

shouldn't be fucking possible but its ingrained in there."

I sniffle, my bear-bear is ripped but I don't know how. Daddy, I want my daddy.

My tears fall harder when Les-Les comes into my room and she scowls making me slink back a bit, she gave me a weird mark on my arm yesterday because I dropped my cup, it hurt bad.

"what are you moaning about now?"

She sounds mad and I sniffle, "bear-bear broken."

She rolls her eyes, "I know you little brat I tore it."

My eyes widen and I start to cry, "I want my daddy."

Her eyes go hard, her face red before she looks at the fire, grabbing something while I get up and go to run to daddy's room until I feel something really hot on my back. I scream as pain shoots through my body. What happened, why does it hurt?

"DADDY"

I fall before Leslie grabs a hold of my arm turning me, anger shines through her eyes and she's holding the fire poker thing, the end is red hot, daddy told me to never go near it. She gets in my sobbing face, "call him daddy again and the next time I'll shove it down your throat, got it, he's Stormy to you".

I sniffle and nod my head before she lets go of my arm and kicks me hard in my stomach causing me to scream louder. We hear banging and running, and she quickly puts the poker back, her face changing from angry to scared as my daddy runs into the room,

"oh my god baby, he just ran into the wall on purpose."

My eyes widen while my daddy furrows his brows at me, but confusion soon turns to anger with her next words, "he said he was going to say I hit him."

I bring myself back out of my memory before looking around the table at my brothers, all looking at me with shock and anger before I look at my father, guilt etches all over him as my next words come out, "it's also the first time Stormy had hit me. He believed a three-year-old could be that conniving."

I hear him sniffle as I look at the crest on the table, I can feel Ink tense next to me, his whole body shaking, "it was like that a lot growing up, she'd either hurt me herself then tell everyone how I'd fallen or purposely hurt myself to gain attention, or she'd lie to the man who was supposed to protect me so he would hurt me instead. Every time my blood brother did something, I was blamed. She liked to see me punished all because her plan had failed, her man had a child with someone else before they were even a couple when it was supposed to be her that fell pregnant. My mom had no idea how she had gotten pregnant, not realizing the condoms were faulty, she wasn't even going to tell Stormy I had even been born, she was going to raise me on her own. The only reason why she decided to tell him was because she was dying and didn't want me to end up in care. But I was lucky in some ways because Leslie didn't want anything to do with me and Jewels returned when I was brought back here and she brought me up, she became my mother."

The brothers are all tense while Axel breathes hard, "brother, when did the-the, fuck." He sighs and drops his head, but I know what he wants to ask,

"I was 10 the first time it happened, I'd just got back from the library because Stormy refused to buy a troubled boy who apparently treated his wife like shit a laptop or computer for his schoolwork. I'd walked into my room when she grabbed a hold of me from behind, hitting my head hard, so hard it knocked me out. When I woke up, I was naked and chained to my bed." Ink stands, kicking his chair over while I remember and encounter my first ordeal with my brothers, the men who all thought I was a liar.

I wake groggy, my head hurts and my eyes feel heavy. I try to move my arms and legs but can't before I open my eyes and see I'm naked and chained to my bed. My breathing picks up, "w-what?"

I hear a chuckle in my panicked state and turn to see Leslie grinning wide, her phone recording me while two men I've never seen before standing next to me, holding their dicks in their hands, stroking themselves and my tears fall, realizing what she's allowing to happen to her husband's child, what she ensured would happen.

One of the men whose brown eyes that seem void of any life starts to trace my body with his fingers all while moving his other hand up and down on his dick, squeezing it tightly, and I start to struggle against the chains, hoping to slip through them while my body trembles with fear and disgust. I hear Leslie cackle as the guy wraps his hand around my limp dick and I sob, struggling to get my hands free while the guy squeezes his dick harder before his cum spurts out all over my stomach and dick. I start to gag, feeling dirty when the next man with even colder eyes gets his knife and starts to slice my skin as he pleasures himself all while Leslie films it laughing.

All I can think of though is 'I want to die'.

I'm brought back from my memories as Ink storms out of the room, I hear Mel shout him, but my eyes stay locked on my fathers. His tears glisten his eyes, falling down his cheeks while the brothers breathe hard.

I shake my head looking at each of them, seeing their guilt but can't bring myself to tell them it's ok, that I forgive them because its not ok, they heard my pleas but ignored them. Sighing I stand before leaving the chapel and head to my woman who instantly rushes towards me when seeing my pain. She wraps her arms around me with Bella at our feet before whispering not realizing how true her statement was,

"let's go home."

I nod before guiding her out of the club's backdoor with our dog right on our heels, finally taking my girl home, to our home where I'll never let her go again all while the brothers watch us go hoping I don't leave the brotherhood.

Chapter 25

Melanie – one month later

I've just walked into a cubicle in the E.R and I freeze in shock, not knowing what to do. The couple clear their throats while I just gawp. What the actual fuck?

"I uh, um" I stutter, I'm speechless. Like seriously speechless. The man, who I'm guessing to Mr. Blaze smiles awkwardly,

"we uh, kind of got ourselves into a little problem."

I blink again, "uh, did you uh come in like this? I, uh, I mean is this why you are here?" shit, I can't get my professionalism out, I'm dumbstruck.

The woman shakes her head causing the man to gasp then moan in what I think is pain, making her freeze as his member hardens. He clears his throat, "I uh came in because I have some massaging beads stuck in my rectum and well, we well you know."

I nod trying to be understanding which is really hard, "got bored."

He nods while the woman clears her throat.

I swallow and clear my throat, "I'm, uh, just going to page the doctor on duty, I'll, uh, need his help but uh, I'll be right back."

I turn and leave the cubicle so fast you'd think my ass was on fire. I ensure to shut the curtain before I bite my bottom lip, shit, I cannot laugh, I cannot laugh. I try to chant the words in my head but it's difficult. I look down the corridor to see Doc and I shout him causing him to stop and turn towards my voice. He grins, "well, if it isn't my favorite nurse." I grin back. I'm definitely not going to be his favorite nurse in a minute especially if I tell this story to Trav who will most likely tell everyone else for a kick.

I clear my throat and nod my head towards the cubicle, "can I uh, get a consult in here?"

He furrows his brows but nods his head walking past me before saying, "knock, knock." He walks in then freezes making my whole body shake with silent laughter. He turns his head slightly to look at me and I quickly bite my lip. He narrows his eyes as I walk in and clear my throat,

"Dr Thomas, Mr. Blaze here came in because he has some massaging beads suck in his rectum, while waiting he and his wife here got a little bored and as you can see, her tongue piercing is stuck to his prince Albert piercing."

He nods while side eyeing me, making it obvious that payback will be a bitch. I try to hide my smile as we get to work freeing them both which was a lot harder than expected and things only got worse when Mr. Blaze ejaculated on Doc's chest. Doc glares at me when myself and Mrs. Blaze try to hold in our laughter while her husband is red from embarrassment. Doc shakes his head and requests me to book Mr. Blaze in for a transanal endoscopy to remove the beads while he showers. As he leaves the room myself and Mrs. Blaze burst out in laughter while her husband smirks.

Travis is going to love this story.

A little while later I'm dodging Doc when I meet up with Meghan outside for lunch. She raises her brows at me wondering why were not in the cafeteria and I just laugh making her furrow her brows before I clear my throat and explain my morning. When I get to the part in conning Doc into the cubicle and my patient ejaculating on his chest she's nearly pissing herself laughing too.

I shake my head, "I'm officially hiding from Doc, I think Travis may need to teach me self-defense."

She laughs harder making me grin before I take a bite out of my ham salad sandwich.

She sighs, and starts to play with her food and I tilt my head, "what's up Meg? Is Lilah ok?"

She smiles sadly at me, "she's good, already planning her birthday even though it's in six months."

I grin, "then what's up?"

She shrugs, "she's only asking for one thing, one thing I can't give her."

I furrow my brows while a tear slides down her cheeks before she rasps,

"Her father."

I sigh and close my eyes. Meghan has tried for years to find him with no luck.

She sniffles, gaining my attention again, "I'm starting to think he never existed at all."

I lean forward and grab her hand, squeezing it, "let me speak to Travis. Please. I know you said you spoke to someone from his MC, but he may know him from club meets, there can't be that many Noah's in the MC world, let me help you make her birthday wish come true."

She sniffles her eyes conflicted before she nods in agreement, and I sigh in relief. Leaning forward I hug her to me, "you're the best mom, don't forget that." she nods against my shoulder before I lean back and wipe her eyes. My friend deserves happiness, and so does her little girl. I'll do everything I can to help her gain it.

A little while later I'm leaving Mr. Blaze's room after doing his observations when my phone vibrates. I pull it out knowing it'll only be one person and a grin lights up my face when I see a picture of us from our first date show on my screen before I answer,

"Hey you."

I hear the smile in his voice, "you still mad at me precious."

I hum, he's lucky he still has his balls. Over the past month he's come up with excuse after excuse to keep me at his. He even went to my apartment to grab some of my clothes before suddenly more of my things were showing up at his big light blue Victorian house behind the clubhouse, bit by bit all of my clothes filled the other side of his closest in his master room then my little trinkets filled the black dresser before my kitchen equipment filled his cream and grey kitchen that's got to be a chefs dream. The fucker had moved me in bit by bit then let go of my apartment without consulting me first. I finally confronted him last night about it where he tried to act innocent. I didn't get a chance to shout at him though when he admitted to letting my apartment go because he sort of distracted me. His body is very mesmerizing and don't get me started on his tongue, it would have distracted anyone, so don't judge me.

"Precious, admit it, you love living with me plus your my old lady, you should have known I wouldn't let you go once I had you in our home."

I smile wide, 'our home', this man. I shake my head "you're lucky I love you Trav."

He hums back, "not as much as I love you baby."

I grin wide before I see the back of Meghan's head, our conversation from lunch coming back and I clear my throat, "hey Trav can I ask you something?"

"Anything baby but it'll have to be quick, I've got to get going on the run in a minute, it's why I called, I'll be back in eight hours just as you finish your shift."

I smile again loving how he always keeps me updated. I'm so proud of him, despite his brothers not investigating his 'stories' growing up, he's still trying to be a brother to them. He did talk about possibly moving away from the clubhouse which everyone panicked over, especially Stormy, Ink and Axel but I managed to convince him to stay, to work on forgiveness even if it's just one day at a time.

I clear my throat, "do you, uh, know a brother called Noah? He's roughly 30 years old and does a run to Wincher."

"yeah Precious I know a Noah," he chuckles, and hope builds in my chest, "so do you. We're the only club that do the run to Wincher, it's where I'm off to now."

My eyes widen and I grin wide, "really?"

He chuckles, "yeah baby its..." he's cut off when someone shouts his name,

"Fuck, I've got to go baby, I'll message when we leave Wincher."

"But..." I need the brothers' name, yes, I can tell Meghan Lilah's father is a part of the Untamed Hell fire's, but I want to selfishly know which one it is.

"We'll talk when I get back, I promise then you can tell me why you want to know as well."

I smile, "ok, thank you Trav."

"always baby, I love you."

I grin wide, "I love you too."

He hangs up and I look up while putting my phone back into my pocket still seeing Meghan near the nurses desk and I rush over to her grinning. I bump into her back causing her to gasp before I wrap my arms around her, squeezing her tightly. She turns when I let her go smiling at me, "someone's happy."

I nod, "and so will you be."

She furrows her brows at me, but I just grin wider,

"I just spoke to Trav, and not only does he know a Noah, but apparently so do I and he is in his club."

Her eyes widen, hope glimmers through them before it diminishes, "but that doesn't mean it's my Noah."

I just grin wider, "his club is the only club that does the Wincher runs."

Tears well in her eyes as a sob breaks through before she grabs a hold of me, hugging me tight while rasping, "but that woman?"

I pull back and hold onto her arms, "was lying, she was most likely one of the sweet butts not wanting someone else coming into the club taking the men they want. Trav had to go but he's going to talk to me later and tell me which brother he is. When he does, I'll take a photo and send it to you to confirm."

She smiles wide, relief shining through her eyes before my pager goes off. I squeeze her arm before hugging her, "eight hours Meg, just eight hours and you'll have your answers, and your girl will have her birthday wish." She nods, her eyes shining, and I run off to my next patient smiling wide for my friend and her gorgeous little girl who wants nothing more than to have her daddy in her life. I'm still smiling on cloud nine hours later as my shift is nearly coming to an end. I have ten minutes left before I get to see my man and find out which brother is Lilah's dad for my friend.

My pager goes off and I furrow my brows seeing I'm being paged to triage and rush over there expecting an emergency. When I rush into the room I find it empty, and I start to feel a pit in my stomach. The dreading feeling from a month prior coming back in full force when the door opens again and Cassidy walks in. I swallow hard seeing a gun in her hand. This past month she's become more and more aggressive. A shove here, a warning there from her lover, her always glaring at me, trying to ruin my reputation within the hospital walls but this, this is new. I've felt being watched every day and now it makes sense. The woman has gone insane, Trav barely fucking touched her once months ago and this is what she's resorted to, fuck.

She points the gun at me, and my breathing picks up, "you think you can take my man and get away with it."

I swallow, "he was never your man Cassidy. He never really wanted you; you know this."

She sneers at me, "I would have won him over you stupid bitch, he is mine, I have had my eyes on him for years, fucking years and you think you can come a long and take him, well guess what, your stupid bitch ass..."

She's cut off on her rant when the door opens and fuck, Meghan walks in with some bits for the trolleys. My breathing becomes harsher. No, no, no, no. She's a mom, her little girl needs her.

She looks up and gasps as Cassidy points the gun at her, "well, look who's unlucky day it is. Move now over to the wall." Meghan is frozen, not moving but soon jumps when Cassidy shouts, "NOW."

Meghan looks at me as tears fill her eyes and she walks over to the other side of the room while Cassidy keeps the gun trained on her, completely forgetting about me. An idiotic idea comes to mind, and I swallow hard, looking into my friends eyes and I know I have to do this, for Lilah. She sees the decision in my eyes, and she gasps, shaking her head before I mouth, 'Lilah' making her tears fall fast down her cheeks and I rush forward, towards a distracted Cassidy. Meghan sobs as I tackle Cassidy to the ground. I hear Meghan scream for help before the alarm goes off while Cassidy grunts and we fight for the gun in her hands. Her eyes are wild and crazy like she's not even in there as she grins at me, her finger on the trigger. I manage to knock it out of her hands, and it goes flying across the room. She punches me hard in the face, splitting my lip before going after the gun and I scramble to follow her. She grabs a hold of the gun, pointing it at me and I shove into her, knocking her over while her head hits the corner of the desk in the process, knocking her out after the gun goes off.

Chapter 26

Dagger

I hang up the phone with my girl and shake my head grinning while Slicer walks over to me. Fuck, I love hearing her voice.

"Get your loved up ass on your bike brother." He snaps me out of my goofy state, and I chuckle, "yeah, yeah."

I climb on before turning back to him, "do you anyone who would mention to my old lady your birth name?"

He furrows his brows in confusion, "no, why?"

I just shrug, "she was asking me if I knew a 'Noah' that does a club run to Wincher. I told her I do and so does she but didn't get a chance to tell her it was you before I had to hang up. She seemed really interested."

He furrows his brows some more, "strange."

I just chuckle, "it's my old lady, of course its fucking strange."

He still looks confused, and I shake my head, "don't worry brother, I'll ask her later, we'll get to the bottom of it." He nods and puts his bandana on around his mouth, his eyes still unfocused as Ink walks out of the clubhouse towards us scowling. I sigh and shake my head. He's gone off the rails this past month after the revelations about his mom came out. He barely stays in the same room as me and it's starting to fucking piss me off.

As he gets to his bike, I bring Slicer out of his head who smirks at my words, "what's pissed you off brother? Sophie decided you're not pretty enough for her?"

He scowls, refusing to look at me still making me want to punch him, "I fucked up."

I snort while Slicer shakes his head and we both talk at the same time,

"Seriously? Again?"

"Whatcha do this time, wear her favorite underwear?"

He finally turns to us and glares, his cold eyes meeting my amused ones. I grin wide while Slicer chuckles and Ink sighs, rubbing a hand through his hair, "I kind of, might have took my anger over 'her' out on her." He clears his throat, "I called her a whore."

My eyes widen in shock, my mouth hanging open while Slicer spits out his drink that he's just took a sip out of all over his bike causing Hawk to chuckle next to him as he curses, trying to wipe the coke off his handlebars. Ink clears his throat trying not to smile, but his lips twitch before it fades again, realizing he fucked up big time. You never and I mean fucking never call the woman you want a whore. I shake my head at the idiot.

"Alright little brother, here's what we're going to do. You're going to get your shit together on this little road trip, then you're going to drag your fucking ass over to her apartment and fucking grovel, grovel like you've never before and pray, fucking pray that she doesn't rip your balls off because believe me, it's where she'd be aiming for."

He winces before looking at me, his eyes full of guilt. Sighing, I just shake my head, "you didn't know brother because I didn't want you to know. She's your mom, your only fucking mom and I didn't want to take that away from you. Was I wrong? Probably, but I'd still make the same decision brother to protect you, my family. Don't ruin the good thing you have going with Soph all because of your guilt. If you have to, tell her. Tell her my story and I can guarantee she'll forgive you. As long as you didn't fucking cheat because believe me, my woman may have forgiven me, but she hasn't forgotten. I still see the uneasiness in her eyes every day, wondering if I've gone to someone else. I now have a lifetime of groveling. If she wants her favorite meal for tea, she has it. Bella needs a new collar to go with her fifty others, it's hers. She wants to watch some chick flick; I make the fucking popcorn. I grovel everyday so she realizes how much I fucking love her and how I'd never hurt her like that again." I look at him again and see his eyes wide in shock and I furrow my brows, "you didn't cheat did you?"

He scowls, "fuck no, I'm not THAT stupid brother." He raises a brow at me, and I give him the finger causing him to smirk back at me making me grin. He shakes his head while Slicer chuckles as Gunner finally comes out and I raise a brow at him, "about time brother, finally finished doing your make up?"

He looks up his eyes unfocused and we all sit up straighter in confusion but expecting the worst.

He clears his throat, stupefied, "I, uh, Leah, she, uh, she has a date."

I bite my bottom lip, relaxing again while the other brothers clear their throats, trying to contain their laughter, the fucker is finally opening his eyes. About time if you asked me though. He shakes his head and goes to his bike before climbing on. I chuckle and start my girl up,

"ALRIGHT FUCKERS, LET'S FUCKING GO, I'VE GOT A SEXY NURSE TO PICK UP LATER."

They all chuckle and Ink and I take front formation with the van behind us then Slicer and Gunner behind it. Hawk stays besides the van until the end of town before waving us off heading back home while we floor it to our allies in Wincher who will then take the guns to the Italian Mafia.

It doesn't take us too long to get to Wincher, do the exchange of the vans before heading home again with no problems. The run was smooth as ever and I'm excited to go see my girl. When we get back into town I veer off from the group to the right, heading towards the hospital, Ink veers off to the left with Gunner, both heading to the clubs bar where their women apparently are while Slicer continues to the clubhouse with the prospects following in the van. Ten minutes later I'm grinning like a loon walking into the E.R when I bump into a scowling Doc. I raise a brow at him, and he just shakes his head, his voice cold,

"Your fucking woman is a menace and is lucky I haven't taken her off of my service."

I jerk my head back in shock about to rip him a new one but laughter bursts free when he speaks again,

"The fucking woman decided to con me into dealing with a couple who came in because the husband got anal beads stuck in his rectum only for them to get bored waiting five fucking minutes for a nurse to come and get busy. The wife had gotten her tongue piercing stuck to his prince albert."

Holy fucking shit. My mouth drops open before I'm nearly on the floor, dying in laughter while Doc tries to keep a straight face but loses it, laughing right along with me.

"fuck brother, you should have seen how quick she ran from me when we left the cubicle. You'd have thought her ass was on fire."

I chuckle some more while he smirks, shaking his head,

"please tell me you have pictures?"

He grins wide, "you bet your ass I got pictures."

I laugh again. Fuck their job must be good at times.

"If you're looking for your old lady brother then she's still in hiding, not even Meghan would tell me where she was, especially after she decided to tell Meghan that the man ejaculated on me."

I laugh again but its soon cut off when someone screams out in terror from down the hall causing me and Doc to look at each other. An alarm goes off and his eyes go wide, "fuck, it's the alarm for a shooter."

Panic enters me and only one thought comes to mind,

Melanie.

Both Doc and I run towards where the scream came from just as another appears while the rest of the hospital goes in lockdown.

When we turn into a room we come to a halt as the sound of a gunshot rings through it, the sound almost deafening. I look to my left when I hear a sniffle and see Meghan, slouched down with tears running down her face near the side wall, her hand still on the emergency alarm.

"Fuck." I hear Doc mumble in shock, and I look to see the bitch I fucked, lying on the floor, unconscious with blood pouring from her head but that's not what's gotten my heart rate up. No, it's my girl standing in front of Cassidy.

"Mel." I rasp.

My girl turns towards me, her face pale, "d-did I k-kill her?"

She's in shock, I hear Meghan gasp while Doc tenses next to me, but I ignore them as my whole world tilts. Blood, so much fucking blood is pouring from her chest, and she hadn't noticed, her concern on Cassidy.

No, no, no, no, no.

She looks down as if only feeling the pain now as she places her hand on her soaking chest, her knee's starting to go weak. I rush towards her roaring out in pain as I manage to grab her before she hits the floor.

"MEL"

Pain like no other fills my body as her tear-filled eyes latch onto mine.

Please no.

Chapter 27

Melanie

Pain shoots through my chest as I look down. Blood stains my navy-blue nurse's dress. My legs start to get weak; my breathing becomes more difficult. I start to fall when someone roars out in pain before two strong arms go around me, carefully lying me down. I look up to see my man, my world staring down at me with panic on his face. Our watery eyes connect as a sob leaves his throat. My tears start to fall,

"I-I'm s-s-sorry."

He sniffles and shakes his head as Doc skids next to me with Meghan right after him. He puts pressure on my chest while Meghan cries out,

"why, why did you do that?"

My eyes feel heavy as I slur in response, "be-because-cause Lilah."

She lets out a sob while she connects a heart monitor to me. I look back at Trav, his tears fill his cheeks, "I-I I-love yo-you."

He lets out another sob before leaning down, kissing my lips gently, "not as much as I love you precious."

I smile a little before closing my eyes.

I don't know how long I've slept for but when I wake, but I'm still on the floor and the rooms full of colleagues with Doc is shouting orders,

"WE NEED MORE UNITS NOW."

He looks down at me, panic lacing his eyes, "you're going to get through this, you hear me."

I nod slowly before my eyes move to the other side of the room and I panic, no longer seeing her. I look back to Doc,

"Cas-Cas."

Someone squeezes my hand and I turn to see Trav, his cheeks full of tears, "she's alive baby."

I breathe a sigh of relief before I struggle to catch my next breath.

My eyes get heavy again and Trav squeezes my hand tighter, "don't close your eyes precious, stay with us, stay with me."

I can't breathe properly, my body's gone numb, and a tear falls down the side of my cheek and I rasp on my last breath before everything goes black.

"I love you."

Chapter 28

Dagger

"I love you."

She whispers before her hand goes limp in mine and her eyes roll back.

"SHE'S FLATLINED, DEFIBRILLATOR NOW."

My heart stops as Doc starts CPR, no, no, no.

Someone pulls me out of the way, and I look up to see Meghan gripping my shoulders, tears staining her cheeks while her eyes stay on the scene. I look back in time to see Doc shock my girl,

"CLEAR."

Everyone moves out of the way as her body jolts.

They look at the monitor, nothing.

My breathing picks up, please baby, don't leave me.

"AGAIN, CLEAR."

They shock her again but still nothing. Meghan sobs and I grip her hand, not taking my eyes off my lifeless girl, blood staining her chest.

'come on precious, come back to me' I mumble as Doc tries one more time. He presses the button and her body jolts again.

Beeping enters the room, and we all sigh in relief as Doc scrambles up, "O.R NOW. MOVE, MOVE, MOVE."

They all rush as Meghan pulls me back, helping me stand before they rush my girl out of the room leaving nothing but a puddle of her blood on the floor.

"Come on, l-let's wait in the w-waiting room, we n-need to get-get you out of this r-room."

I nod with my eyes still on the blood making her pull me out of the room before leading me to the same waiting room we sat in waiting for Annalise. We round the corner just as my uncle David comes into view. He furrows his brows when he sees me and the state I'm in before excusing himself from the conversation with some nurses who he's trying to take statements from. He grips my shoulders, his grey eyes looking at me with concern, "you know the victim."

My tears fall hard, my pain showing over my face and his eyes go wide with realization while he shakes his head, "no, not Mel." I nod as a sob pulls from my throat and his grip tightens as he pulls me into him, holding me tight. Him and Mel have gotten close this past month, much to Stormy's dismay. She's still pissed at him and rightfully so.

My sobs rip from my chest,

I can't lose her, I can't.

We pull back when we hear a sob coming from Meghan and I

pull her into my arms, tensing with her touch but trying to ignore it. David squeezes my shoulder, "I'm going to call your dad ok." I nod before I rasp, "call Gunner first." He nods back and goes to make the call before I help Meghan sit.

"what happened Meg?" I need to know. I need confirmation that this is my fucking fault. It doesn't take a genius to know the gun belong to Cassidy.

"I-I went into the room to stock it and Cassidy, she-she put the gun on me, she looked crazy, kept going o-on and on h-how you were hers, have been for y-years." Her tears fall harder when she looks at me with pain and guilt, "I saw the decision in Mel's eyes straight away. She-she, oh God. She mouthed Lilah to me then tackled Cassidy, she wouldn't let-let her take me a-away f-from my-my daughter...." She lets out another sob and I wrap my arm around her, "it's not your fault Meghan." I try to comfort her because it isn't her fault, it's fucking mine. I did this but she doesn't believe me, she just sobs harder.

I don't know how long we sit here before the door opens and Stormy rushes in with Butch and Gunner. Meghan sits up, wiping her tears while mine start to fall again. I stand just in time for my father to grab me into a hug. I grip him tight back and start to sob again, my guilt crushing my chest. If I lose her then I'll be joining her. I need her, I can't breathe without her.

When he pulls back, he gives me a hard stare like he can read my mind, "she'll make it son, she's strong, do you hear me, she won't leave you, she won't abandon you, not like I did, she'll fight, just like she has all this time for you." I nod back before placing my forehead to his shoulder while he grips me tight. I sniffle as the door opens again and Axel rushes in with

Ink and Flame.

Axel's eyes are wide while Flame looks ready for murder.

"Any news?"

My dad shakes his head to Axel's question as more tears fall from my eyes. I hear Meghan sniffle and I turn towards her to see her sitting on the chair where I left her, her legs pulled up and her whole body shaking.

Fuck.

I walk over to her and kneel, "Meghan."

She shakes her head, "s-she's m-my best friend, s-she saved me, I can't l-lose her, Lilah c-can't lose her."

I grip her hand, "she's strong Meg, we won't lose her, she'll fight."

She sniffles, wiping her cheeks with the back of her hand while gripping mine with her other. I help her stand when the door opens again and Doc comes in, covered in blood and I pale. Meghan takes a step back her eyes wide while Butch shakes his head, chanting 'no' over and over but all I can do is stare at the man I see as an uncle, covered in my woman's blood.

He walks over to me while scrubbing a hand over his head, "she survived." My whole-body sags while Meghan sobs. I see Gunner kneel, his hands gripping his head while his dad's tears fall. My own father walks over to me and grips my shoulder as Doc continues,

"we lost her three times in the O.R, she'd lost a lot of blood and the bullet was stuck in her chest cavity. We gave her a blood transfusion and finally managed to pull the bullet out."

More tears fall from my eyes as I nod, she fought.

"When I can see her."

Doc takes a deep breath, "brother, there's a chance, its slim, but there's a chance she may not wake."

I go still and Stormy grips me before I fall, "she lacked oxygen each time she coded and we couldn't, we couldn't…shit. We couldn't bring her back quick enough each time. Her body was weak. If she does wake, there's a chance she'll have memory loss and there's also a chance she could have brain damage."

That does it.

Meghan screams out in pain as I fall to the floor with Stormy and Doc following me. Stormy grips me tightly as Doc grips my cheek panic in his eyes as the blood rushes from my face while Gunner destroys the waiting room with my Uncle David holding Butch back from joining. Flame quickly grabs Gunner, restraining him while Doc continues, "have fucking faith brother. We need fucking faith." I nod in a state, "she's in an induced coma at the moment, we'll ween her off the medication in 48hours and see if she'll wake. Now get your ass up and come see your girl."

I nod as they help me up while Doc grabs a hold of Meghan, helping her up before wrapping an arm around her. He guides us all towards Mel's room just as Butches wife Hazel rushes in with tears staining her cheeks. I ignore her and continue with Doc and Meghan. I understand she'll be upset but as much as

I love Hazel like an aunt, I need to see my girl, plus Hazel has fucked up a lot lately where my girl is concerned.

When we get to her room, Doc opens the door and I freeze, all the air from my lungs disappearing while my ears feel like they're full of water. I feel people move around me, but my eyes stay on my girl's form. She looks tiny in the hospital bed. Her hairs fanned out over the pillow, her face pale with dark shadows around her eyes. She has a tube down her throat helping her breathe and a tear falls down my cheek. I hear Hazel let out a scream when she walks around me and I squeeze my eyes shut, not able to do this. I want to run.

"Dad take mom out now; Dagger doesn't need this."

You can hear the anger in Gunner's voice as he speaks but his dad doesn't seem to register it.

"She has every right to be in this room son."

I shake my head. No, she doesn't and he knows it, he just doesn't want to rock his perfect fucking boat.

Gunner voices my thoughts,

"no, she doesn't. Mel hasn't wanted anything to do with her at the moment and you know this dad. Mom is partially the reason why she was abused growing up, she's also the reason why everyone knows what her mom tried to do. Just take her outside to stop her screaming dad, none of us need this, you should never have called her until we knew more."

I don't open my eyes, but I do hear Butch sigh before there's a scuffle and Hazel's protests before the room quietens with only Meghan's sniffles. I squeeze my eyes tighter, my hands forming fists when I hear Axel,

"Trav?" concern lacing his voice.

I can't, I fucking can't.

I feel someone get right into my face before they grip my shoulder, making me tense and I open my eyes only to look deep into ones just like my own that are full of compassion.

"You can do this son."

I shake my head, calling him something I haven't in a very long time making his eyes mist, "I can't dad. I can't breathe without her."

He nods, "I know son, but she needs you to be strong for the both of you. You can do this Travis and we'll all stand behind you like we should have done all those years ago."

I sniffle and nod while he grips the back of my neck, placing his forehead against mine, "together son." I nod again before he pulls back and guides me deeper into my girl's room. The brothers stand back while Doc keeps a hold of an inconsolable Meghan. I walk round her bed before taking her hand gently in mine, a lump forming in my throat at how still she is.

I lean down, placing a gentle kiss on her cold lips as a few tears fall from my eyes, landing onto her perfect cheeks. I rub my nose along her before I rasp quietly, "please come back to me precious. Where you go, I go, remember that baby."

I hear several intakes of breaths while Meghan lets out a sob, but I ignore them all, focusing on my girl.

She's so pale. Is that normal?

My eyes trace her face, every little freckle.

I can't lose her, I can't. We haven't lived yet.

Chapter 29

Melanie

Pain. So much pain.

Why do I hurt so much.

I try to open my eyes, but I can't. My breathing picks up. Why can't I open my eyes? Oh God, am I dead?

I feel something light touch my lips before wetness hits my cheeks. Something soft goes along my nose, his woodsy scent instantly hits me.

Travis.

So no, not dead. A coma maybe? But why?

"Please come back to me precious. Where you go, I go, remember that baby."

No, no, no, no. Blackness starts to hit, no. Please. He sounds in so much pain, please, why is he in pain, I don't want to leave him, he needs me, please.

I sense myself coming back again when I hear talking. Something heavy is leaning against my side and I don't know how but I know it's Travis. He's holding me tight, his body making mine tingle.

I try to open my eyes, but they just won't budge. Seriously, why in the fuck can't I wake up!

"He's not left her side in two weeks brother."

Gunner?

"I know. He needs her Gun, I mean, fuck, after everything my egg doner put him through, Mel is the only reason he didn't return back to the seals. They wanted him back, offered him his job back with more pay but she's the reason he stayed. If he loses her then we don't just lose her, we lose him too. You heard him. Where she goes, he goes."

Ink! He sounds heartbroken.

"we won't let that happen brother."

I hear a sniffle, "we won't have a chance Gun. She's his universe like Sophies mine. I understand where he's coming from, I mean fuck, look at Flame, he's dying bit by bit inside without Star. When we love brother, we love hard."

I hear Gunner sigh; Ink clearly gave him a look.

"I don't love Leah."

I'd snort if I was awake. He so does love her, but he's too fucking stubborn to open his eyes, I mean I've met her a few times now and every time those two are in a room together, it's like a fucking furnace.

I hear Travis snort making me want to open my eyes so badly so I can see his handsome face and beautiful grey eyes.

I hear him rasp, "so you'll be ok with the fact she's now

dating someone."

I hear rustling, "what? No, she fucking isn't, she hasn't wanted anything to do with anyone after I rescued her from that prick three months ago."

I hear Ink clear his throat while my man traces a finger over my face, "well, I don't know what to say then brother because she is, Cammy set her up with someone last week, I heard they hit it off."

I hear a bang,

"THERE'S NO FUCKING WAY CAMMY SET HER UP WITH ANYONE. WHEN WILL THAT FUCKING WOMAN STOP MEDDLING."

I hear Ink snort before something light touches my forehead, "I'll come see you later sis, I have a woman to go fucking confront."

I really want to laugh right now. These men are so clueless about women.

I hear a door bang before Ink starts to laugh while Travis continues to trace my face. Blackness starts to come again. NO, come one, I was having fun. Please.

"come back to me baby,"

Everything goes black on his rasp.

I hear a sniffle.

"Please wake up Mel. It's been a month. Dagger, he's struggling without you. His dad had to force him out of your room this morning, he's barely left your side and Lilah, she wants her favorite aunt back."

I want to reply I'm her only aunt but yet again my body refuses to fucking listen. This is starting to get boring, and I still don't know what even happened to me.

Meghan sniffles again, "she asked about her dad again today. I told her I may have found him, but we need you to wake up. My little girl loves you so much Mel. She said she'll give up a thousand daddy's to have her auntie back. Please wake up."

I feel my heart rate pick up. She may have found Lilah's dad?

My heart hurts for my family, they need me.

My body goes weak again. COME ON!!

"Look, I know your still pissed with me Soph, but can you just sit with her until we get out of church? It's the only way Dag was willing to attend. We need to discuss what to do with Cassidy."

Cassidy?

I hear a sigh, "yes, go."

I hear rustling before he rasps, "thank you pixie." There's a click of the door before another sigh enters the room, "alright girlie, you need to open your eyes and soon. Dagger's losing it."

Sophie?

"Here, I'll make a deal with you. I'll forgive Ink for taking his anger out on me over his crazy ass mother if you wake up.

How's that?"

I want to laugh. I met Sophie when Travis was away and she became our vet, she's absolutely lovely, Ink's an idiot for screwing things up with her. Although didn't she just say…. hmmm.

"Come on Melanie, wake up for us, wake up for me. I need a reason to forgive the idiot without him gloating. The man is a pain in the ass, and he called me a whore but I'm ready to give in here, I miss him."

I feel her touch my hand as I try to open my eyes. She has a fucking point; he won't let her live it down if she forgives him.

Come on body, comply. Ink would owe me big time.

I hear her sigh, "come on Mel, Dagger needs you. Bella needs you."

Oh my sweet puppy, how could I forget about her.

I feel my heart rate pick up and I manage to move a finger. I need to wake, they need me.

"Mel?"

I hear rustling but I ignore it, trying to open my eyes. I manage to move my finger again and I hear her gasp before she shouts, "MEGHAN, SHE'S TRYING TO WAKE UP."

I hear more rustling before someone touches my face, "ok, come on Mel, open your eyes, please, it's been two months, wake up for me."

I blink, yes. I blink again, the light blinding making me squeeze my eyes tight before I slowly open them and look around the room and see both Meghan and Sophie with tears in their eyes. I can still feel the tube in my throat, and I go to touch it, but Meghan stops me, grabbing my hand,

"don't touch Mel, I'll page Dr Thomas now ok."

I nod, tears falling down my cheeks as Sophie comes into view. She leans forward and kisses my forehead before rasping, "Ink is so going to owe you big time."

I manage a small smile around the tube and a small nod before I close my eyes for a few seconds, happy to be back but confused as to what happened to me.

Chapter 30

Dagger

I lean back in my seat and sigh as Ink goes over the books for the tattoo shop. They've doubled in business, which is great, I just couldn't give a fuck though, I should be with my girl, not here.

"I have another back piece next week while Hawk here has the minor to contend with still."

The brothers laugh while I shake my head, ok this I have to hear. We all look at Hawk to see him scowling at Ink who just grins then nods his head to me making Hawk sigh. The brothers laugh,

"alright fine, jailbait whose now just turned 18 had decided to break into the shop."

We all sit up, fucking pissed while he just shakes his head,

"I found her butt naked, lying on my tattoo chair, fingering herself," he shudders in disgust, "she said she's now of age and wants me to take her virginity."

My eyes widen while Axel tries to hide his laughter.

"I called the chief and he picked her up, said something of the lines of, she can't keep throwing herself at business owners thinking she can be a kept woman. Turns out she fucked a few guys a few towns over and decided I was her next victim. It apparently helped that I was good looking, Davids wife's words not mine."

That does it, we all burst out in laughter while he sulks making us laugh harder. I can't wait to tell Mel; she'll piss herself laughing. My laughter dies off when I remember; my girl can't laugh because she's ventilated. Fuck. I sigh and rub a hand down my face while Axel looks at me with concern. I look at him, my eyes showing him that I need to get back to the hospital and he nods,

"Alright brothers, Cassidy. What do we do about her. David can only keep her as missing for so long."

The brothers all scowl at the mention of the bitches name while Stormy speaks up, "I'll fucking end her if none of the brothers want to hurt a woman. She nearly killed my daughter in law."

I look at my father, he's looking at me while the brothers all nod in agreement to end her life, but I clear my throat, "my woman. She'll want to show compassion. When she thought she'd killed her, the look in her eyes" I shake my head, "we need to go by the law with this one." Stormy goes to say something, but I just put my hand up, "get her into the state jail, have one of our women we have in there sort her out. At least then my woman stays guilt free because if she goes 'missing' she'll believe she killed her, and it would completely destroy her."

Stormy grins and nods his while Axel stands, "all in favor."

Every man bangs the table once before shouting 'AYE' when Doc's pager goes off. None of us think anything of it until he stands suddenly, his chair falling over as he looks at me and I tense, panic enters my body,

"she's awake."

The air leaves my lungs as everyone freezes.

Awake. She's finally awake.

I quickly snap out of it and jump from my seat, running towards the door. All the brothers in the main room stand and stare at us as we rush out of church. Axel shouts behind me on our way out, "SHE'S AWAKE" causing every chair to scrape. I don't wait for anyone as I jump on my bike with Axel hot my heels to the hospital.

It takes me less than ten minutes to get to the hospital before I'm rushing into the doors towards the stairs, refusing to wait for the lift. Axel and Doc are right behind me as I rush into Mel's room, slamming the door open making Sophie jump. She grins when she sees me but my eyes lock on ones I've missed so much, fuck. My tears start to shine through my eyes as they fall down my cheeks. I bend forward, placing my hands on my knees as a sob breaks through from my throat.

She's awake. She's really awake.

Doc goes around me and rushes towards her before looking around the room with furrowed brows while Axel and Slicer stand next to me, placing a hand on either shoulder, making me tense. They squeeze knowing my discomfort but refuse to let me go, knowing I'll end up on my ass otherwise.

"Where's Meghan?"

Sophie smiles a sad smile while my girl has a tear falling down her cheek, her eyes on mine. It gets my ass moving and I walk towards her, grabbing her hand before squeezing it tight while rubbing her tear away with my other hand.

"She uh, she went to go collect Lilah and well, she's still struggling." Sophie struggles to get her words out as Ink walks in and heads straight for her. She goes into his arms willingly as she explains.

I sigh and slowly close my eyes before I lean forward and gently kiss my girl's forehead, mindful of the tube while Doc does his checks. Meghan's held guilt over the incident ever since it happened. I just hope my girl doesn't lose her friend over it because I know she's already started distancing herself from her. She's barely been in here and hasn't been around us much since.

"Alright Mel, I'm going to remove the tube, ok?"

I stand straight but don't remove my hand from hers as another nurse walks in to help after Doc paged her. Mel nods her head but keeps her eyes on mine as Doc slowly removes the tube from down her throat. Once it's gone she coughs and I bite my bottom lip hard, waiting, impatiently, to hear her voice while Doc gives her sips of water.

Her eyes never leave mine before they narrow causing everyone to holds their breath and I start to panic. She does remember me, right?

"I-If you…ever…threaten to j-join me if I had died again…I'll skin you…alive."

Everyone sighs in relief while I let out a watery laugh before I lunge forward and wrap my arms around her. She lets out a sob into my neck, matching mine, "I-I missed yo-you." I shake my head, "not as much as I missed you precious, fuck, don't ever do this to me again."

I feel her nod against me as she squeezes tighter.

I pull back and sit next to her on the bed, making her lean against me with my arm wrapped around her when Doc speaks while Axel, Slicer, Stormy, Ink, Gunner, and Butch all lean against the walls with Sophie leaning against Ink. The others are in the waiting room, patiently waiting for news on my old lady.

"Alright Mel. I need to know what you last remember."

She furrows her brows trying to think as I massage the back of her neck.

"I-I remember getting my cut."

I suck in a breath, fuck, that was three months ago.

"Ok sweetheart. What else do you remember?"

She furrows her brows again, frustration etches over her features, and I smooth out her forehead, "don't force it baby."

She nods, "I-I remember." She stops then looks at Doc before biting her bottom lip wanting to laugh while everyone looks at her in confusion, "I-I remember Mr. and Mrs. Blaze."

I burst out in laughter while Doc scowls at her then narrows his eyes at me in warning but I just grin and look at the others before telling them in detail how my devious girl decided to con Doc into taking the case and what the case entailed causing everyone to laugh their asses off.

Mel looks confused and I move her hand towards my mouth, kissing it, making her smile at me, "what's on your pretty mind precious?"

"I ca-can't r-remember anything after t-that. How did I-I end u-up in here?"

I look at Doc and he nods for me to tell her.

"Cassidy. She paged you to triage and pointed a gun at you." Her eyes widen but I continue, "Meghan walked in the room to stock it while it was quiet, and Cassidy turned the gun on her. You made a decision and tackled her. That was two months ago."

Her eyes slowly close as tears fall, and I wipe them away.

"Lilah."

I nod, "yeah baby, you saved Meghan for Lilah."

More tears fall and she looks around the room, noticing the one woman not here and she sniffles, "s-she feels g-g-guilty."

I nod, "she'll come around baby. I'll make sure of it."

She nods then leans into me before her eyes start to get droopy.

"Sleep baby. We'll be here when you wake."

She nods before closing her eyes and I sigh in relief, closing my eyes while I relax against her pillow finally having her back in my arms again.

Chapter 31

Melanie

I wake up to voices and slowly open my eyes to see Slicer sitting on the chair next to my bed while Travis holds me tightly to him. They're both talking quietly trying not to disturb me. I close my eyes again and just listen, letting their hush whispers sooth me.

"How long will you be gone for?"

Slicer shrugs, "maybe a month. I don't know. Snake still can't trust his men, so he's come to Axel for help, they believe that's where Hairy is hiding and to be fair, we don't want Star home until the fucker is found."

Travis sighs, "alright brother. Just stay in touch yeah?"

I hear some rustling as Slicer stands before something soft touches my forehead, "will do brother. Take care of your girl yeah."

I feel him nod before the sound of a soft click enters the room and I slowly open my eyes again before looking up to my man who is playing with my hair which is probably rank and greasy.

Shit.

I sit up a bit gasping a little in pain making him scowl at me,

"Melanie."

I giggle a little before rasping, my throat still sore from being intubated, "oh hush you. My hair is probably gross, and I most likely stink, I need a shower."

He just shakes his head at me and grins, "baby, I've been giving you bed baths so don't worry."

My eyes widen comically no doubt while a blush hits my cheeks making him chuckle before he slowly leans down and kisses my lips gently, once, twice, three times, like always, before pulling away a little as I lean against him again, relaxing.

He smiles at me, "alright precious, I have a question which has driven me crazy for the past two months."

I look at him and raise a brow and he grins, shaking his head, "fuck I've missed you. Alright baby, how do you my brothers legal name Noah?"

I furrow my brows at him in confusion. When did I mention Lilah's dads name? He sees the confusion on my face and smirks, "you rang me that day and asked if I knew a Noah that did a club run to Wincher. I told you I did know one and so do you. I also told you we were the only club who did that run."

My heart stops. Oh god, that's why Meg needed me to wake up, I had found out Lilah's dad is in Travis's club. I sit up even straighter, ignoring the stiffness and pain and grab Travis's arm tightly,

"Who is he?"

He tilts his head, "it's Slicer baby. But why did you want to know? Should I be jealous here because I feel like I should be."

My eyes widen ignoring his humor, "oh my God."

"What? Mel?"

My mouth hangs open. All along my suspicions were right. He is Lilah's dad, its why he looks so familiar to me, fuck, the eyes, it's the eyes and the hair, she's a spitting image of him, shit, shit, shit. How did I not put it all together. Dammit I'm so dumb!

"Where is he now? Slicer?" I know he was just here but maybe he can get him to come back.

Travis just raises a brow, "baby, explanation first please because as of right now I want to murder my brother!."

I wince, oops, my bad.

I gently reach up with my hand and trace my finger over his brows making his face soften before he grabs a hold of my hand and kisses my palm making me smile at him. "alright baby, explain."

I sigh knowing I'm about to shock the shit out of him. "Lilah's father, the man Meghan has been in love with for years is a biker whose legal name is Noah and is in a club that does club runs to Wincher." His eyes widen in shock, and I nod as he sits him a little, taking me with him.

"Fuck, he's now on his way to Seattle to do a job for another club. Fuck."

I gasp, no, no, no.

"Can you get him back here?"

He sighs and shakes his head, "no baby, the plane left five minutes ago, and this isn't something he needs to hear over the phone. He's been looking for Meghan for years Mel, fucking years. When he went back to the café where she worked the woman told him she was just passing by."

I sigh, "nope, she was just off that day, she stayed there for another year before moving on when she realized he wasn't showing back up."

He runs a hand through his hair, "fuck." I nod agreeing before his eyes turn sad, "precious, he turned into a man whore when he couldn't find her."

I close my eyes, squeezing them tightly before placing my face into his neck. Dammit, I know for a fact she hasn't been with anyone since him, this is going to destroy her.

A few hours later after Doc did a check up on me, telling me I'll be here for a few days before being discharged, I had managed to convince Travis to go home for some better food and a shower. He didn't want to go but I have to talk to Meghan. I know she's been avoiding me but if I had to do it all over again, I'd still try to save her for that beautiful witty girl of hers. I had Doc page her 911 for my room and just on time she rushes in looking frazzled and I smile wide at her while she looks at me with panic before she realizes she'd been set up. She narrows her eyes at me, but I speak before she can give me a lashing,

"if I have to do it all over again, I wouldn't change a thing. Ok, well maybe not being shot and losing two months of my life and part of my memory would be good but otherwise, I wouldn't change a thing. Lilah needs her mom alive and well, not in a coma or in the ground. Don't feel guilty because I chose to save you, if anything kick Travis's ass for half fucking her in the first place." Her eyes go from narrowed to comically wide then to amusement within seconds and I grin before tears start to fall from her eyes as she launches herself at me, hugging me gently but tightly while sobbing on my shoulder while I gently rock her whispering that it's ok.

My friend is all heart.

A little while later she's lying on the bed next to me after Doc gave her the afternoon off when Travis walks in. He grins seeing Meghan, her head on my shoulder and relief shines through his eyes before walking over to the chair and taking a seat. He looks at me while taking my hand, "you told her yet?" Meghan sits up a little and looks between us with furrowed brows while I shake my head no before I look down and clear my throat, "so before Cassidy turned into crazy lady, I asked Travis if he knew a Noah." I turn my head to look at her to see her eyes widen in shock, showing me that she had forgotten which I can't really blame her.

"Slicer, in our club, his legal name is Noah. He's about 6"1, hazel eyes, and brown hair that he keeps in a man bun on top, the rest short back and sides. Sound familiar to you?"

Tears pool in her eyes before they fall down her cheeks as she nods while a sob comes out. She places her hand over her mouth as Travis continues, "he's gone out of town for a little while to help out another club. When he returns, I'll speak to him. He's been looking for you for years Meghan, he never stopped, he did lose his way, struggling but he never gave up hope. Your daughter will know her father, I promise and in the meantime, she can get to know her favorite uncle before the rest of the club find out and try to take the title."

She lets out a watery laugh before laying her head on my shoulder sobbing and I squeeze her tight with tears shining my eyes while smiling wide at Travis who looks at me full of love.

A few days later I'm tapping my finger on my leg waiting for Travis to pick me up. I'm finally being discharged, and I could use a good bath as well as a good dicking but he's flipping late and when the door opens and Butch walks in with Gunner I scowl harder making them both chuckle.

Butch lifts his hands up in surrender, "he got held up by a catfight at untamed girls, we're here to take you home."

My eyebrows shoot up in surprise before I scowl again, "and he didn't film it?" because let's face it, that would be hilarious to watch after being stuck in the hospital for two flipping months. They both laugh before Gunner shows me his phone and yep, sure enough two strippers in only their thongs are slapping the shit out of each other making me smile which turns into a laugh when I hear Travis,

"CAN YOU TWO SERIOUSLY NOT JUST FUCK THE GUY TOGETHER, I'VE GOT TO FUCKING GET MY GIRL FROM THE HOSPITAL, I DON'T NEED THIS SHIT."

I hear a lot of laughter in the background as Gunner shakes his head while Butch grins. He's been in here a lot the past few days. Now, I doubt I'll ever call him dad, I mean, he did chose his wife over claiming his daughter and said wife decided to out my mothers mistaken drunken night causing my life hell, but I did promise to try and be his friend for Gunner's sake. We watch as the two woman start shoving each other causing them to bump into a very pissed off Travis.

"I SWEAR TO FUCKING GOD, GUNNER GO PICK YOUR SISTER UP AND BRING HER BACK TO THE CLUBHOUSE WHILE I SORT THIS SHIT. I SWEAR IF MY WOMAN IS MAD AT ME FOR THIS YOUR BOTH DONE FOR."

I laugh harder at his scowl and the way the women freeze at the sound of his hard and angry voice.

"Alright little sis, you heard him, let's go."

I grin and do a little dance causing them both to chuckle before leading them out of the room. I head to the nurses desk when I see Meghan and kiss her cheek making her grin wide at me, "I'll come and see you tomorrow with Lilah." I nod and give her a hug before saying bye to everyone and head for the exit like my ass is on fire. I may love working there but being a patient fricking sucks.

Fifteen minutes later we're parking up near the front doors of the clubhouse and I smile wide as Shane runs over to us, helping me out before giving me a gentle hug, "its good to have you home Mellie." I grin at him, "it's good to be back Shane." He kisses my cheek before going back to his post while we head inside and as soon as we open the door a loud cheer greets me and I smile wide seeing everyone, glad to have me home but my eyes only want one man and as the crowd separates I see him, my man walking towards me and I rush over to him, ignoring my discomfort and jump into his awaiting arms causing everyone to chuckle. "I've missed you baby." I squeeze him tighter at his rasp, my eyes starting to water.

"Let's get you home precious, yeah?"

I nod, placing my head in the crook of his neck, breathing him in while he turns and walks out the backdoor while shouting, "LATERS FUCKERS" making everyone laugh. He walks all the way to our home with me in his arms without breaking a sweat all while my nose is in the crook of his neck. He opens the black front door where we're greeted by Bella, and I sob while he lets me down. I kneel in front of her before she licks and nips at my chin. Travis chuckles before grabbing her and picking her up making me look up at him and pout,

"Alright Bella let's get you fed; Mel get your sweet ass upstairs; a bath has already been ran for you." He winks at me before heading to our kitchen while I look at him in awe. He's already ran me a bath. God I love that man. I climb the stairs to our master room before heading into our his and hers bathroom that's full of blacks, dark blue's and greys and see all the candles that are lit, and I smile wide. The man has thought of everything. I quickly undress out of my sweats before climbing in, not looking at my scar in the mirror. I lay back and sigh in relief, letting the water surround me when the door opens and Travis walks in smiling gently seeing me all relaxed, I smile when I notice he's let his hair down.

I watch on as he undresses, ensuring to hang his cut up before removing his jeans. His body on full display. His tattoo's stand out hiding his scars and he smirks noticing me checking out him out. I can't help it, he's a work of art. He walks towards me, and I scoot forward so he can climb in behind me. Once he's in I settle behind him while his arms come around me with a sponge in his hand. He starts to wash my body while I lean my head against his chest, feeling content.

I feel him rub his nose along the shell of my ear before he rasps, "I love you precious."

I smile, "I love you too."

I close my eyes and smile until a memory of Cassidy pops through my head, she's standing in front of me in triage, pointing the gun at Meghan. I sigh knowing I need to know.

"What happened to Cassidy?"

I feel him tense but his hands continue to wash my body, "she was arrested. Sentenced to 45years in prison."

I sigh in relief. When my memories started to come back, I honestly thought I had killed her. The thought when I saw her lying there, not moving that I took her life, I felt sick to my stomach. I became a nurse to help people, not end their lives, even if she was crazy and nearly killed me. It's just not who I am.

"Don't get me wrong baby, it was hard. I wanted her blood for what she did, so did the brothers, but I knew you wouldn't be able to live by that."

I smile, loving how honest he is with me and how much he knows me and my heart. I turn my head slightly looking at him, my eyes shining with love while running my fingers through his lush hair causing him to lean down and kiss me.

The kiss starts gentle before our passion takes over, lust pouring from my veins, my body needing to feel his to feed our connection.

He brings one of his hands down my body, going between my legs that I have shamelessly opened for him while his other kneads my breast before lightly twisting my nipple causing me to moan. I gasp into his mouth when his fingers find my clit and he starts slow, hard circles against it before he dips two fingers inside me. He teases my body, driving me wild before he finally curls his fingers inside me, finding my g-spot and rubs hard as his fingers on his other hand twist my nipples. I come moaning into his mouth, my body arches as my orgasm washes over me. He waits until my orgasm has ebbed away before removing his fingers. He breaks the kiss to suck them into his mouth, ensuring to get all of my juices making my pupils dilate. His eyes turn smoldering before he rasps, "turn around baby." I listen and turn in his arms before he gently lifts me so I'm hovering over his hard dick, his head already turning purple with the need to come.

He gently lowers me onto him and we both groan as he fills me up before he places a hand behind my neck pulling my lips down to his while his other grips my hips, helping me move up and down on him. Our breathing mixes as our lips stay infused while my hips move faster, I grind down each time I move down towards him, making my clit rub against his pelvis. My stomach starts to clench, my next orgasm building, I climb higher and higher before he moves his hand off my hip and down towards my clit, he pinches it, hard and I see stars, my eyes blacken, "that's it baby, squeeze my cock, come for me."

And I do, I come hard before he thrusts up into me two,

three, four more times before he cums, shooting his seed into me with a groan. He places his forehead onto my shoulder, lightly kissing me there while keeping me infused with him, his dick still inside, keeping his cum from coming out of me.

We let our breathing come down before he leans back, smiling lovingly at me, "why don't we continue this in bed precious, we have two months to make up for."

I grin wide before nodding my head and he smiles wide back before leaning forward and taking my lips again. He continues to kiss me passionately as he stands up from the bath, taking me into our bedroom completely wet and not giving a crap, where he spends the rest of the night showing me how much he loves my body.

When we fall asleep in each other's arms the only thought that comes to mind is how grateful I am for giving him another shot.

Epilogue – One Month Later

Dagger

I'm pacing the clubhouse driveway while Shane laughs at me the fucker.

"I just think this is ironic is all, I mean, I was having this same talk with your woman all those months ago about just ripping the band aid off and all that and here we are again."

I point at him, "it's not the fucking same and you know it."

He just laughs as Flame walks out with Gunner and Hawk. They all look at me, raising a brow and I just shake my head at them before looking back at Shane. I hold my arms out, "what if I'm wrong and she says no? what if doing it at the hospital where we met is a bad idea and all it does is bring that bitch back up?"

I hear the men clear their throats while Flame chuckles, making me glare at him and he puts his hands up in surrender, "brother firstly, the bitch is dead. Our informant did her job making it look like suicide so Mel doesn't get suspicious and secondly, if I could, I would turn back time and make Star mine instantly. I'd tie her to me in everyway possible. Don't make the same mistakes I did. Get your ass on your bike and go and fucking propose."

I sigh, placing my hands on my hips, compassion shining through for my brother who misses his girl, "still nothing?"

He shakes his head, "she's talking to Annie, that's the main thing right now. Go get your girl brother so we can give her some more good news that would hopefully convince her to come home."

I smile and nod before walking over to him, hugging him tight, managing not to tense. I've been getting better at that; it helps that my woman forced me into therapy. I sigh, a fucking biker in therapy. Just as we pull apart Gunner and Ink grin wide when Stormy comes out and opens his fucking mouth,

"Still not gotten the balls to go and propose huh. What kind of kids have I brought up."

Flame chuckles while I shake my head at him, "thanks for the push dad."

He smiles wide at the endearment while I climb on my bike. I rev her up before roaring out of the clubhouse parking lot, pulling my middle finger up at a laughing Shane, heading to the hospital, hoping she doesn't fucking tell me where to go.

I stay seated on my bike for a good ten minutes before I get the nerve to go in. Doc texted, letting me know she's now near the nurses desk in the E.R and I swallow hard. I walk in and Meghan grins wide, giving me two thumbs up making me smile a little and shake my head at her. I look around the room and notice its full. My smile turns into a scowl making her giggle before she bounces on her toes with excitement, proving to me she had something to do with this. I shake my head before I look around the room again and finally notice my girl; her back is to me, and I smile before walking up behind her conscious of all the eyes on us. Fucking Meghan.

I place my hands on either side of her on the desk and she leans against me, making me smile into the side of her neck while I rasp,

"Now, how did you know it was me?"

I can hear the smile in her voice as she talks making my smile grow wider,

"I always know when your near, my body pulls to yours like we're magnets, bound for each other."

I kiss her gently on the side of her neck, "you've been apart of my body and soul for over seven months now baby, even when you didn't want to. We met here at the hospital and my body and heart has needed yours ever since."

She turns in my arms, wrapping hers around my neck, completely oblivious to everyone staring at us, waiting anxiously for me to drop on one knee and I would bet my bike Doc is currently live streaming this to the clubhouse. She leans on her tiptoes, kissing my lips gently before rubbing her nose against mine making me smile, "to what do I owe this surprise visit?"

I smile, gently caressing my lips against hers, "I wanted to see me girl."

She grins at me, "best excuse going."

I chuckle before rubbing my hands along her hips before I look into her beautiful eyes that sparkle with love for me, how I got so lucky to catch and keep her is beyond me, but Flame is right, I can't wait any longer. I need her tethered to me in everyway possible. First I'll put my ring on her finger then I'm putting my baby in her belly, she's mine and I'm hers. We may be married by the laws of the club, but I want her married to me by the eyes of the fucking law and then every mother fucker will know she's mine.

I take a deep breath before I kiss her lips lightly then take a step back making her look at me in confusion, but I just smile gently at her,

"you blew into my life precious. I didn't want you; I didn't even want to be in this town. I was planning to leave again, rejoining my team and never look back but there you were shocking the shit out of me and my heart." She smiles at me, her eyes still holding confusion, "you were and still are the light I needed to overcome my demons. You brought me back to life and became my universe and I cannot even imagine a life where your not in it. You center me, you complete me, and you make me feel whole."

Her eyes start to shine with each of my words before I finally get down on one knee. She gasps, placing her hands over her mouth as her tears fall and I smile wide while getting my mothers blue halo sapphire diamond ring out that used to be her grandmothers. Mel's tears fall faster while I hear a few sniffles in the background.

"your my whole universe Mel, your all I see and need, and I want to do everything in my power to tether you to me forever because without you there is no forever for me.

Marry me precious. Marry me and complete me.

Become tethered to me so we can create more memories together and grow old.

Marry me."

She lets out a sob before nodding her head frantically and I grin wide while the whole room erupts in cheers making her jump back looking around. Everyone chuckles at her while I stand and place my mothers ring on her ring finger before I pick her up, placing my lips on hers in a passionate kiss. She wraps her arms around my neck, her fingers gripping the bottom of my head while her legs dangle down because of her dress.

I smile into the kiss as the room claps before I slow down the kiss, rubbing my nose along hers and she gives me a watery laugh,

"I love you."

I grin wide,

"not as much as I love you precious."

She giggles while I put her down, but not moving my arm from around her waist as we're swarmed by everyone. Meghan grabs us both in a hug while Doc slaps my back,

"about time Dag."

I chuckle and shake my head while he shows me his phone, "wave brother."

I chuckle again and give a one finger salute as a cheer can be heard in the background, but I furrow my brows because I swear I could hear Budgie which is impossible because I'm pretty sure he told me they had another mission until I hear Sparrow speak.

"About time you grew a pair and locked her down Sniper, we've been waiting for his mission for months".

I laugh looking at Doc, but he just shrugs, "I made sure your whole family could witness this." Mel grins wide while I hug Doc, feeling fucking grateful before I kiss my girl again making everyone cheer louder.

Finally, I feel at ease, like I'm where I'm supposed to be.

A few hours later I'm leaning against the headboard in my room at the clubhouse with Mel asleep with her head on my naked chest while her leg and arm are thrown over me. Her warm breath fanning over my skin, sending warmth through me as her ring sparkles in the moonlight on my chest.

After we spent a good few hours partying with the brothers and my squadron who showed up, I brought my girl back to our room in the clubhouse where I loved on her body until she could no longer keep her eyes open. It was fucking perfect. I gently rub her back with my fingers making her sigh in her sleep when my phone pings. I furrow my brows and pick up before a smile shines through my face when I see who it's from.

Starfish - Congrats Dagger, I'm proud of you xx

I message back straight away,

Me – thanks Starfish. Weddings in a month? xx

I hold my breath, hoping and praying.

Starfish – I'll try and come back for it. love yah Dag's xx

I grin wide before replying then screenshotting the message, sending it to Flame and Axel,

Me – love yah too. Miss you girlie xx

Flame messages back straight away then Axel soon after,

Flame – fuck yes!!

Axel – well done brother.

And I chuckle making Mel hold me tighter and I grin. Everything finally feeling fucking right.

I got my girl and hopefully soon, we'll have a family.

Dear reader

Thank you so much for reading the first book of my second series! I hope you consider leaving a review to let others know what you thought of this book, this is the first book of the series, and I thoroughly enjoyed every second of writing it. This story is based on fictional places.

Book 3 Inks story next.

If you haven't yet, please check out my first series, Bound Mafia Series which is made up of three books that can be read individually but better reading altogether.

Dagger: An MC Romance

ABOUT THE AUTHOR

C L McGinlay is a full-time mum to two boys, but also a full-time carer for her youngest who was born with a medical condition and requires more care than the average child and had to leave her job to care for him.

Writing is something that she's always wanted to do but never had the courage to pull through with it, she's loves to read and creating stories is a passion. With much self-doubt she didn't think she could do it but with the support and encouragement from her husband and her family she decided to try and write to see what she can come up with, and the bound series was born. When she's not taking care of her family or spending quality time with them then she's reading, then writing in the evenings, hopeful a career might be born with her stories and people can fall in love with the characters and laugh and cry with them just like she does when she reads books.

Printed in Great Britain
by Amazon